"The female lead is a resourceful, powerful woman, and we're already looking forward to hearing more about her in the future Underwater Investigation Unit novels."

—Yahoo!

"*The Girl Beneath the Sea* continuously dives deeper and deeper until you no longer know whom Sloan can trust. This is a terrific entry in a new and unique series."

—Criminal Element

THE NATURALIST

"[A] smoothly written suspense novel from Thriller Award finalist Mayne . . . The action builds to [an] . . . exciting confrontation between Cray and his foe, and scientific detail lends verisimilitude."

—*Publishers Weekly*

"With a strong sense of place and palpable suspense that builds to a violent confrontation and resolution, Mayne's (*Angel Killer*) series debut will satisfy devotees of outdoors mysteries and intriguing characters."

—*Library Journal*

"*The Naturalist* is a suspenseful, tense, and wholly entertaining story . . . Compliments to Andrew Mayne for the brilliant first entry in a fascinating new series."

—*New York Journal of Books*

"An engrossing mix of science, speculation, and suspense, *The Naturalist* will suck you in."

—*Omnivoracious*

THE
FINAL
EQUINOX

OTHER TITLES BY ANDREW MAYNE

THEO CRAY & JESSICA BLACKWOOD SERIES

Mastermind

UNDERWATER INVESTIGATION UNIT SERIES

The Girl Beneath the Sea
Black Coral
Sea Storm

THEO CRAY SERIES

The Naturalist
Looking Glass
Murder Theory
Dark Pattern

JESSICA BLACKWOOD SERIES

Angel Killer
Name of the Devil
Black Fall

THE CHRONOLOGICAL MAN SERIES

The Monster in the Mist
The Martian Emperor

Other Fiction Titles

Station Breaker
Public Enemy Zero
Hollywood Pharaohs
Knight School
The Grendel's Shadow

Nonfiction

The Cure for Writer's Block
How to Write a Novella in 24 Hours

THE FINAL EQUINOX

A THEO CRAY AND JESSICA BLACKWOOD THRILLER

ANDREW MAYNE

THOMAS & MERCER

Text copyright © 2022 by Andrew Mayne
All rights reserved.

Published by Thomas & Mercer, Seattle

www.apub.com

Amazon, the Amazon logo, and Thomas & Mercer are trademarks of Amazon.com, Inc., or its affiliates.

ISBN-13: 9781542033992
ISBN-10: 1542033993

Cover design by Shasti O'Leary Soudant

Printed in the United States of America

THE
FINAL
EQUINOX

PART ONE

THEORIST

CHAPTER ONE
MURDER EXPERT

The suspect's body lies on the table before me. Dr. Radu is using a digital microscope connected to a monitor to go over every millimeter of it in search of a clue—a drop of blood, a hair, or a fiber from a shirt, anything that could tell us what happened, because neither the victim nor the suspect is talking. I look from the screen to the body—average height, no visible injuries, inscrutable face—and suspect I may be out of my depth. I'm in a damn science-fiction movie.

The suspect is a robot called mu2, and its victim, Jason Zhao, currently in a coma in the ICU with a fractured skull, is one of the engineers who created it.

An accident (attempted murder?) with a machine like this was bound to happen, but I never imagined I'd get a front-row seat, let alone be asked to provide expertise.

Some people claim the first time a robot killed a human was at a Ford Motor plant in 1979 when a man named Robert Williams got in the path of a parts-transfer machine that didn't have appropriate safeguards. He'd crawled up into a section of the vast infrastructure and was struck. It took his coworkers half an hour to realize what had happened.

In my opinion, from a systems point of view, there's not much separating the functionality of the mobile machine that killed Williams and the guidance systems in missiles like the V1 flying bombs and V2 rockets the Germans lobbed at London in World War II. They're all devices with automated processes that can sometimes make choices that kill people.

Fortunately for Zhao, he was found in time and has a good chance of recovery. While everyone waits for him to be able to tell us what happened, assuming he'll remember, AtlantaRobotics, Zhao's employer and mu2's manufacturer, has launched a full-fledged investigation alongside OSHA and the other federal and state agencies that get called in when something like this happens.

AtlantaRobotics CEO Iris Newell is looking at me for an answer. She's in her midfifties and possesses piercing hazel eyes that don't let go of you. She called me in a state of near panic. Newell is friends with an investor who helped me launch a company a few years ago—back when my reputation was strong enough to allow me to raise money and attract top talent. Before people started whispering that all the serial killer stuff had driven me crazy.

Now, no one will trust my reputation with a 401(k), let alone a term sheet to fund a biotech or machine-learning start-up—well, no one outside of some crazy bitcoin millionaires with sketchy schemes I want no part of. People do seem to trust my expertise, though, which is why I find myself getting asked to consult secretly on projects and problems.

When Iris Newell called, I explained that I had no practical knowledge of robotics and it was a field I'd barely been able to keep up with. She replied she didn't need a robotics expert, she wanted a "murder expert," as she inarticulately described it in her panic.

So here I am, the "murder expert," staring at the body of a bipedal robot that may have been responsible for a grave injury to a living person.

Newell has her arms crossed as she looks from the robot to the screen to me, waiting for me to shout "Aha!" and point out what actually happened like a detective in an Agatha Christie novel.

All I can think to say is, "Yep, that's a robot all right."

I feel a twinge of guilt for accepting the job. Usually, I'm asked to look at issues with potential laboratory contamination or help start-ups focus their data-labeling and training methods for building neural networks. Occasionally I get a call from an intelligence agency.

I used to be more discriminating about the jobs I took, but given that I'm approaching forty and living largely off the charity of my girlfriend and her government salary, I've decided to say yes if the money is right and the job's not too ridiculous.

I decided my pride needed to keep its mouth shut when I was at a fancy steak house in Georgetown with Jessica and realized I couldn't put the bill on my credit card. I gave everything I had to the last woman I loved when I knew things weren't going to work out, leaving me with nothing for the next one. Neither of them ever asked me for anything, which only makes the guilt all the more painful.

"Your thoughts?" asks Newell.

The rest of the AtlantaRobotics senior management team is standing in the back of the workshop, watching me. Between worrying about their colleague, their creation, and the future of their company, this has to be a nerve-racking experience.

I have no idea what to tell them, so I do the next best thing to make myself look smart—I ask a question. "Explain to me again what mu2's capabilities are and what kind of data is recorded?"

A young female engineer steps forward. Her name tag reads "Tilly Goodswain."

"Mu2 is able to accept basic verbal instruction and navigate different environments to accomplish tasks. We record all the visual and IMU readings. But its data has been wiped," she explains.

So, the suspect has amnesia, too. Which is suspiciously convenient and the reason why Newell asked for me. As far as OSHA is concerned, this was an accident. She fears otherwise.

"Magnetic disk or SSD?" I ask. A magnetic disk can be wiped with a strong electromagnet. An SSD is much harder to erase.

"We use SSDs because of the vibrations," replies Goodswain.

I should have known that. "Could I see where this took place?"

Newell points to a lab bench work space in the corner cordoned off with yellow tape and a big sign that says ACCIDENT SCENE: DO NOT ENTER.

I walk to the section for a closer look. There's an office chair in front of a computer surrounded by papers, gears, a lighter, machine parts, and tools.

"What was Zhao doing?" I ask Newell, who followed me over to the section.

"Working late on a visual system."

Hmm, working late, the number one cause of office-related homicide in murder mysteries.

Newell points to the chair. "Our security guard found him on the ground next to the chair. The doctor said it appeared he was struck from behind."

"And where was mu2?"

"Standing next to the body."

Of course. "And your security system?"

"We don't track people inside the building. There was just Zhao and the guard in the facility. And we have the guard on the lobby camera at the time it happened," she explains.

"Could someone have been hiding in the building?"

"We have cameras on the lobby and the loading dock. We checked to see who had entered and left the building."

"What about there?" I point to an exit at the end of the room.

"That's a fire escape. It's wired with an alarm," says Winston McCauley, the head of security.

I walk over to the door. There's a magnetic sensor at the top of the frame that's triggered when the door is opened. A tall tool chest is next to it with photos and fridge magnets stuck to its sides.

I glance at the people in the back of the room. The project manager, Michael Landrow, is leaning against the wall, looking uncomfortable. So far, he hasn't said anything.

I step to Zhao's workbench and study the tools and parts. I pick up the lighter and flick it. The flame lights and I study it for a moment. "Was Zhao a smoker?" I look at Landrow.

He looks from side to side, waiting for somebody to speak first. No one does. "Uh, yeah. He was trying to quit."

"Interesting." I walk back to the emergency exit.

A little metal robot toy is stuck to the side of the tool chest at waist level. I pull it free and stick it to the magnetic sensor on the door. When I push the bar, the door swings open onto a gravel-covered roof.

Amid the deafening silence, I ask, "Is it a silent alarm?"

Newell stares at McCauley. "Did you know about this?"

"People aren't supposed to do that," he says defensively.

"People aren't supposed to do a lot of things," I point out.

There's a coffee can with cigarette butts on the other side of the door, along with a large cinder block. I pick up the coffee can and show its contents to the group. "And yet here we are."

"There's no stairway access on the roof," snaps Landrow. He's aware that as project manager it would be ridiculous for him not to know about this, yet he never spoke up.

I walk to the edge of the roof toward the back of the facility. A few feet below lies the roof of a utility closet. Next to that is a dumpster.

"Want to race me to the lobby?" I ask Landrow, pointing out how easy it would be to go from here to the first level using this path.

He shakes his head. "I told them they can't use the roof," he explains weakly.

Newell stares at the man, clearly ready to bite his head off.

I hold up my hands. "This kind of thing is more common than you may realize." I turn to McCauley. "You work with engineers and scientists; finding exploits is what they do for a living. Do you think a sign's gonna stop them?"

McCauley's face turns red, but he has the sense to keep his mouth shut.

Goodswain looks around at everybody. "I'm confused . . . are you saying one of us did it? I thought the fracture matched mu2's hand?"

"I'm just pointing out that your security isn't so secure. As to who did it, I'd like to take another look at mu2."

CHAPTER TWO
THE THREE LAWS

"What would you like to see?" asks Dr. Radu, leaning over mu2 in his grease-stained lab coat. "Do you want to take a look at the GPUs? The reinforcement learning system?"

I can't tell if he's throwing jargon at me or being sincere. Either way, I'm pretty sure what I need to know isn't going to be in the software or sticking to the surface like a racetrack ticket on the bottom of a shoe.

"When mu2 was found, the battery still had charge but the memory was wiped, correct?" I ask.

"Yes," replies Radu.

I point to a cabinet of computer servers in the corner. "Is mu2 totally autonomous, or does it connect somewhere?"

Iris Newell answers for Radu. "We keep training data on the servers and download them to the machines. We then upload their environmental experiences back up to our cloud to be incorporated into model training. Most of the training happens virtually. We use real-world data as a test, mostly."

By *virtually*, she means that they have a computer cluster running simulations of millions of virtual mu2s doing different tasks, like a video game. That's how the robot learned to walk and pick up objects like Coke cans without pulverizing them.

The challenge with virtual training is that it can only take you so far. Eventually you have to test it in the less-than-perfect real world and find out if all that theory has any value.

"Was mu2 ever trained to . . . harm people?" I ask.

"Absolutely not!" says Radu. "We have harm avoidance built into the system."

That's all good in theory, but a simple system can make simple mistakes. A robot programmed with real rules, or fictional ones like Isaac Asimov's Three Laws of Robotics, can only follow them so far as they understand them. If you ask a robot or a person to press a switch, they have no way of knowing if it's going to turn on a light or electrocute the guy in the next room.

The robot that killed Robert Williams in 1979 didn't want to kill him. It didn't want anything. It was just a simple machine following a simple routine.

Mu2, while a million times more sophisticated, is a robot designed to pick up and move things, not a general artificial intelligence capable of ruminating on life and death or the trolley problem. Whether mu2 is responsible for Zhao being in the hospital has no more relevance to morality in advanced AIs than V2 rockets raining down on London do.

Though Radu protested that mu2 is incapable of harming someone, Newell remained quiet.

"Have you looked into other applications for mu2?" I ask her.

"We're constantly looking for different use cases," she replies.

"What about military or crowd control?"

Everyone looks at her. Apparently, this is a hot-button topic. There's a lot of sensitivity among tech workers about using artificial intelligence in military applications, even to the point that some tech giants have officially announced they won't pursue them so as to avoid an internal employee revolt.

"We haven't ruled out any applications," she answers.

I'll take this as a yes. From the reaction of her employees, it's a big update.

"What are you saying, Iris?" asks Radu.

"We've talked about this."

Radu shakes his head in disgust, then turns back to me. "What else can I show you?"

"Can you take it apart?"

He shakes his head and wipes his hands on his coat. "That takes days."

There's something odd about his lab coat. In the corner, there's a rack with six more of them hanging from it. All the others are bright white and clean.

"Could you take off its arms?" I ask.

"That could take a few hours," he replies.

"Just use the quick-disconnect bolt," offers Goodswain.

"But that's attached to the shoulder servos," says Radu.

"I'll do it." Goodswain grabs a pair of rubber gloves from a table and slips them on. I notice Radu's hands are bare.

Goodswain pops open the chest cavity and uses a hex wrench to unfasten three bolts. The left arm comes free in less than a minute, followed swiftly by the right one. She lays them on the workbench.

I put on a pair of gloves and pick up the right arm, the opposite of the one that allegedly brought down Zhao. It's lighter than I expected. I can pick it up by the shoulder and lift it with ease. It's heavy, but not too heavy.

I take the arm and go back to Zhao's workbench. I bring mu2's arm up and swing it at the space where his head would have been.

"Interesting." I rest the arm on my shoulder like a baseball bat and turn to Newell and her team. "I think it's time to call the Atlanta Police Department."

"You can't be serious," says Radu as he reaches for the other robotic arm.

"Don't touch that. You already made a show of getting your fingerprints all over the robot. No need to add any more."

He raises his hands defensively. "I'm not sure what you're trying to insinuate."

Actually, I'm not trying to insinuate anything. Sure, Radu's looking pretty suspicious, but I've been exactly where he's standing with all the fingers pointing at me.

Landrow looks suspicious because he didn't want Newell knowing he let his engineers take smoke breaks on the roof. McCauley looks suspicious because he didn't know about a basic flaw in the building security.

Goodswain doesn't look suspicious because she's been extremely helpful . . . which makes me extremely suspicious.

Everyone here is brilliant. Some are smart in one sphere, others in several. Goodswain strikes me as all-around smart. Smart enough to know what a guilty person would look like and what an innocent person would do.

That doesn't make her the real suspect . . . only suspicious.

When Newell invited me here, there was talk about industrial espionage, a virus infecting the robot, and all the other paranoid concepts that come with an advanced robotics start-up.

"Are you saying mu2 didn't do it?" asks Newell.

I can tell she's calculating the valuation of her company if an employee was knocked comatose by a fellow employee wielding a robot arm versus a scenario in which one of its robots nearly murdered a researcher. She likes where this is heading.

"I'm saying this should be treated like an attempted-murder investigation and that this is a crime scene. If anyone has a story to tell, now is the time to come forward and tell it before it gets worse," I tell the group.

Actually, if they're smart, now is the time to shut up and hire a lawyer. But I don't say that, because I want the guilty party or parties found out.

Unfortunately, real life isn't like a dinner party murder mystery where the detective lays out the facts and the killer confesses to—

"It was *her* idea," Landrow blurts, pointing at Goodswain.

"You prick. It was Zhao's idea," she shouts back. "And if you weren't such a pansy, you could have just knocked him out instead of loosening your grip and fracturing his skull!"

11

Correction: apparently, they don't know life isn't a dinner party murder mystery. I shut up and let them talk.

Goodswain pleads to Newell, "We told you we didn't want this to be used as a murderbot."

"So you decided to *fake* that it's a murderbot?" Newell asks, trying to process what just happened.

"We wanted the board of directors to get cold feet," interrupts Landrow. "Zhao volunteered. He offered to take one for the team. Only . . . It was an accident."

Newell turns to me. "What now?"

"It's a convenient story. Until Zhao wakes up, it could be true; it could be bullshit. You need to call the cops in either way."

"It was an *accident*," says Goodswain. "We don't need to make this into something that it's not." She points to me. "Why, of all people, are you listening to this guy anyway? Everyone knows he's batshit crazy."

Now *that* hurts.

"Have you been offered employment at another company, or are you in the process of forming a start-up?" I ask her.

"You're not the cops. I don't have to answer any of that," says Goodswain.

"No problem. I'm just going to add that to the list of questions I give the detectives when they try to determine the real motive."

I'm not buying her "no murderbots" defense. She's up to something. I don't know if Landrow and Zhao were fully on board, but Goodswain's too smart for her own good.

The only thing she lacked was experience. Being smart is not enough to get away with a crime . . . you have to spend time getting good at it.

Newell takes out her phone and stares at it. Probably wondering whether she should call the company lawyer or the police.

I decide to leave the premises before things get any more heated. I'll do what I do best: create chaos and slip away into the night.

Maybe I don't so much create chaos—I simply point out what everyone else has been trying so hard to ignore.

CHAPTER THREE
ADVISER

When you've had several hack books and a bad TV movie made about your life, the world starts to form an opinion of you that, while not entirely accurate, represents a kind of funhouse-mirror version of you. And when your name is connected to the capture of some of the most prolific serial killers ever, you meet a lot of weirdos. Most harmless, some scary.

Then there are the conspiracy theorists . . .

My favorite was the Uber driver who randomly brought up the Grizzly Killer, the topic of a recent NPR podcast that was mostly okay. I had different thoughts on the case, seeing as how I was the one who caught him.

The Uber driver, a young man with close-cut hair and enough cologne for a Marine Corps battalion weekend leave, explained with no idea who I was that he thought the Grizzly Killer was actually Dr. Theo Cray . . . *me*. He went on to detail a theory popular on YouTube about how I was also the killer behind several other murder streaks.

At the end of the ride, I thanked him and out of a cruel sense of humor handed him my business card. I got a kick out of the expression on his face in the rearview mirror. He probably pissed himself. (Lucky he had all that cologne on.)

Jessica would have given me a talking to if she'd seen me do that. She's had more close calls with real psychos then I have and multiple stab and bullet wounds to show for it.

When I arrive at my hotel, there's a blinking message on my phone, and my gut sinks at the thought that someone has gotten through.

I pick up the receiver and play the message, hoping it's room service telling me that more towels are coming.

"Hello, Dr. Cray? This is Philip Martinez. I've sent you an email, actually several. I'm sorry to bother you again, but this is an urgent matter. My client has requested your services and time is important."

This guy sounds a lot like a lawyer, which is not a plus. I try to stay as far from attorneys as possible.

"Just let me know what your retainer fee is and I will wire you the money."

Okay, this sounds somewhat legit, or at least serious. I take out my laptop and respond to his last message with payment information, then go take a shower. I'd avoided him before because his emails were written like a paranoiac worried about secrecy.

By the time I step out, there's a notification on my phone that I just got sent five thousand dollars—the made-up price I told him for a phone consultation. There's also an email asking if I could call him right away.

Fine, let's get this over with. I'll tell him I can't track down his junkie son or explain why it's unlikely anyone will ever find out who killed his long-lost whatever. Then I'll give him back his money and move on with my life.

"This is Theo Cray," I say when he picks up.

"Dr. Cray? Thank you so much for returning my call. I know you're quite busy."

Actually, I have nothing on the books, but I'll let him think otherwise. "How may I help you?"

"My client has requested your services."

14

"Okay, you have them."

"No, Dr. Cray, we need you in person. We can't discuss this over the phone," he explains.

Oh brother. "And why is that?"

"Again, I can't explain that. What I *can* tell you is that we're requesting you as an adviser for several days, along with several others."

"Who else?"

"I can't tell you that, either. I apologize, but I assure you that it will all make sense."

This is smelling very fishy. "How do I know this isn't something illegal or involving technology transfers to a foreign government?"

"It's not, Dr. Cray."

There's another scary possibility. "Does this involve consulting on a criminal matter?"

I sometimes get asked to serve as a professional witness for the defense teams of people who are clearly guilty. I'll do anything to stay out of a courtroom, so that's a flat no.

"This has nothing to do with that," he assures me.

"Are you a company building something?" I press.

"No. All I can say is that this involves a serious scientific inquiry. I'm very sure you will find it interesting, but we want to avoid public attention."

All right, now I'm curious. "When do you need me?"

"I need you on the next available plane. We'll pay you a day rate in addition to what I sent you as a retainer."

"How many days again?" I probe.

"Possibly a week. Maybe more."

"And where will I be going?"

"I can only tell you once you accept, Dr. Cray. Those are the conditions."

I need to talk to somebody cleverer than me. "Let me call you back."

"Okay, but please do hurry."

I hang up and call Jessica.

"How's Atlanta?" she asks.

"Full of ghosts." The last time I was here, I was hunting a child killer. "Quick question . . . got a minute?"

"Yeah, I'm just walking through the woods with my flashlight looking for a ghost called the Tree Man that may have kidnapped two girls."

"Okay, cool . . . wait, *what*?"

Jessica's sarcasm is as sharp as a razor. We've been together for a year, and I still can't tell when she's serious or joking. Sometimes I suspect she can't, either.

"Long story. I'll tell you later. I don't think he's going to show. What's up?"

"I've been offered a large sum of money to go to a mysterious place for some unknown rich guy to do something they won't tell me."

"Is it porn?" she asks.

"I forgot to ask."

"Always ask. I was once handed a contract when I was in Japan for what I thought was a game show. It wasn't for a game show. Thankfully my translator explained what was up."

Before becoming a Miami police officer, then joining the FBI, Jessica was a teenage magic prodigy who toured the world with her father and grandfather, the famous Blackstars. She lived more before turning thirteen than I have my whole life.

"I'm pretty sure it's not porn. They said it was scientific. A scientific inquiry."

"Uh-huh. And they told *me* it was going to be artistic. Did the guy making the offer have Yakuza tattoos?"

"It was a phone call. They paid me five thousand dollars up front for the consultation."

"Was he breathing heavily?"

"Um . . . what? No. It's not porn. It's probably some rich guy who wants to explain how evolution is all wrong or needs me to validate his grand unified theory of whatever."

"Sounds like easy money."

"Would you take it?"

"No. But you should."

I don't know if this is a reference to my finances or Jessica trying to break me out of my bubble. I had a bit of a breakdown before we met, and I'm still trying to learn how to process life, the universe, and everything.

"Fine. If it's some rich weirdo thing or he tries to hunt me down in his game preserve, you won't hear the end of it from me."

"Not if you're mounted on a wall," she replies.

I think that was a joke.

CHAPTER FOUR
THE PANEL

Philip Martinez left out one little detail when I agreed to hop on the next flight to New Mexico—apparently, I have to go through some kind of vetting process before I get to the next step of whatever this is. Now I'm sitting across from my interrogators in a conference room inside the Santa Fe Marriott.

I suspect Martinez didn't tell me because he was afraid I'd bail. Staring at the serious expressions on the man and the woman sitting on either side of him, I'm getting flashbacks to defending my PhD thesis and wishing this chair were an ejection seat—or better yet, theirs.

Back when I presented my doctoral research on using machine learning to predict the growth of Enterotoxigenic *Escherichia coli* in petri dishes, I knew I had at least one skeptic in the room. I was able to plan for that and supply answers for every single contingency I could imagine. Computational biology was still an emerging science, and many of the professors I encountered were still stuck in the mindset of using antiquated methods instead of today's artificial-intelligence techniques like deep learning.

Here, I'm having trouble determining if Claire Chambers or Ronald Urbina is the skeptic, based on the questions they've asked so far. Both seem not to hold me in high regard.

"Dr. Cray, could you explain to us how you got your government security clearance revoked?" asks Chambers, going for the throat and making her my prime suspect as the designated skeptic.

It's a leading question, but exactly the kind I'd throw at me if I were on the other side of the table and wanted to cut me off at the knees.

"I didn't have my security clearance revoked. It expired and I decided not to renew it." This is mostly accurate.

"Was this related to funding being pulled from your lab by the Department of Defense?" asks Chambers.

"We had a difference of opinion. I felt our research wasn't being used . . . sincerely." This is still a delicate topic for me. I'd worked closely with DoD officials when they threw me a lifeline after my academic career came to an abrupt halt.

The problem with DoD was, while one person has good intentions and wants to use your methods for making the world safer, someone else has different ideas and asks you to do things like make biomarkers to track the children of suspected terrorists. I had no confidence that there was any proper oversight applied to the people making these requests and decided to extricate myself from the situation altogether.

That and the fact that one of my lab employees tried to kill me with a pathogen made me suspect my management skills left much to be desired.

I used to think my hard knocks went along with being an introverted loner, but then I saw Jessica, equally introverted and a fellow loner, run a class of FBI cadets through a field exercise like an actual response team and realized that wasn't the case. She is a leader. I could hold a group of students captivated for a few hours; she could get them to follow her out the door and try to save the world.

"How would you define your expertise?" asks Urbina.

"I'm a computational biologist. I study the use of computer modeling to understand how biological systems function."

"Studied," says Chambers, emphasizing the past tense.

"Study," I respond. "This is something I'm still actively pursuing."

"Can you direct us to any recent research papers that you've published?" she asks.

"Well . . . nothing I've submitted. I'm still working on the details." Procrastinating is more like it. I think I have some novel approaches using deep neural networks, but I'm not sure how well they'll be received—or more precisely, how well *I'll* be received.

"Can you describe what you've been working on?" asks Urbina.

"Sure. It's a computer model that tries to predict what's missing in an ecosystem. Let's say you do a survey and find a hundred different species and it roughly matches another ecosystem, say, a jungle in Belize and a jungle in the Congo, and in Belize you notice there's a kind of ant that digs tunnels and aerates the soil, but in the Congo there's no such ant, yet the soil and plant growth is similar. The model points this out and suggests what else to look for. Is there a termite performing the same function? Does the soil have some chemical property that went unnoticed? Or did something recently go extinct and the entire ecosystem is at risk of collapsing?"

From Urbina's nod of approval, I sense the explanation helped save me a little face. I stop short of explaining that I based this entire model on my research into tracking serial killers through data on vulnerable sex workers.

Is there a killer working the I-95 corridor? Do the locations of Instagram posts made by prostitutes change in that region when they start to feel unsafe? All of it's fuzzy data, but if you add enough correlating information, sometimes you see a signal.

So far, this tribunal has felt more like a grant review than an interview for whatever supersecret project they want me on.

"Would you say your research has applications outside of biology?" asks Chambers.

"In a narrow way. I have to always remind myself that being knowledgeable in one area doesn't automatically make me an expert in everything adjacent. I try to bring the same discipline to everything."

"I wish more experts thought like you," replies Urbina. "How do you approach unusual claims?"

"Unusual? How do you mean?"

"There are some who think science isn't able to explain or understand a number of phenomena. Do you think science can explain everything?"

"Yes," I reply.

"Yes? That simple?" asks Chambers as she leans forward.

"Of course. Science is our attempt to understand the rules of the universe. Nothing more. Nothing less. Either the universe follows rules or it doesn't. If there are no rules, then nothing makes sense." This was my stock line back when I taught college freshmen.

"And science understands those rules? Physics is just a matter of deciding the details? The human brain is a bunch of cells and that's it?" asks Urbina.

I'm noticing the tide change. Urbina was the more friendly interrogator; now he's on the attack.

"I didn't say any of those things, out of due respect. Relativity could be wrong or just a rough approximation. Evolution could have some other bizarre explanation that's beyond my ability to understand. The rules of the universe aren't what we observe . . . they're what we believe we're observing based upon the best evidence.

"Science isn't a book of explanations. It's a process. A process we're continuing to refine and make more precise. Despite setbacks and wrong turns, nobody has ever seriously said the problem with science was its demand for more precision and deeper understanding."

I cut my impromptu TED Talk short because I'm sure they've heard this before. The heart of what they're getting at is science versus scientism. The former being the process and the latter being putting the discoveries of the process, and the people who made them, on a pedestal that's beyond reproach.

"What do you think of phenomena like UAPs that are pretty well documented?" asks Urbina.

"Unidentified aerial phenomena?" I reply, referring to the footage of strange flying objects caught by military aircraft systems.

"Correct."

"I don't know why they don't still call them UFOs."

"UFO is prejudicial and assumes a flying craft of some kind," Urbina explains.

"UAP is just as prejudicial and presumes that it's actually aerial and not some behavior of the observing equipment that's not well understood. I've seen some of them explained as bokeh effects on infrared sensors, others as submarine-launched balloons, and yet others as the conflation of different observations into one event." I shrug. "I don't know *what* to believe, but I have very low confidence in the people who are actively promoting them and not much more in the agencies investigating them."

"Some of the most knowledgeable experts in the world treat these as serious phenomena," replies Urbina.

"Experts on what? Is the pilot that sees it on his screen more qualified than the Raytheon engineer who built the system to explain what the sensor is showing? Is the person who wrote down the witness observations a better expert than a trained criminal investigator who understands how stories can change and conform over time? I don't know."

"So you think it's all bunk?"

"I don't know what to think. If I took this as seriously as these experts say they do, I wouldn't be here talking about it; I'd be out there trying to find the answer to the greatest mystery of our time. Instead of tweeting that someone else should look into it. It's like a flat-earther that can't be bothered to take a trip to Antarctica to find out if the world is indeed flat. Do they cherish the notion more than the fact?"

I'm suspecting my rant hasn't helped me win over Urbina, who I now believe to be the real skeptic.

"So you'd say you consider the idea of aliens ridiculous?" asks Chambers.

"Aliens? I'd say they are inevitable. While I can't speak to the likelihood of intelligent life, it's not outside of what I think is possible. The universe is big and old. Why not?"

"But you don't think we've been visited?" asks Urbina.

"I don't think we have any evidence for visitation, but an uncontacted tribe in the Bay of Bengal wouldn't have any evidence that a satellite flying overhead is photographing them, much less that there's a space station filled with people whizzing two hundred and fifty miles overhead every few weeks."

"Ninety minutes," says Urbina.

"Pardon me?"

"The International Space Station makes an orbit every ninety minutes."

"Correct, but it takes six weeks for the station to pass over the same spot. It's rotating around the Earth as we rotate on our axis."

I don't think I won any points by correcting his correction. I simply had to let them know I was the smartest person in the room, didn't I?

I can imagine Jessica shaking her head. I've gotten better about correcting people, but I'm so horrible about it that the improvement is probably invisible to most.

Chambers speaks up. "So, you think it's possible we've been visited by aliens?"

"Possible. Sure. Life on Earth could have been seeded by extraterrestrial rocks. Some of the viral fragments in our DNA could have come from life outside our solar system. It could be raining down on us now."

"So, to put it succinctly, despite your skepticism of UAPs and other phenomena, you put the possibility of extraterrestrial intelligence as high?"

"I wouldn't qualify it as low, medium, or high, but certainly worth investigating."

Chambers glances at Martinez and he nods. Urbina makes a non-committal wave of his hand that I assume means "whatever."

"Thank you, Dr. Cray," says Martinez. "If you wouldn't mind waiting outside while we have a discussion?"

"No problem. Just one question: Are you investigating UAPs? Is that what this is all about?" I imagine a gaggle of crazy rich dudes gathering to stare at blurry footage and watch videos of abductees talking about being probed.

"No, Dr. Cray. That was just to find out about your open-mindedness," he replies. "We should have an answer shortly."

Open-mindedness? What's next, a haunted house?

CHAPTER FIVE

QUANT

It took them thirty minutes to decide. I spent the time sitting at the hotel bar drinking a beer while watching a soccer game between two European teams whose names eluded me. I wasn't really paying attention as much as trying to take apart the conversation we'd had.

I googled both Chambers and Urbina, hoping that would tell me more. Chambers has an academic background with a PhD in political science and a work history with various nonprofit organizations. Ronald Urbina is more of a mystery. No LinkedIn, no social media. There are a few mentions of him in articles discussing philanthropic efforts in developing countries, but that's it.

Martinez enters the bar with a large folder under his arm as I'm finishing my beer.

"Dr. Cray," he says, smiling. "Welcome aboard."

I shake his outstretched hand. "Welcome aboard what?"

"First I need you to sign some papers. I've already arranged for your bags to be brought down."

"Brought down? I only got here two hours ago."

"I apologize for the cloak-and-dagger. We do the interviews here and then bring people to the facility if they pass the interview," he explains.

"Facility? You know this is sounding more and more like a 1970s science-fiction horror film." If I end up getting killed in the desert by a robot gunslinger, I'll only have myself to blame.

He pushes the folder toward me. "I apologize, but I think you'll understand. Once you sign these, we can head to the airport."

"Airport?" I ask as I pull the papers out.

"We'll be taking a helicopter. It's a three-hour drive otherwise. Do you have any questions about the NDA?"

I flip through the document. It's fairly standard, not much different from the hundreds I've signed before. I'm tight-lipped about what I work on and know the difference between what a lawyer can threaten you with and what they can actually do. In a case like this, they're more afraid of me saying something in the short term to a competitor or the media as opposed to years later.

I sign the documents and hand them back. "All right, talk."

Martinez laughs. "I wish I could." He checks his watch. "We only have another hour and all will be revealed. Well, rather, it will begin. I have to collect two more people and then we'll be on our way."

"To the cloning facility," I supply.

Martinez grins. "Nothing so sinister."

"Can you at least tell me who's paying for all this?"

"In time . . ."

I'm losing my patience. "Let me phrase it this way: If you want me to get in that helicopter, tell me what you promised to tell me when I came here, or at the very least reassure me that I'm not going to get interviewed by the FBI a month from now because I walked into a Chinese plot to steal intellectual property."

"Dr. Cray . . ."

I point to the hotel front desk. "If I asked them for the name of the firm that reserved the conference room, how long would it take me to find out the name of your client?"

Martinez glances at the desk as if it's harboring a trade secret. "Okay. Fair enough. You signed the papers. Thomas T. Theismann. Have you heard of him?"

I nod.

"Is that helpful?" asks Martinez.

"I'll get on your helicopter," I reply, my curiosity piqued.

Theismann is an interesting figure. He's known to most of the world as a billionaire investor who avoids attention, but to math nerds and people like me, he has a different reputation.

In the 1970s, when the use of computers to trade stocks started to ramp up, Theismann was a graduate student at MIT who took a side job helping a financial firm build software to determine at what price to buy or sell currencies. Traders would input the latest data and look for trends and then make decisions. While electronic trading didn't exist yet, private institutions would use teletype time stamps to verify when an execution was made, allowing for an almost real-time trading network like the one that came about a decade later.

Currency traders looked for trends to see if a price was going up or down. With real-time data, traders using computers and software could spot a trend and buy into or sell before other less-adept firms were able to make decisions.

While working on an IBM mainframe installing trading software, Theismann noticed the way the system—and every other computer like it at the time—handled floating point operations, the math used to handle really large numbers or numbers with lots of decimals. It was rounding decimals either up or down after four places.

This meant that if a German mark was trading for $.46436 US, it was actually rounded to $.4644. While these differences didn't seem significant in small numbers, over billions of exchanges going back and forth in a matter of days, they added up.

The firms and even the programmers working for them ignored this because electronic trading was profitable, and everyone assumed that you couldn't get more precision out of the computers at the time. Theismann dug into the code and the hardware and discovered a way to get the computers to do the math with even greater precision and in less time.

He talked a small Cambridge financial firm into a venture, dropped out of MIT, and started one of the first and most successful quantitative-analysis trading operations ever. Theismann was also smart enough to keep the method secret. It wasn't until years later, when programmers were pushing the capabilities of PCs, that they stumbled upon the same solution Theismann had come up with and profited from a decade earlier.

By that time, he'd hired teams of mathematicians, engineers, and computer programmers to squeeze even more performance out of state-of-the-art systems to maintain a competitive edge.

Beyond that, I don't know much about the man other than he does a lot of charitable giving. But the fact that his mathematical algorithms were quietly chipping away at the financial system while nobody noticed amuses me. Instead of burying the math in an academic paper that would be forgotten, he put it to use, making himself wealthy and supporting causes he found worthy.

I'm waiting outside the hotel with my still-unpacked bag when Martinez joins me with a man who looks like he's in his midthirties and has a nervous smile.

"Dr. Cray, this is Dr. Barker," says Martinez.

"Theo," I tell Barker.

"Trevor," he responds, shaking my hand.

He's got a good grip with rough hands. His boots are made for hiking. I assume his doctorate has something to do with pulling things out of the ground. Either rocks, bones, or antiques.

Trevor is dressed in a fleece jacket over a T-shirt and has a thicker jacket tucked between the handles of his duffel bag. This suggests he's used to layering—going from warm to cold climates in a single day. That implies either climbing mountains or spending time in the desert.

His boots are waterproof and similar to the ones I use when I go traipsing through mountain ponds looking for bacteria. I notice his fingernails are trimmed as precisely as my own when I do lab work.

"Archaeology?" I ask.

Trevor glances over at Martinez, then back to me. "Yes . . . did Mr. Martinez tell you?"

"No. Just a guess."

"I can see why you're here," he says with a smile.

"That makes one of us."

"This way, gentlemen," says Martinez as a black Land Rover pulls up. "We have to pick up one more person at the airport, and then we'll go to the helipad. Please, um, wait until we get there before discussing anything, um, relevant."

"We'd have to know what's relevant to know how to avoid discussing anything relevant, wouldn't we?" I reply.

"You have a dry wit, Dr. Cray," says an exasperated Martinez.

I grin and pretend it was a joke and not a Theoism, as Jessica calls my observations.

So, a computational biologist and an archaeologist board a black SUV owned by a reclusive billionaire obsessed with mathematics. It's anyone's guess who we pick up next.

CHAPTER SIX
THE BASE

I have Dr. Anna Kosinski down as either a linguist or a sociologist the moment she gets into the Land Rover. As I climb into the third row of seats in the back, I notice that her carry-on bag has several books stuffed into it, including French and Farsi versions of the same science-fiction novel.

"I'm Anna," she says to Trevor, then turns to shake my hand and make eye contact.

"I'm Theo."

"I know. You're almost as good-looking in person as the guy who played you on television," she says matter-of-factly.

I can only smile. I don't have clever responses to this kind of thing like Jessica does.

Anna is about forty and speaks very clearly, as if each word is appearing before you in a subtitle. I'm curious if she had a deaf sibling or parent.

She leans forward and taps Martinez on the shoulder. "So this is the real thing? Not a dry run?"

"Dr. Kosinski, please," says Martinez, flustered. Clearly, they've interacted in the past.

She sits back down and half turns to me. "This will be interesting for you. I guess you're the backup for Andrea."

"Andrea?" I ask.

"Andrea Hoffman," she replies.

"Dr. Kosinski, I'm begging you. Hold all conversation until we get to the base," Martinez pleads.

She makes a zipping motion with her hand across her lips and rolls her eyes. "Yes, Philip."

Kosinski is quite a character. She feels comfortable enough to push whatever rules Martinez is trying to enforce. I don't know how much of it is practical versus him struggling to enforce instructions given by someone else.

The mention of Andrea Hoffman is interesting. I've heard her speak at several conferences and read several of her papers. She's a neuroscientist-turned-AI-researcher who's made some interesting advances using computing systems to replicate entire nervous systems.

Hoffman pioneered a method that follows cellular growth in fruit flies for mapping out a virtual version of their brain. This has led to some important ideas about layer sizes and depth.

We're not in the same field, but I can see how someone might think we're interchangeable based upon our overlap of machine-learning usage. To be honest, her research is much timelier and more relevant than mine. She'd be my pick for whatever we're about to embark upon.

The driver stops the vehicle at the fence on the edge of a tarmac. Martinez hops out and ushers us all to a waiting helicopter.

"It's not too windy at the base, so we're good to fly in," he says over the whine of the engine.

The sun has just set, and the sky is a brilliant palette of crimson and orange. I'm appreciating the colors when Anna grabs me by the arm and pulls me toward the helicopter.

Out of earshot of Martinez and under the rush of the whirling blades, she whispers to me, "If this is what I think it's about, you're in for a real ride."

We climb inside the helicopter and I take the opposite window seat from Anna with Trevor between us, looking somewhat nervous. I take it he's not a fan of helicopters or once had a bad experience in one.

You haven't flown until you've taken to the air in a third-world country on board a craft with visible rust and a pilot who keeps the manual in his lap. Fortunately, our pilot seems to know what he's doing, and the helicopter looks brand new.

We head south and are soon flying over the desert, which is fading into long shadows as the glow of the setting sun begins to fade. Headlights from cars and pools of lights around homes become sparser and sparser.

Mountain ranges loom on either side, and the landscape begins to look as if humans had never touched it, which is kind of ironic, considering that somewhere on the eastern horizon is the location of the first Clovis archaeological site, which yielded evidence of the earliest known North American culture.

Thirteen thousand years ago, things would have looked a lot different. This region would have been wetter and filled with plant life, not the desert it is now.

Who knows what ancient dwellings and artifacts we're flying over now? In some parts of the desert, all you have to do is throw a rock and start digging. Your spade will hit something important eventually.

Soon, the only light is the illumination of the pilot's dashboard and the occasional flicker of a beacon on a distant antenna. Anna points to the windshield.

A large grid of red and green aircraft warning lights blink on top of what I presume is a field of wind turbines.

"That's the base," says Anna over the helicopter intercom.

"We don't call it that," replies Martinez.

"What is it called?" I ask.

"Field Research Station Alpha."

As we draw closer, a cluster of buildings becomes visible. Most are single story, but there's a large facility with a massive dome in the center.

A parking lot sits near an airstrip and a small hangar. A Gulfstream jet is parked near the open entrance.

Our helicopter begins its vertical descent and comes to a rest on an elevated landing pad that keeps the dust from flying back at us. The pilot powers down, and Martinez motions for us to exit.

"We'll take your bags. We're heading straight to the auditorium," he explains.

"How about a restroom pit stop first?" asks Anna.

Martinez checks his watch. "Fine. But please hurry. This way."

We follow him along a stone path toward the building with the huge dome. The facility is architecturally unusual and looks like it was designed in the 1980s. It reminds me of EPCOT.

The one feature I notice as we head for the main building is that there are absolutely no signs indicating what this place is or what each building is for, other than a number. In this case, the number one.

We enter a reception hall with a high ceiling and a light fixture composed of different planes of colored glass that make it resemble a prism. Eight other people are gathered in the center. I don't recognize any of them.

I follow Martinez's hand gesture to a table, where I have to surrender my phone to a guard and have it sealed inside a bag that's then placed in a locker during the presentation. The guard ushers me into a seat in a short row of chairs facing a small stage with a table and lectern.

It's a strange room. It's completely round, and the ceiling fades into darkness. Sound echoes here in a peculiar way.

It reminds me of a James Bond villain's conference room. I check the floor below me for a trapdoor just in case I say the wrong thing and find myself dropped into a shark tank.

A tall woman dressed in a white blazer and pants walks to the center of the stage and smiles at us. She looks like she's in her late fifties; I suspect she's older but extremely fit.

"Good evening, everyone. For those of you who don't know me, my name is Fiona Joss. I'm director of this research station. Lights, please."

The entire auditorium goes pitch-black. Not even an exit sign. Pure darkness.

"Get ready for the show," whispers Anna, sitting behind me.

"This all started when our benefactor had a vision," Joss begins.

An instant later, the ceiling is filled with a million stars, and I realize this isn't an auditorium, it's a planetarium.

"He developed a series of algorithms and predictions we call the Theismann Hypothesis. And for nearly two decades, we've been pursuing them, testing them, and trying to find out if it's more than a theory."

The stars above begin to zoom around us, and one grows larger in the center of the dome. We zoom in even closer to a blue speck orbiting the star, and I realize this is our solar system and the speck is Earth.

The dot grows larger and continents become visible until we zoom into New Mexico, literally showing our place in the universe.

As we get closer, I recognize the facility from the air, the only difference being that what I thought were wind turbines aren't wind turbines.

They're radio telescopes.

Joss continues, "Theismann's vision is that to find intelligent life, you have to look for it intelligently. And you all have been brought here today because we think we may have found it."

There's a shush of clothing as half a dozen arms shoot into the air to ask questions.

Joss holds up her hands, a signal for everyone to wait. "Trust me, we'll have plenty of time for questions. And we're going to need more of them. You're here to help us confirm or explain what we think we've observed."

What have I walked into?

A glance behind me shows Anna with a smirk on her face. "I told you it would be interesting."

CHAPTER SEVEN
SIGNAL

After the initial commotion dies down, Joss introduces someone else to the stage—a man who looks a little older and has a bushy beard and a bald head that scream "scientist."

"Hello, everyone, I'm Norman Rood, director of the signal array here at the station. As Fiona said, we'll get to questions, but first let me tell you what we've found so far.

"As a few of you know, Station Alpha has been conducting a search for extraterrestrial signals for over two decades. We've preferred to keep our efforts private to avoid any distraction. Due to the generosity of our benefactor, we haven't had to seek any public or private funding. That, along with the effective management of Fiona, means we've been able to investigate the Theismann Hypothesis to the best of our ability.

"What is the Theismann Hypothesis specifically? It's actually quite simple. Most of you were flown in here and probably observed Santa Fe and Albuquerque. While quite obviously those cities are inhabited by intelligent life, where are the radio transmitters?"

An image of a tall radio tower on the top of a mountain appears behind Rood. He aims a laser pointer at the top. "In places like this."

The slide changes, and an image of a communications satellite in orbit appears. "And out here."

A new slide appears, showing a radio telescope inside a crater on the moon. "Some people have even talked about putting a transmitter and receiver on the moon, or better yet, beyond Earth's orbit.

"Notice a trend? As we become more technologically civilized, we either use smaller transmitters like your cell phones or larger ones that we keep far away because of signal reach and interference.

"Two directions: closer or farther out. Theismann believed the search for extraterrestrial intelligence was fundamentally flawed—no offense to those of you working in that field," he adds.

Another slide appears, showing a list of star names. "Most candidate locations are star systems we think might be hospitable to life. Meanwhile, would anyone care to tell me the population of geosynchronous orbit or Sandia Peak?" He holds up his hand to make a zero with his thumb and first finger.

"Theismann's theory, and one I have subscribed to ever since I met him as a young grad student working on signal processing, is that you have to look for intelligent life in places where intelligent life would want to be found.

"Think lighthouses, not population centers. Locations that have special significance. We build our radio antennas and our churches in places that stand out. The Statue of Liberty isn't in the middle of Manhattan—it's out in the harbor so it's the first thing you see.

"So, for the last several decades, we have been cataloging potential points of interest and looking for signals in places other searchers wouldn't even consider.

"And now, if what we've detected is accurate, and I'm having a hell of a time disproving it, we've found proof of this hypothesis, and more importantly, we may have made contact."

"Fast radio bursts?" shouts a man to my right as he comes to his feet, determined to jump-start the question-and-answer session.

"No, Dr. Sexton," says Rood.

"Pulsars?" asks Sexton.

Rood politely shakes his head. "In a minute. In a minute."

"You can't just throw this out there and not expect questions," Sexton protests.

"Maybe if you sit down and let me continue, some of them will be answered."

Sexton takes a seat but keeps shaking his head. I can't tell if he's excited or thinks this is all one big screwup that he'll be able to disprove by shouting out perspicacious questions.

I'm out of my league when it comes to astrophysics. And Rood doesn't strike me as a crank or someone likely to make simple mistakes. The fact that this whole research operation has been going on for several decades and kept a complete secret is impressive enough and an indication that they take this search seriously.

I don't know how much I subscribe to the so-called Theismann Hypothesis, but it does have a point. We choose candidate stars mainly because of their likelihood of harboring life, but would really intelligent life remain stuck there or feel the need to signal where their home planet is located?

"Other institutes have looked for so-called lighthouse locations, too," says a man sitting behind me and to my left.

"Yes, they have," replies Rood. "I'm about to get to that."

The slide changes, and the dome fills with a view of the night sky and all of its constellations. Rood waves his laser pointer around the Milky Way.

"Where would you look if you weren't fixed on habitable stars? A pulsar? The outer edge of a black hole? Those are possibilities. Of course, the problem is, when we see *this*, we think that's *space*. Whereas the reality is, it's something more like this . . ."

Millions of new points of light fill the sky. "This is just an estimate of the number of rogue planets drifting within a thousand light-years of Earth. Between our sun and Proxima Centauri, there could be dozens of wandering bodies or barely captured objects that are Earth-sized or larger."

Lines fill the dome, displaying trajectories, and the stars start to move. "Our own solar system has made several revolutions around the center of the galaxy since life began on Earth. What would a vastly older civilization make of all this? Where would they place beacons? That's the question we've been asking all these years.

"Then we decided to look in our own backyard and started scanning the outer edges of our solar system. Not for civilizations but for a beacon, meant just for us."

The slide changes and is replaced with the image of a signal flag on a sailboat. "How do you signal your intentions from afar? How do you avoid dangerous missteps? First, you maintain distance; second, you try to make your intentions as clear as possible. This is what a civilized culture would do.

"In the outer edge of our solar system beyond the orbit of Neptune, in an orbit predicted by Theismann, we've received a message. And because of the close proximity, we've been able to talk to it." He takes a dramatic pause. "And it has talked back."

CHAPTER EIGHT
ORBIT

Rood motions for the people with their hands raised to put them back down, then directs our attention to a diagram of the solar system. "Let's first establish the origin point of the signal." He uses his pointer to indicate a region near the orbit of Neptune. "This appears to be the source."

"From Neptune?" asks Sexton.

"No, it's in a region near there. We haven't identified an object or determined its complete orbit yet. We only detected the signal a few weeks ago."

"How do you even know that's the right part of the sky?" asks Sexton. "Have you confirmed the position with other observatories?"

"We've confirmed position with our two sister research stations. We've done an off-axis search and everything else from the textbook as well as a few things that aren't in it," replies Rood.

"Except reach out to other organizations," says a woman sitting to my right.

"We have our own methods of verification before we do that, and we expect you to respect that," Fiona Joss interjects.

Rood nods. "You're here to help us verify this before we reach out to other organizations. We want to double-check everything, and there's the added factor I mentioned—this entity is not only transmitting, it's also receiving. We don't understand what or how, but we want to take this carefully."

"Entity?" scoffs Sexton.

"We're going to let you look at the data and come to your own conclusions. But yes, for the lack of a better word, that's what we're calling it," says Rood.

"An alien?"

"We haven't said that. My suspicion is that it's some kind of intelligent probe and not an actual living system."

Behind me someone whispers, "That would make more sense. Easier to send a machine a thousand light-years than a person."

I have nothing to contribute. I can't imagine what we'll be capable of one hundred years from now, let alone a civilization ten thousand years more advanced than we are. I feel very out of place in this discussion. Maybe if they had an alien body for me to look at . . .

A graph showing a waveform appears behind Rood. "This is the signal. It's in the thirty gigahertz band, which is at the outer edge of what you can pick up on a planet with a thick atmosphere. When we examine the signal, we see these pulses spaced about ten milliseconds apart. The entire burst is eighty-three seconds long. The pulses are either a long or a short burst."

The graph dissolves, showing a long line with tall and short bars. "We examined this data using different methods and found that it fits nicely into a 94-by-94 matrix. This number is interesting for a reason: it's the number of naturally occurring elements. Now, we don't want to read *too* much into that, but that's one of the numbers suggested by the Theismann Hypothesis. He assumed that intelligent life would try to find common understanding with other species using universal facts."

Sexton raises his hand and speaks before being called upon. "How do you know this signal is intelligent?"

"We have our reasons, but if it's not intelligent, can you suggest how a radio signal like this could be emanating from some inanimate object?" Rood asks.

"A chunk of iron ore in a planetary magnetic field; ionizing gas from the surface of a comet; a piezoelectric effect from an icy mass of gravel," replies Sexton.

"We'll give you the opportunity to examine the data for yourself. All of those are considerations, but it's the signal itself that's significant. Allow me to show you," says Rood.

The image of the mystery signal changes to a graph as the values are used to fill up the blocks. Squares begin to fill at random spots until a blocky image appears: it's a map of a solar system with eight planets.

"No love for Pluto," whispers someone.

"This is the position of our solar system at the time of the transmission. The distances aren't correct, but the orbits are accurate," says Rood.

There's a square where Earth would be.

"They use abstraction like we do," replies Anna.

"I don't know how you get to an advanced level of technology without it. Abstraction is essentially a form of compression. If you can't compress information, it's hard to do anything useful," offers someone next to her.

"Symbolic representation," says someone else.

"Yes, but even symbolic systems start as abstractions. The letters and numbers we use once had pictographic meaning," Anna replies.

Rood lets us stare at the image, trying to make sense of it. I glance around the audience trying to make sense of them. I'm not in a position to say if it's real or fake, but the room has definitely taken a turn for the serious.

Even Anna, who was taking everything lightly, is leaning forward, scrutinizing the image, seemingly trying to grasp what it all means.

"This signal was followed by another one ninety-four epochs later . . . an epoch being the unit of time it took them to transmit an image like this. Approximately six minutes per epoch. We don't know if that has special significance to them or not. Most people today have no idea why a second is a second or why electrical outlets have one hundred and twenty volts," says Rood.

An image appears of a different solar system. This one has eleven planets and a square in the fourth position.

"We think this is where the probe came from," explains Rood as the two diagrams appear side by side. "This could be their way of saying hello."

"You've made a lot of assumptions," says Sexton. "What makes you so sure this isn't a hoax or some terrestrial signal?"

"We've pinpointed the part of the sky where it came from. We're fairly certain of that. As far as it being a hoax or something else we haven't thought about, that's why you're here. It's also why we ask you to please keep this a secret until we've had a chance to confirm this."

"Did you say you tried contacting it?" asks a woman behind me.

"Yes," says Rood. "We transmitted a pair of images to the probe."

"What gives you that right?" the woman demands.

Fiona Joss stands. "What gives you the right to ask us that question, Dr. Kelstrom? What gives any thinking creature the right to have a dialogue with another?"

"This should be a global decision," says Dr. Kelstrom.

"And how good is the world at making decisions? Should the Taliban have a say in the message? Should we wait for the president of China to engage with them?" Joss fires back.

"What was the message you sent?" asks Sexton.

"First, we sent a single 94-by-94-pixel image," says Rood.

An image appears of a spiral galaxy with a box where our solar system lies at an outer edge.

"They responded with this." Rood points to a new image that shows a different box a small distance away from ours in the same spiral galaxy. "By our estimate, it's about nine hundred light-years away. We have about three hundred candidate stars in that region."

"Has there been any other contact?" asks Sexton.

"Yes. One message," replies Rood.

"What was it?"

"We sent them more data. They responded with this image," he explains.

An image of our solar system appears. Some of the planets appear to be in slightly different positions from before.

"We believe this shows our solar system twelve days from when we sent the data. I think they were telling us to wait," he says.

"Wait for what?" asks Dr. Kelstrom.

"We gave them a lot of data. Basically, we sent them an entire encyclopedia—one we've prepared for a situation like this. It's a primer to help us understand one another," Rood explains.

"I helped work on that," Anna whispers to me.

"Did you know about all this?" I ask.

"Hell no. I thought it was a joke."

"Are you laughing now?"

"I don't know *what* to do."

The very vocal Sexton speaks up. "When did you send this?"

"Ten days ago. We're expecting a response tomorrow or the day after," replies Joss.

Well, that's certainly suspenseful. No matter what anyone in this room believes right now, I don't think they'll be getting any sleep for the next several days.

CHAPTER NINE
RESPONSE TEAM

I'm sitting at an outdoor fire pit near the visitors' apartments at the research station. Anna Kosinski, Glen Sexton, Riley Kelstrom, Trevor Barker, and a few others I've only just met are drinking and taking in the warmth of the fire as we try to make sense of what we'd heard an hour ago.

Norman Rood is also with us, patiently answering questions as we come up with them. I watched him and Sexton engage for a half hour of technical talk. Half the time, Rood answered Sexton's questions with, *I'll let you check the data and examine the equipment.*

Rood is convinced. He seems to be enjoying the moment but also doesn't strike me as the type of person to make any kind of announcement without being absolutely certain, let alone about something this momentous.

"Errant space probe?" asks Sexton, still thinking up explanations.

"You can check the deep-sky database for yourself. Then you can find out why it's talking to us like this," says Rood.

Sexton shakes his head. "It's just—"

"You don't need to tell me, Glen," Rood says gently. "I want a practical explanation almost as much as I want this to be true."

"When do you plan on notifying the other institutions?" asks Riley.

"After you have had time to confirm or debunk this," says Rood. "Joss wanted to make an announcement, but I begged her to hold off. Once we tell one of them, everyone will know."

"And you can't control this anymore," Riley points out.

"It's not that, not at all. I'm excited but cautious. Our reputation hangs on this. That's why we've trusted you to keep it quiet while you help us investigate it."

"And if one of us talks?" asks Riley.

"Joss will put you on the first van out of here. That's not a fun ride. You'd also miss out on the excitement, not to mention contributing to the paper."

There's an interesting angle—bribing academics with the potential of having their name on the most important research paper of all time.

"Why do you think it's a probe?" asks Trevor.

"It would need to have been there for a long time and probably took forever to get there," says Rood.

"I can only imagine the power source that could last that long," replies Sexton.

Rood nods at me. "Dr. Cray, I expected you to have the most questions. You haven't asked any."

"I can't think of anything more intelligent than the ones already being thrown at you. I'm more curious about what they have to say," I reply with all sincerity.

"Come on, Theo. Do you buy any of this?" asks Anna, prodding me.

"I believe there's a nonzero chance this could be true, but I have no reason to accept anything at this point."

"Interesting. What would convince you?" asks Rood.

I get the impression that he wants to convince me more than anyone else.

"I'll need to think about that. But understand, from my point of view, I've never met any of you before today. For all I know you could all be actors and this is one giant practical joke," I reply.

"All for your benefit?" says Rood.

"Certainly not for my benefit. But if you asked me which was more likely, we just received a postcard from an alien civilization or someone is having a bit of fun, I'd go for the latter over the former."

"So, no opinion?" asks Trevor.

"Why does everyone feel the need to have an opinion about everything? 'I don't know' is a perfectly respectful position from where I'm sitting."

"It was too much for me at first, too," says Rood.

"I don't know that it's too much," I say. "I believe in the possibility of extraterrestrial life. I believe that it could become highly advanced. I believe that there could be millions of advanced civilizations, and one or more of them could send out probes to find others.

"None of that bothers me on an existential level. I also believe that tyrannosaurs once ran across the plains beyond where your radio telescopes now stand. But I don't believe one is waiting inside my room. It's not impossible, just highly unlikely. Though I put the odds of *T. rex* slightly higher than this probe. No offense to the efforts you've made."

"None taken," Rood responds with a knowing smile.

At first, I thought he was completely convinced. Now I suspect he's waiting for me or Sexton to sign off on this so he can finally accept what he wants to be true.

"Okay, let's pretend it's real. Then what?" asks Anna.

"We have to notify the other institutions," says Riley.

Sexton turns to Dr. Kelstrom. "Do we?"

"It's the responsible thing to do."

"Is it?" replies Sexton. "I'd put it differently than Joss, but her point still stands. It's one thing if we only detected a signal that had been making its way across the galaxy. This is different. Rood says they've talked to it. Do we let everyone with a transmitter blast it with questions?"

"I don't think we should be the ones to decide," Riley responds, echoing what she'd said earlier.

"And who are the adults in the room going to be? The head of NSF? The NSA? The president of the United States? Are you serious?" Anna says with a laugh.

"I'm not comfortable with a private institution having this much control over what could be the most important event in human history," says Riley.

"Right . . . and politicians would be a better choice?" asks Sexton.

"I didn't say politicians. I mean scientists," she replies.

"Scientists like us," offers Anna.

"Well, no . . ."

"Scientists selected by politicians?" counters Sexton.

I feel a bit sorry for Riley as she's being ganged up on, albeit in a collegial manner. Science is, in theory, about sharing discoveries. But what about a discovery where one bad actor could ruin everything?

What happens if our president decides to ask the alien probe its position on abortion or to take sides in a trade war?

I don't think anyone is really bothered by the notion of aliens or first contact; it's the idea that an advanced civilization might say something we don't agree with. What if they say sexism is totally fine or the secret to a successful culture is in sacrificing your elderly as they become a burden? What if they tell us social media is rotting our brains and will bring about the downfall of our civilization?

People would riot. Facebook would start building space battleships.

A dusty old message of goodwill that takes an eternity to respond to isn't frightening. But an alien entity in our backyard that we can start a text chat with—and all the potential miscommunications that go along with that—is terrifying.

Assuming any of this is true . . . which I put much closer to zero in my nonzero response than I'd let on. Rood wanted to know why I didn't have questions. Actually, I have plenty, but not the kind he could or would answer.

My questions involve making observations and seeing how people behave. I also have one huge question that I keep thinking about: Assuming this is all a hoax, who is perpetrating it, and what's their angle?

CHAPTER TEN

ARRAY

I'm standing on a platform overlooking the sixteen radio telescopes that make up Research Station Alpha's array. I'm told that there're two more like this, one in Argentina, the other in Australia. Kaz Patel, the engineer in charge of the array, has been explaining it to me as we tour the facility.

I understand the physics and the basics of radio astronomy, but Glen Sexton has a much deeper knowledge and is asking most of the questions. He's also been to the station before and taken this tour.

Occasionally I ask about the signal processing and diagnostic tests they use to check their equipment, but mainly I keep silent and observe.

Radio astronomy is a fascinating field to me. Some of the biggest discoveries were right in front of us. The "noise" we hear between AM radio stations can be anything from a hair dryer in the next room, to lightning bursts somewhere in the world, to sources from space, including our own sun.

In 1932, a physicist and radio engineer named Karl Guthe Jansky built a large rotating antenna system to try to locate the source of interference with radiotelephones. Aside from lightning strikes and power lines, he noticed another signal that appeared at the same time every twenty-three hours and fifty-six minutes—the length of time it takes a celestial object to return to the same part of the sky.

He realized he was listening to radio noise from the center of the Milky Way. Thirty years later, a Bell Labs antenna would detect the cosmic background radiation predicted to have been left behind after the big bang.

A radio telescope is kind of the inverse of the microscope in my lab. Whereas I want the precision to observe individual cell functions, radio telescopes can observe the entire known universe.

Arrays like the one we're standing in use a group of radio telescopes to act as a much larger one. By combining the signals they receive, it allows you to see farther and in much greater detail.

As we look over the field of antennas pointed at the same part of the sky like Labrador retrievers fixated on a bird, I ask Patel why I'd never heard of this facility.

Patel leans on a railing. "Because that's the way Theismann wanted it. We had to sign secrecy agreements to work here, and technically this is a radio-transmitter testing lab. We do some work for the government, which makes it easy to explain why we're trying to be so anonymous.

"Mostly we're left alone, but we get the occasional flyover or a small airplane with Chinese or Russian tourists holding cameras with huge lenses. Carly Nicholson, our head of computer engineering, will tell you about the almost daily intrusion attempts we have on our network."

"But why the secrecy?" I ask. "Paul Allen didn't hide the fact he was financing a good part of the search for extraterrestrial intelligence." The late Microsoft cofounder was one of the world's most generous benefactors in the search for life in space.

"Theismann is from a different time. He began all this in the 1980s when he was still working his wonders on Wall Street. I don't think he wanted his fund investors knowing he was a UFO nut," says Sexton.

"Theismann is anything but a nut," replies Patel with the same reverence I've seen other staffers refer to him.

"My point stands. It's different now with the world's richest man building rockets to Mars and getting into Twitter spats," says Sexton.

"But we *do* work with other organizations on a quieter level. Most of the people invited here have been to conferences we've arranged and visited this facility," replies Patel.

Sexton nods. "Under an NDA the size of a phone book. But the per diems are amazing."

"I'm going to check on a transformer at the north end. I keep finding bird's nests full of fishing line. Who fishes out here?" asks Patel as he heads back down the ladder, leaving Sexton and me alone.

"You're the quiet, deep-thinker type," says Sexton.

"It's a lot to process, wouldn't you say?"

Sexton throws up his hands and shrugs. "I'm curious to see the signal processing and check the data from the other stations, but I don't know what to make of it all. It's both over- and underwhelming at the same time. In movies, first contact is supposed to be a lot more profound. We got a postcard. A low-res one, at that."

"You ever read Lewis and Clark's accounts of their expedition?" I ask.

"Not since I was a kid."

"What was interesting to me was the farther they went into the West and away from the Native American tribes they were familiar with, the harder it became to communicate. Even their own Indian guides were often baffled at the languages and dialects they encountered."

Sexton nods for me to continue.

"A simple message doesn't surprise me. I'd be even more suspicious if it was something complex. That and the fact that they say this probe is talking back to them. It actually seems logical to me. Which worries me, to an extent."

"How is that?" asks Sexton.

"I have a hard time believing in aliens that are behaving in the way I believe aliens would behave . . . I would think they'd be more . . . alien."

"Maybe it's a symptom of a really advanced civilization—like how downtown Tokyo looks a lot like London or New York City?"

"Maybe." The huge globe of the main facility is visible in the distance, along with the rest of the campus. "Theismann sure went through a lot of effort."

"His people are top-notch. He pays them above and beyond what they could get in the private world, way more than in academia. They've sent me an offer letter more than once."

"Why did you turn it down? You don't like the desert?" I ask.

"They've got another facility in Virginia where they do computation. It wasn't that. I like to talk about what I find . . . with everyone. If I wanted all the cloak-and-dagger, I'd be working for the NRO or some other agency."

"So, what's next?" I ask.

"I want to check the data, make sure it's coming from where they say it is. Ideally, I'd like to get a friend at a separate array to independently verify the point of origin," replies Sexton.

"I don't know if they're going to go for that."

"Without that, there's no sign-off for me. But there are a few other private arrays that do government research. I think I can talk Joss into working out an arrangement with one. They'll keep their mouths shut. This is the kind of thing they do."

"Look for aliens?" I ask.

"No. Spy on Russian and Chinese satellites. We don't just let them sit up there without trying to figure out what they're doing."

"And what happens if they say the signal is coming from where Rood and the others say it is?"

Sexton sighs. "Then it's out of my hands. It's up to Anna and the others—and you—to figure what it's doing here."

CHAPTER ELEVEN
EXTRAORDINARY PROOF

Glen Sexton is holding the telephone receiver to his ear while he types away on a computer. The phone, like every other phone at the station, is a landline. Our cell phones are useless when the Wi-Fi is shut down because there isn't a cell tower for a hundred miles.

This makes keeping everything secret a lot easier, but I don't think anyone in our group is about to break the embargo. Even Riley, who has protested the secrecy, seems to understand that we should have our chance to verify the results before contacting other institutions.

Sexton is bobbing his head up and down as he listens to the voice at the other end, the director of Sierra Sky Watch, a private radio telescope facility in Utah that has been given the coordinates of our signal.

Joss didn't take too much convincing; she even said she'd considered using the Utah company before. Sexton's assurance that they'd treat it with complete secrecy and his personal trust in the director was enough to persuade her.

Rood was open to the idea from the get-go. He understands there's only so much we can accept at face value without outside confirmation.

Their openness to outside confirmation makes sense: there could be a thousand other explanations for the signal if there's no independent evidence. The transmission could be something as simple as an old test routine that somehow is sending information into their signal processor.

On a more sinister level, they could have been hacked.

I followed Sexton from telescope to telescope as he physically inspected them to see if there was a small transmitter or some other device that was creating the signal.

Although he was satisfied there wasn't, I'm not convinced there couldn't be something wired into the underground cabling that would be almost impossible to find. The entire array could be hacked.

When I voiced my concern to the others, it elevated their interest in having Sierra Sky Watch confirm the signal.

We've reached the window during which the next transmission is supposed to arrive. It takes light approximately four hours and thirty minutes to make its way from Neptune to Earth, so there's some fuzziness about when exactly the signal will reach us.

The fact that it only takes eight minutes for light to reach the Earth from the sun gives you some idea how far away Neptune is from us. Our nearest stellar neighbor, Proxima Centauri, is about eight thousand times that distance. Which either sounds like a lot or a little, depending on how big the universe feels to you.

While Sexton is at his station waiting for the signal, the staff of the facility are all at their workstations, checking their systems to make sure everything is ready. I'm sitting in a row of chairs with the other members of the team, watching the bustle.

We were quite chatty until the clock started getting closer to the window. Now nobody has anything to say, nor do they dare walk away to the bathroom or kitchen for fear of not being here when what could be one of the most important moments in history takes place.

Who wants to tell their grandchildren they were getting a Fresca when we started talking to aliens?

Deep down, I don't believe we'll be talking to aliens or that Joss and her team have actually made contact, but I can get carried away by the thought from time to time.

Carl Sagan's famous quote, "Extraordinary claims require extraordinary evidence," echoes in the back of my mind.

It's a perfectly logical point of view, although I've heard softer-minded people object to it, insisting that unusual claims, paranormal or otherwise, should have the same threshold of proof as anything else.

But they miss the point. If a claim is extraordinary, it's because there's overwhelming evidence that says it isn't likely to be true. Sagan wasn't saying we shouldn't accept unusual claims simply because they were out there; he was saying that they were extraordinary because they contradict existing evidence.

You shouldn't believe someone is a reincarnated Egyptian pharaoh based upon their word alone. You'd need way more evidence than them parroting information found in a history book.

It's fascinating to me the number of people that will take something like this as proof. In claims of reincarnation, you'll see phrases like "this person couldn't have known about that" or some other rationalization that the information didn't come from a public library or a TV documentary. Claims aren't proof until proven. How about telling us where the pharaoh's gold is buried? *That* would confirm your story.

As I wait for the signal, I try to think of what extraordinary evidence I'm going to need to believe there's something to this claim. There has to be something; otherwise I'm not a skeptic, I'm a dogmatist who refuses to change my worldview.

Belief isn't zero or one for me. I think in terms of probability. I'll never have enough information to say something is absolutely one way or the other, but I can be persuaded that something is vastly more likely to be true than not.

I put clothes on every morning because I think it's likely the weather will call for it and I know that society didn't convene while I was sleeping to make clothing optional. I'm not one hundred percent convinced, but enough so that it seems a reasonable way to function.

I try to make a mental checklist of what I'll need to be convinced this is likely to be true. Then I realize I need a flowchart instead.

No single person in this room can convince me. Sexton understands radio telescopes and the physics, but he doesn't get that this system could be hacked or vulnerable to some other exploit. The others can weigh in on their expertise, but each of us has our blind spots.

In theory, all of us working together should compensate for each other's blind spots and come to a general consensus—assuming we have good data to work with. So far, the only data we have is what the researchers at this station have provided us.

Even if their intentions are genuine, it's a lot to ask. If they have a motive to deceive us, well . . . that makes things even more complicated.

"We're getting signal!" shouts Rood as he observes a readout on his monitor.

A waveform appears on a large screen behind the workstations. Lines shoot up for every pulse. Somewhere, a speaker makes a staccato sound.

We all stare at the waveform as if it'll reveal its secrets to us without any kind of signal processing.

"What about Sierra?" asks Rood over his shoulder to Glen.

Glen nods his head excitedly. "They have signal! Same location! They're going off-axis to confirm."

This means they're momentarily turning their radio telescope away to make sure they have the right point of origin.

"Confirmed!" he shouts.

"Confirmed they have signal off-axis?" asks a confused Rood. This would mean the signal is coming from somewhere closer.

"No! Sorry. No signal off-axis. It returned when they fixed on the point of origin," says Sexton.

"Jesus, Glen," replies Rood, who clearly feared he'd made some huge mistake.

"Let me talk to them," says Joss as she walks over to Sexton.

The waveform vanishes and the sound ends abruptly. We all turn to Carly Nicholson, the head of computing and the person responsible for the processing algorithms.

"This will take a little while. It's very different than before," she explains.

Joss hangs up the phone and addresses us all. "Let's let them do their work while we move to the cafeteria."

Reluctantly, we move to the spacious hall and grab cups of coffee to make us even more anxious as we sit around a table trying to make sense of it all.

"Penny for your thoughts," says Joss, sitting across from me.

She has a charismatic presence, but I can't get a true sense of her the way Jessica would. At the moment, though, Joss is dedicating all her brain power to reading me.

"It's a lot to take in," I tell her.

"How does the confirmation of the probe from the Sierra group change things?" she asks.

"Signal," I reply.

"Signal?"

"They confirmed a signal. Not a probe. We don't know what it is. Maybe we know where it's coming from, but that still doesn't tell us *what*."

"I'd be curious to know what you think could be at the outer edge of our solar system sending us this information," she asks. "Maybe NASA or Roscosmos playing a prank with some secret spacecraft they managed to launch without anyone noticing?"

She's still acting friendly, but there's an edge to her voice. The subtext is, *What more proof do you need?*

Sexton comes running into the cafeteria. "I just spoke to Sierra Sky Watch again. They won't explain how, but they picked up another signal!"

"What?" asks Joss.

"Same bandwidth, only it was directed *at the probe* . . . from Earth. At the same instant the probe stopped."

"Is someone else talking to them?" asks Rood, who I now notice has been sitting at a far table.

"That's where it gets weird. Follow me!" says Sexton as he rushes back to the control room.

Overhead on a screen is a large map of what looks like a jungle. Glen points to a crosshair at the center. "Somewhere around here."

"There's nothing there," says Rood.

"That's what's weird about it," says Sexton. "This is in Guatemala."

"And they're certain?" asks Joss.

"This is what they do. If they say a signal came from here, then I don't doubt it."

"Who's talking to our probe?" demands Rood.

"*What* is talking to it?" asks Trevor.

Rood turns to the archaeologist. "You know the region?"

"Some of it. That's deep jungle. There are a lot . . ." His voice trails off.

"A lot of what?" asks Rood.

"Ruins. Unexplored ruins."

I overhear Joss whispering to Rood: "That's in the Theismann Hypothesis, too."

CHAPTER TWELVE
FIELD TRIP

Joss sends us all back to the apartments while her team works on the message and plans next steps. Our group gathers back at the fire pit to discuss things, but I'm feeling restless and start walking around the campus.

There's a single-story building next to the main hall, and I use my ID badge to see if it will let me in. The panel turns green and the door unlocks.

Inside, it looks like all the modern faculty buildings I've visited and worked in. Rows of wooden doors with name plaques and bulletin boards with notices about picnics and other events.

Most of the staff live in a small town about forty miles away. Some live on the base, and there's another set of apartments nearby for the full-timers.

The building appears to be empty, which makes sense with all the excitement in the control room. I walk by Rood's office and see a messy desk covered with papers—about what I expect.

The titles on the plaques are interesting. There are astronomers, linguists, mathematicians, and physicists all grouped in one building.

I recognize all the names as belonging to on-site scientists and staffers except for one: David Ikeda, head of computational biology.

I vaguely remember his name from some research papers a while ago dealing with rates of genetic mutation and population growth. He'd be an interesting guy to have on a project like this. If anyone could answer the question of the probability of life in the universe, it'd be him.

Intelligent life may not simply be a product of time and environment; other factors like the rate of DNA mutation from the host star and other nearby cosmic objects could drive adaptation.

If our atmosphere had been a little bit thicker and blocked a few percentage points more of alpha particles, life may have taken longer to become multicellular, and the dominant species now might have been giant clams.

A few more particles? Velociraptors could have been building colonies on Mars by the time the asteroid hit.

Nature is weird like that. Rock strata show gradual environmental changes over time, accelerated occasionally by a volcanic eruption or meteor strike. Similarly, evolution tends to be a long, slow process. But external factors—like stars going supernova or our sun spitting out a solar flare—can suddenly change the pace of things.

Thinking about this, I realize that, strictly speaking, the first radio telescope wasn't built in 1932. It was the telegraph system that in 1859 got struck by the Carrington Event, a powerful geomagnetic storm caused by the sun. The sky lit up so brightly in some parts of the world that people thought night had turned to daylight. We didn't fully understand what was going on at the time, but all those telegraph wires strung up on wooden poles across the US and Europe acted as antennas and absorbed a huge amount of energy, frying electrical equipment and electrocuting telegraph operators.

Nature is weird and unpredictable. I'd love to talk to Dr. Ikeda about all this.

I peer inside the window to see if he's at his desk, but it's empty. A cardboard box stands alone, and the rest of the office looks like it's been cleaned out.

Did he leave the facility? I'll have to ask.

I make my way out of the building and head across the parking lot back to the apartments. I stop when I see everyone hurrying to the control center.

"What's going on?" I ask Anna.

"They've got a message!" she says, urging me along with the others to the control center, where we take up our seats from before.

Joss stands near the midpoint of the table, hands folded. "Before we begin, I want to explain what was in the primer we sent to the probe. To give you some context." When everyone settles down, she continues. "Part of the Theismann Hypothesis is that any sufficiently advanced species we encounter should also have an understanding of information theory on par or superior to our own. The same applies to computation and signal processing. Look around the room: we not only have computers, we can handle a variety of signals, from sound to high-energy transmissions, and in a variety of patterns, from images to binary data. So can they.

"So we should in theory be able to provide them with enough context to understand the intent and meaning behind our language. To understand how we perceive the physical world. And presumably to decode our many human languages and communicate back to us intelligibly.

"So, in our primer, we simply included a vast array of images and illustrations, along with text and their phonetic counterparts. Structured the same way you'd teach any newcomer to a foreign world."

If nothing else, Theismann was considerably ahead of his time. This is the same way you'd teach a deep neural network in artificial intelligence. Whether a brain is made of protein or silicon, some rules are generalized when it comes to information theory.

Joss presses a button on a keyboard. "Along with the primer, this is the message we sent."

The words appear on the screen behind her.

Hello from Field Research Station Alpha on Earth

"It's a simple message, but we thought it would be a polite one to start with," explains Joss.

"Did they understand it?" asks Anna.

"I think so. I'll let you decide for yourself. This is what we just received."

> Hello Field Research Station Alpha. It's nice to meet
> you. My name is Seeker 453,212. I am a machine.
> My makers sent me to find others.

"Pretty loquacious," Trevor observes.

"Our primer was quite comprehensive on language and meaning. Seeker is probably assembling its responses from sentence fragments. Although it's possible it already understood by listening to our radio transmissions," she adds.

"Like you said," I suddenly chime in, "they have vastly superior computation to ours. If you processed sound and video being broadcast from Earth for any amount of time, you'd learn a lot."

Rood nods. "Yes. We actually did some research on that."

"Was that David Ikeda?" I ask.

He nods again. "Yes."

"I'd be curious to hear what he has to say about this."

Rood sighs. "Us too. Unfortunately, David passed away."

"And he is missed," says Joss, "but he'd be proud to see his work finally coming to fruition."

"What does Seeker mean by 'others'?" asks Riley. She has her arms folded and seems agitated. "And why did you say this message was from Field Research Station Alpha and not everyone on Earth?"

"Because it was from us and not the entire planet. We already covered this. We believe in complete objective honesty." Rood slides his chair around from his console to address us all. "What we need to focus on is how we're going to respond to Seeker. What are we going to ask it? What's its purpose? Is it just here to collect data, or is it the initial step in first contact?"

"Or is it a neutron bomb set to go off when it decides it doesn't like our religious views," Sexton puts in.

"I put that possibility at zero," snaps Joss. "If it had harmful intent, we would have known by now."

"Would we?" asks Trevor. "The Jesuits came to the Americas offering peace and eternal salvation. A few generations later, entire cultures were wiped out. And how resilient *are* we, really, to a much more advanced civilization?"

It's easy to dismiss the impact when you're the culture doing the vanquishing. On the other hand, human history shows a persistent tendency for pluralistic cultures to exist—even in places devastated by past colonization. In the long term, neither identity nor culture is fixed. Despite difficulty and risk, humans tend toward social networks, bigger cities, environments where it's easy to come in contact with new ideas.

Assuming for a moment that Seeker is real, that could be its actual purpose—not as an emissary but a probe to see what interesting ideas we have.

"Dr. Kelstrom," Joss says to Riley, using her honorific, "I want you and Dr. Kosinski to make some suggestions about how we should respond, and how to learn its purpose. Dr. Sexton, I invite you to go through our computer systems and make a full audit."

"What about the thermal images from Guatemala?" asks Trevor.

This is the first I've heard of this. "What thermal images?"

Trevor turns to me. "I was able to get a satellite company to do a survey of the area with a precision camera. There's something down there where the signal came from."

"Something?" I ask.

"Could be a structure, a ruin. I don't know. There's a logging road about a kilometer from the site. I want to see it firsthand."

"I don't know if that's a priority right now," says Joss.

"It seems like a priority to me," Rood interjects. "I think Trevor should go."

Joss hesitates. "I don't know . . ."

"Fiona, come on. This is straight out of the Theismann Hypothesis. It was the part I was most skeptical about, but here we are," says Rood.

"Which part is that?" asks Sexton.

"If you have an advanced-enough civilization, they might send multiple probes. We use satellites, drones, and buoys to monitor various spaces . . . why would they be any different? Theismann suggested that we look on Earth for evidence of that." He holds up his hands. "Now I *don't* mean to imply that we're after buried spaceships. None of that bullshit. We're looking for things like craters, impact sites, natural antennas."

"Natural antennas?" asks Sexton.

"If you were an alien civilization and you wanted to send signals back to your home planet without any of the advanced beings on the host planet knowing, you might do it with coordinated lightning strikes. It would seem just like sferics to us—atmospheric electrical activity," explains Rood.

"So, a spy probe?" says Sexton.

"Not exactly. It could be from before there were people here. Maybe it was meant to capture ecological data."

"Or harvest DNA," says Trevor. "If something *is* transmitting back to the probe, we need to know what it is."

Trevor is normally reserved, but he's forceful in this matter. And for good reason. They just dangled the possibility of evidence for alien contact in a region that an archaeologist like him would already have a keen interest in and a fair bit of knowledge about.

"All right. We'll send Trevor down there," Joss concedes at last.

"Dr. Cray, too," says Trevor. "He has more field experience than anyone. If this thing is a machine or biological, I can't think of any person I'd rather have there."

"We need Dr. Cray here to help Sexton do the audit," says Joss.

"I think I'm good," says Sexton. "And with Sierra Sky corroborating the signal, it's only gonna be so useful. I am interested in the earth-bound signal in Guatemala, though . . ."

"Okay, Cray and Trevor it is," Joss says with finality, putting a stop to things before the entire group demands to go.

Great, I'm going to the jungle. Last time I was in a rain forest, people died. A lot of them. Some of them because of me. Let's hope this plays out differently.

I couldn't tell if Joss's reluctance was sincere or an act. What I do know is that as more parts of the Theismann Hypothesis are confirmed, I feel like I'm witnessing a huge show with multiple acts . . . but I don't know for whose benefit.

Part Two
Detective

CHAPTER THIRTEEN
THE TREE MAN

It's my second night of walking through this forest outside Lynchburg, Virginia, searching for the "Tree Man." So far, I'm zero for two in finding this elusive entity.

What started out as an internet meme in the surrounding area got deadly serious when two teenage girls went missing after trying to find him. They reportedly left their houses in the wee hours of the night, specifically 2:22 a.m.—the time when he's supposed to be visible—and never came home.

Searchers found a sneaker belonging to one of the girls and bloody handprints that were a DNA match of the other girl. The handprints led to a small clearing where even more blood was found collected in glass jars and cans on the ground.

Part of the Tree Man legend said that if he catches you after dark, he'll "drain you of all your sap." Since the connection between the meme and the missing girls made the news, everyone has been in a tizzy.

Although this is a local matter, I am here on behalf of the FBI with two new agents, Rhonda Parry and Denise Elliott. Rhonda and Denise were two of my better students. Gerald Voigt, my former coworker at the bureau who runs special investigations, decided to send me into the field with them. Ostensibly to give them hands-on experience with my methods, but also, I suspect, to get me out from behind my desk at the academy.

I was not wild about the assignment. I've never liked the spotlight. Well, not since I was young. Unfortunately, chasing serial killers and techno-terrorists brings you the kind of attention you don't want. Hunting down a TikTok meme with a billion views also didn't sound particularly low profile.

Gerald's pitch was basically, *Train them to think like you do and I won't have to send you out there every time something weird happens.*

It wasn't quite a threat. It was more of a compromise. Gerald knows that I've been unhappy at the FBI, but leaving is hard. This was his way of giving me an excuse to move on while knowing that there will be others here to fill the odd void that I occupied.

Denise and Rhonda aren't me. They don't have my background or experience, but they're unique in their own way. Rhonda studied biology before joining the FBI and reminds me a little of Theo—my computational-biologist slash freelance-serial-killer-hunter . . . boyfriend. I guess that's the word.

Denise doesn't have Rhonda's mind for science, but she's highly perceptive of people and social cues. She can sit in the front row of a classroom and tell whose shoe is untied and the reason why two people decided to sit next to each other.

I can see their flashlights in the distance as they walk along a ridge, trying to find the Tree Man. I don't have mine on. I'm walking in the dark, trying to keep as quiet as possible. I'm not stalking them—I'm trying to see if anyone else is stalking them.

Denise and Rhonda are well armed and perfectly capable of handling anything that comes their way. I just hope they don't become startled by me and open fire.

While I don't take the story of the Tree Man all that seriously—after all, the meme began in Australia and surely isn't connected to whatever happened here—I do believe that some of the sightings may have a basis in reality.

Whether that's a mythical man-tree that murders and exsanguinates lost teenagers as an act of revenge for humanity chopping down forests or someone who has taken the story a little too seriously . . . that's beyond me at the moment. What I do know is that Charlene Parnell and Pauline Davey haven't been seen in three days.

The students in their high school and the residents of River Crossing, the suburb of a town where this occurred, have all kinds of stories about what happened. Sorting fact from nonsense is nearly impossible.

The initial suspicion was the girls ran away; then the sneaker and blood were found. Teenagers came forward with all kinds of stories about the mysterious goings-on in the woods, from UFOs to alleged orgies involving the football and wrestling teams—a rumor spread only by members of the baseball team, I should point out.

For most people it's still kind of a joke—River Crossing's moment to stand at the center of a Netflix crime documentary series. The fact that there are four very concerned parents waiting for any positive news is easily lost. The detachment some people have, even people the families knew and grew up with, is shocking to me.

I mentioned this to Denise, and she made a biting comment: *For some people, their sense of value and purpose just went up. They get to say they knew Charlene and Pauline. Every tragedy is something you can use to create content.*

I don't get this generation any more than I understood my own. I don't think they're fame-seeking sociopaths; they're simply so numb to reality that it's hard for them to understand what's wrong and what's right.

When I told Denise and Rhonda my theory, I got blank stares. They're not much older than the missing girls, and they grew up with YouTube and Facebook.

Now, every time I say something to them, I feel like I'm Grandma Jessica barking at the clouds from my rocking chair. I'm not even forty yet. How did I end up feeling so old?

I hear a branch break ahead of me and freeze. My two protégés are still visible on the ridge, the beams of their flashlights moving back and forth.

I wait for the sound while my hand slides to the butt of my pistol, ready to pull it out if needed but not itching to do so.

A moment later I see something move in the shadows and spot the black-and-white tail of a skunk. Okay, this just got serious.

Do I say nothing and hope she moves along, risking the chance of surprising her and getting a face full of stink?

Although the advantage of dating a mad scientist is that if I came home smelling like a skunk, he'd probably just comment on the species and then go back to whatever project he was working on—which could range from some complex computer program to timing how long it takes for his cereal to lose its crispness.

Zzzzzzzzz

My phone is on silent but out here in the woods, the vibration alert sounds like a jackhammer. The fluffy tail of death vanishes and I hold my breath . . .

My nose hasn't been assaulted, so I assume the skunk hasn't left me with a cloud of stink spray.

Zzzzzzzzz

"Hey. You almost got me attacked by a skunk," I whisper into my phone, already knowing it's Theo.

"I'm sure it was for a good reason," he replies. "How is the ghost hunt?"

"The Tree Man isn't a ghost."

"Oh. What is he?"

"We don't know."

"So you haven't ruled out ghost. Hmm," he says in his annoying way of letting you know that he caught you in a logical error.

Theo will fully admit when you catch him in one—which is rare—but he sure as hell doesn't like admitting it.

"We haven't ruled out a unicorn, a goblin, or the zombie of a computational biologist who was mysteriously strangled in the night," I reply.

"Point taken."

"How is it going out there?"

"We're under a strict NDA. So it's more of an honor system. But I don't want to say anything that would violate that agreement."

I feel a nervous tingle on the back of my neck. "I don't want to say anything" is a code phrase Theo and I came up with. It means: *I think someone could be eavesdropping on the conversation.*

"How do I sound?" I ask.

Code translation: *Are you in trouble?*

"I think the connection is fine," he replies.

I'm not worried yet.

"What's the weather like?"

Are you in potential danger?

"The evenings are pleasant. The hosts are very attentive," says Theo.

I doubt it. They're just paranoid.

"What did you have for dinner?" I ask.

Use Cypher to tell me what's going on.

Cypher is a system Theo came up with to encrypt code in natural language. I told him how my family used to perform mind-reading stunts using a secret index. A few days later he showed me an algorithm that could encode or decode sentences that sounded like normal conversation.

You could input something like "I'm being watched by terrorists with a gun to my head" and it would output a list of phrases you could use to get that original message. You just have to select the one that best fits the conversation.

For "I'm being watched by terrorists with a gun to my head," the shortest phrase was, "Did I drop out?"

When I asked Theo how you could compress eleven words down to four, I got a lengthy lecture on how the Shannon limit didn't apply to indexes that were sorted from small to large based upon a preset prioritization. Obviously.

"The views are amazing. I wish I brought my camera to take photos," says Theo.

Okay, that's a long one. I type it into our Cypher application.

I squint at the translation and my eyebrows go up: *They say they've detected an alien signal.*

"Did I drop out?" I ask.

Is this real?

"Not to me."

They think so.

What the *hell*?

"Anything you need me to do while you're gone?" I ask. Like call NASA?

"If you feel like it, add to my to-do list. I know you wanted some gardening done," he replies.

I type in his response. The translation reads, *Find out what happened to David Ikeda.*

Who is David Ikeda?

"Will do once I get back from this trip."

Is it urgent?

"That's fine."

Do your thing first.

"Okay, let me know if you need anything else."

Anything else?

"Come to think of it, I could use a new pair of sandals," he says.

I'm going to Guatemala to look for a crashed UFO.

Jesus, Theo.

We end our call, and I decide I need to get to the bottom of this Tree Man nonsense sooner rather than later.

I don't think Theo knows what he's gotten himself into. If these people are anything but one hundred percent honest about what they claim, then my experience tells me that they could be dangerous.

And Theo and jungles is not a good fit. The first time we'd met was when he went Rambo in Burma, chasing down members of a death squad who'd killed members of a medical team vaccinating villagers.

The men who did that did not meet a pleasant end.

Theo is the most compassionate man I've ever met and also one of the most lethal.

One of . . .

Sigh. I have a type.

CHAPTER FOURTEEN
SHADOWS

Rhonda is sitting on the floor controlling the motel room television with her laptop while Denise and I recline on the twin beds, watching the screen. I'd called the search off for the night and had us reconvene at our base camp in the Days Inn. A deputy for the sheriff's department sarcastically referred it to as "the Girl Scout Camp."

Rhonda and Denise laughed it off. All they cared about was results. The other investigators could make their jokes about me and my green rookies, but we were out there in the woods looking for any sign of Charlene Parnell and Pauline Davey while they were sitting at home yelling at their TVs as they watched college football.

The secret of my dubious success, as I've explained it to my trainees, is caring more. It's also why I reached burnout before I hit thirty and have more wounds than a combat vet, but that's another story.

"I made a master cut of all the TikTok and Instagram videos the girls made over the last six months. That way we can watch it and see if we notice anything," explains Rhonda.

We'd seen dozens of videos, but this approach might help us pick up on something more subtle. It's a method I use to look for clues.

Theo and I had an interesting conversation about this when he explained that's basically how unsupervised machine learning works.

You let the machine pick up things instead of giving it a specific goal. This also appears to be how our subconscious can sometimes solve problems.

The two girls are both pretty. Charlene is a redhead with dancer's body, and Pauline has dark, short hair and likes to wear ripped-up T-shirts of bands that were around before I was born. While Charlene appears more preppy, they have a similar dark humor and flirtatious attitude.

The videos are from both of the missing girls' accounts, and the pair frequently appears together doing the kinds of things every other teenager does—making fun of their friends, showing off outfits, dancing—all the things I did privately when I was a teenager. Well, almost all.

I started performing magic when I was a child, and my costumes became more risqué in my teenage years, much to the chagrin of my father. I wouldn't say I did it for attention, but the applause seemed to be louder and the bookings better the more I sold my sexuality.

It didn't make me feel more attractive or valuable to get that kind of attention, but it felt like a way to capitalize on something I didn't quite understand.

I spent a good part of my life embarrassed about my past. I'll never forget the day I walked into an office at the FBI and saw the cover of a magic magazine that looked more like a cover of *Playboy*.

It turns out Robert Ailes, the man who would become my boss, my mentor, and my friend at the bureau, wanted to put my brain to use. He considered my past an asset the FBI wasn't making good use of.

I started to feel less embarrassed about where I came from and proud of the fact that my skills allowed me to help people. I also recognize that everyone has self-doubts. Hopefully, if I can do anything for Rhonda and Denise, it'll be to teach them that the thing they're most afraid of could also be what gives them their strength.

"Okay, what have we learned?" I ask my scouts.

"I don't want to be mean, but these are two of the most narcissistic . . . girls I've ever seen," says Rhonda, probably catching herself before using a slang word that an FBI agent shouldn't use to refer to potential victims. "They make the Kardashians look like nuns on a vow of silence."

"These girls don't like themselves," says Denise. "They're both attractive, but they're desperate for attention. The parents seemed normal, but I suspect they have a messed-up homelife. Charlene Parnell's father seemed like a control freak, and Pauline Davey's mother reminds me of the kind of woman that would flirt with her daughter's boyfriend."

"Gross, but accurate," Rhonda agrees.

"I noticed how she changed her posture when she spoke to you, Jessica. Her spine stiffened, like she was in a beauty contest. And Mr. Parnell did not like talking to us at all. He stared at you a lot . . . I think he has a problem with women," adds Denise.

"So, what effect can that environment have on a child?" I ask.

"Risk taking. There's a reason they were willing to go out into the woods at night. Probably drug use. They'd be intrigued by men other girls would consider dangerous," replies Denise. "Not a lot of common sense."

That stings.

"This is the last video they uploaded. Their phones went dead an hour later, near where the shoe was found." Rhonda clicks play on her laptop.

Charlene is holding her phone out for a selfie shot with Pauline. They're illuminated by the flashlight on Pauline's phone.

"Okay, guys, this is our third attempt at trying to find this Tree Man for ourselves," Charlene says in the video.

"And maybe we'll drain *his* sap," replies Pauline.

Charlene giggles. "Once you go branch, you never go back."

"Show us the first video from the edge of the forest," Denise tells Rhonda, who scrolls back to the clip.

Charlene and Pauline are sitting in their car in a parking lot near the woods.

"Okay, it's Charlene and Pauline, your two badass-bitch investigators. We're about to go find out what all this Tree Man bullshit is about," says Charlene.

The next cut is of the girls walking through the woods with Charlene talking into the phone, her face barely lit by the screen.

"Okay, it's kind of scary out here, not gonna lie." She looks up. "Pauline?"

"Right behind you," says Pauline as she puts her hand on Charlene's shoulder. "Damn that's bright."

"If I turn it down, you can't see shit," replies Charlene.

"I'm blind now and can't see shit. If I get raped by the Tree Man because I didn't see him coming, it's all your fault."

Charlene laughs. "Do you even listen to yourself?"

"No, that's what I have you for," Pauline fires back.

"You've never had me, bitch."

Pauline grabs Charlene in a bear hug and makes a thrusting gesture. "We'll see who walks out of these woods a virgin."

"I know who didn't walk into these words a virgin," replies Charlene. "Um, no one."

The two laugh and the video ends.

"Everything they do is sexually charged," says Rhonda.

Denise sighs. "Have you ever met a teenager?"

"I know, but these girls seem very—"

"Thirsty?" I ask.

Denise and Rhonda burst out laughing at my use of the word.

"Sorry, Agent Blackwood," says Denise. "It's just when you say it . . ."

I told them long ago that they could use my first name; Denise only uses "Agent Blackwood" when she's trying to avoid getting scolded.

"Yeah, yeah. Anyhow, what do you take away from this?" I ask, gesturing at the laptop screen.

"Every perv in a hundred-mile radius who saw this would suddenly decide they wanted to take up camping in the hopes of meeting these two idiots," says Denise. "I'm sorry. I shouldn't call them that."

"We have to avoid terms like that because then we start to dehumanize them. But I understand," I tell her.

I give my students a full lecture about how prolific serial killers like Lonnie David Franklin Jr. go undetected because they focus on marginalized people from poor backgrounds. Cops and the media have a habit of considering those peoples' deaths and disappearances a cost of doing business.

A poor black woman or a runaway young gay man goes missing and it's a nonevent. Two pretty girls from upper-middle-class families like Charlene and Pauline vanish and it's national news.

Race is part of it, but it's also socioeconomic. We make jokes about dead hookers and barely bat an eye when a homeless person dies a violent death.

As cops, when we care about some people less than others, it makes us not very good at our jobs. We miss things.

Theo doesn't miss a thing. That's how he was able to catch the Grizzly Killer and the Toy Man—serial killers who preyed upon the vulnerable.

I spend an entire week with my students going through his cases and showing how those men could have been caught sooner if we had more empathy for the victims.

Theo has even come into my classes at the academy to talk to my students. While he doesn't consider himself charismatic or a good speaker, you could hear a pin drop as he goes through his thought process and methods. My students can't take their eyes off him as he speaks.

He's otherworldly.

Some people describe him as robotic, but that's not accurate. He reminds me of a clever child constantly having realizations about how the universe works.

I'm afraid one day he's going to notice what a train wreck of a person I am, do some mental calculations, then move on.

What would Theo make of the videos? He might not pick up on what Denise does, but I bet he'd be able to tell us a lot about where it was shot, list what stars were in the sky, and identify every animal in the entire forest by the sound. What else would he notice?

"What's your best theory right now?" I ask.

"I think these girls attracted a bad guy. Some dangerous perv saw this and went after them," says Denise.

"They could have enemies. Maybe somebody they know. A lot of people hated them," replies Rhonda.

"We have profilers helping do background checks on everyone who commented on the videos, and police have been doing interviews with everyone who knew them. So that's being covered. What else? Tell me more about them."

"Like, profile them?" asks Denise.

"Stick to what's obvious. Don't create a just-so hypothesis."

I have a skeptical view of a lot of the profiling that's done, including by the bureau. Some profilers spew nonsense to sound like they've got a deep grip on the human psyche. It's one thing to say that a suspect fits a pattern and describe the facts of the pattern. It's another to go into some unprovable Freudian analysis about how Tuesdays make the suspect feel sad.

"All right, well . . . these girls aren't well liked by their peers," says Rhonda.

"They really want attention," says Denise. "Their audience is mostly strangers. They're playing characters for them. They don't mind looking like thirsty bimbos because they don't care what the people around them think."

"They've hooked up with guys from their school, but none of the girls have had any lasting relationships. The ex-boyfriends didn't raise any red flags," Rhonda adds.

"Just typical high-school jocks. If one of them killed them, I'd expect it would have been sloppy and we'd have found the bodies," says Denise.

"Unless it was more than one," Rhonda puts in.

"Maybe. But I think someone would have talked or given an extra-nervous interview," replies Denise.

"Okay, what are we not seeing? What's happening when they're not making videos?" I ask.

"We talked to their friends. They keep to themselves. We know who they were involved with," says Denise.

"Do we? What if one of them was involved with someone who didn't tell us?" I reply.

"Would any teenage boy who had sex with either one keep his mouth shut about that?" asks Denise.

"What if it's not a teenage boy? What if one of them was having an affair with an older man?" Rhonda speculates.

"Like what if Charlene's father was having sex with Pauline? She might have a daddy issue," says Denise.

"He might kill the two to spare himself the embarrassment of it being found out," Rhonda riffs.

"Maybe," I say, "but we don't have anything to support any of that. And the local police will be looking into that anyway. What else? What are we missing?"

I watch the videos again. The second-to-last one shows the two girls outside their car at the edge of the woods, putting on makeup.

What would Theo see . . . ?

"Go back!" I shout.

Rhonda replays the last thirty seconds as each girl takes turns showing off her Tree Man hunting outfit while the other holds the phone.

"Did you see that?" I ask.

Rhonda freezes the frame. Pauline is at the edge of the screen while Charlene is mugging for the camera, pulling her skirt high to show thigh.

Denise gets close to the television. "Is there someone in the woods?"

"Look closer," I reply.

Rhonda zooms into the video and moves around Charlene's body, then the trees. "I can enhance this a little."

"You don't need to. It's right there," I assure her.

My students stare at the screen, trying to see what I see. I want them to make the connection so it will be stronger. But then I realize now's not the time for a lesson.

"Look at Pauline," I tell them.

"Her eyes flicker off to somewhere beyond the camera," says Denise.

"An approaching car?" asks Rhonda.

"Look again," I implore.

Rhonda zooms in on Pauline. The shadow of the phone crosses her face. Rhonda freezes the video. "Is that from a streetlamp? We have a location, so we should know that."

"Check the location. There's no streetlamp," I reply.

"Then where's the light coming from?" asks Denise.

"Or, more precisely," says Rhonda, "who's holding it?"

CHAPTER FIFTEEN
VOLUNTEER

Charlene's mother greets us at the door. The poor woman looks like she hasn't slept in days. She apologizes for the nonexistent mess in her elegantly decorated home.

Instead of calling, I drove by the house, hoping she or her husband were up this late. Mrs. Parnell was visible through the living room window sitting on the couch and watching a repeat of a news report about her missing child.

My god, how painful must that be?

She has her daughter's cheekbones, and speaking to her is slightly eerie. I've had this happen before when talking to the family of a victim when there's a strong resemblance.

"I'm sorry to bother you, Mrs. Parnell, but I'd like to talk to you and have a look around Charlene's room. If that's okay . . ."

"Of course. Of course. Thank you for working so late. Can I get you some coffee? Ben is asleep, but I can wake him up," she offers.

"That's okay. We just want to talk to you. I know you've already been asked this, but did Charlene or Pauline have any male friends that might not have gone to their school?"

"Like internet friends?" she replies.

"Maybe, but people they'd know personally."

Rhonda and Denise are back at the motel, looking through dating apps to see if either of the girls was using one with a fake name and age. We realized that it's possible they may have been living a secret life, their friends and family unaware.

"I wish I knew. She was pretty secretive about boys. We didn't really talk much about that. Maybe I should have been more proactive," says Mrs. Parnell.

She's going through a guilt trip about what she should have done differently, blaming herself for everything.

"I didn't talk to my parents about that kind of thing, either," I tell her, leaving out the fact that my mother left the scene while I was still young.

Mrs. Parnell stares at me for a moment. "I realize who you are now." She goes pale. "Is it . . . that bad?"

"I'm just here to help. Can you show me her room?" I ask, trying to take her mind off whatever she thinks it means that I'm working the case.

"This way. We left everything as is. The police took most of her clothes and her computer," Mrs. Parnell explains.

Charlene's room is dark, mainly lit by fairy lights over the bed and a neon-style sign that says DREAM. Her desk has textbooks that look never-opened and an empty space where her laptop went. Two coatracks hold scarves and jackets.

There's a Mötley Crüe poster on the wall that could have been bought at Hot Topic a week ago alongside a poster of Post Malone with lipstick on his cheeks.

Teenagers today live in a weird space. Because of YouTube and music streaming, a band from their parents' generation could be equally relevant as the latest teenage pop sensation.

I remember driving by a group of young boys the day before. They were riding their skateboards in a convenience store parking lot, and I couldn't tell what decade they were from by the way they were dressed.

The pants looked just as baggy as when I was that age and the skateboards just as beat up as the one belonging to the skater boys at my school.

The only sign that this was the twenty-first century was that one of them was filming another with his iPhone. But even that could have happened over a decade ago. While technology keeps moving forward, sometimes I feel like time has stopped.

I examine the items on a shelf over Charlene's desk. There's a bulletin board with class schedules, tickets to concerts, and Polaroid photos of her and Pauline.

Polaroids! It's crazy how those have somehow come back in a world of 5K displays and Instagram. I guess there's something about being able to physically hold a photo.

The shots are either of Pauline, Charlene, or abstract images of trees and clouds, with the exception of two images that show a bunch of teenagers crowded into the frame. Below the photos is a jar with pens and a racquetball with a face drawn across it.

I pick up the ball. "Did Charlene play racquetball?"

"Not that I know about," she replies.

I turn the ball over. Written across the other side are the words, "Now cough."

"What does this mean?" I ask.

Mrs. Parnell shakes her head. "I never got Charlene's sense of humor."

So it's a joke? What's the joke?

I stare at the ball.

Cough . . . ?

Wait, I've had male friends joke about this. When they get a physical, they say the doctor squeezes their testicles and tells them to cough.

How is this funny unless you're squeezing the ball? It's a long joke. Maybe a guy friend inked the ball?

No, the handwriting is Charlene's. She's got a sharper sense of humor than that.

It's a situational thing . . .

"What clubs was Charlene in?" I ask.

"She dropped out of everything a few months ago," says Mrs. Parnell.

"Before that?"

"Gosh, they changed all the time. She was in the Red Cross Club for a long time. My mother used to do that. Charlene takes . . . took after her a lot. When Mother died, it hit her hard."

"Do you have her yearbook handy?"

"Yes. One second."

Mrs. Parnell returns with Charlene's sophomore yearbook. There's a slip of paper in the pages that opens to her photo. She has a pretty smile and a slightly impish grin. At fifteen, she already looked more mature than the other girls her age.

I flip to the back of the book and find the index for the different clubs. On page 132 there's a photo of the Red Cross Club. There are twelve of them wearing blue tunics standing next to a good-looking young man in a paramedic uniform who appears to be in his early twenties. Charlene isn't in the picture.

"Charlene wasn't in the club last year," says Mrs. Parnell.

"Who is that?" I ask.

"I don't know."

"Do you know if the police have talked to him?"

She shakes her head. "I have no idea who he is."

"Okay. Mind if I take a photo of this?"

"What's up, boss?" asks Rhonda.

I waited until I was back in my car before calling my team at the motel.

"I need you to check the files for a young man who may have volunteered at the school for the Red Cross Club," I tell her.

"One second."

I can hear her fingers typing at an insane pace.

"Thomas Cameron. The police talked to him yesterday. He stopped volunteering at the school about three months ago," says Rhonda.

Around the same time Charlene dropped out . . .

Coincidence?

"Where did they interview him?" I ask.

"It says at his place of work."

"EMS?"

"No. A supermarket. It doesn't mention anything about that," says Rhonda.

"Check the EMT records. I believe he was licensed."

"One second." Rhonda types away. "He lost his EMT license. It seems he failed a drug test."

"Tell Denise to get ready. We're going to pay him a visit."

"You think he did it?" asks Rhonda excitedly.

"I think he did something."

CHAPTER SIXTEEN
Shut-In

Thomas Cameron answers the door in boxer shorts after Denise and Rhonda knock on it for a minute. It's past 4:00 a.m., but I didn't want to waste any time.

To make sure he answered, I had Denise and Rhonda wear their street clothes and look like normal young women, not FBI agents.

"What's up?" he asks, making a yawning motion without actually yawning.

I step into the doorframe and hold up my badge. "Hello, I'm Agent Blackwood. We could use your help with Charlene and Pauline. Time is really important."

Behind him, a television shows the pause screen for *Call of Duty*. There's a pillow on the couch and a blanket. Beer bottles are on the side table, and the coffee table is filled with empty take-out containers. There's a closed door to his right.

Cameron realizes that he just opened his door to the police and blinks. "Could we talk again in the morning? I already said what I know."

"This is new information about a suspect," I reply.

If Cameron is already a prime suspect, I may be screwing things up. However, if the local police were taking him seriously, they would have tried to interview him at home, not at work. You never know what you might observe or someone might reveal.

"Yeah, sure. I didn't really know the kids that well. But what can I do?"

"Let's go inside. It's cold, and Denise forgot her jacket." I point to Denise, who's wearing only a T-shirt and jeans.

Cameron steps aside as I enter. He doesn't know what to do in this situation, but—importantly—he has given us permission to enter his apartment.

"I've got work in the morning. But what do you need?"

I show him a mug shot on my phone of an older man with a black mustache. "Do you know a Theodore Ronson?"

Cameron thinks, then shakes his head.

Of course he doesn't know him. I made the name up. The photo is of a bank robber in Oregon. For now, I mostly need Cameron to relax.

"Can I see the photo again?" he says, trying to be helpful, then pretends to study the image. "No. Maybe he's come into the store, but I've never seen him."

"Hey, I hate to do this, but I have to take a pee," says Denise. "Is this the bathroom?" she asks, pointing to the closed door.

"That's my roommate's room," says Cameron urgently. "He's sleeping and the toilet is broken. Use that one." He points to a door near the kitchen.

"Thanks. I'm sorry," Denise tells me.

I roll my eyes. "Sorry, Mr. Cameron. We've been chasing down leads since this afternoon. So, when was the last time you spoke to Charlene?"

Cameron blinks as he tries to figure out what to say. "Um, I don't remember. Ages ago."

"Did anyone else in the Red Cross Club know that the two of you were involved?" I pull out the blue racquetball and show it to him like a murder weapon.

"Uh . . . I'm not really sure what you're talking about," he stammers.

"You know, sex."

Cameron is starting to sweat. He looks at Rhonda, expecting her to say something, but she's quiet. She knows how awkward silence makes a guilty conscience try to fill the void with words, even at the risk of self-incrimination.

"I don't like where this is headed," says Cameron. "I think you should go now."

"You can talk to me now or I can put Agents Parry and Elliott outside your door twenty-four seven while I get a search warrant."

He shakes his head. "You're barking up the wrong tree if you think I killed those kids."

"Kids. You say that, but it sounds rehearsed. You mean girls. Like Charlene, the one you were sleeping with. But you have the right to ask us to leave. Just answer one more question and we'll go. Otherwise, I leave my agents outside your door."

Cameron's eyes move around the room as he tries to think of a way out of this.

My phone vibrates with a text message. "One second while you think about that," I tell him.

Denise has texted me several photos from the bathroom, along with a message: This place has been wiped clean! Call forensics? Get a warrant for the rest of the place?

My suspicion has just been confirmed. I have a different idea.

"What's the question?" asks Cameron.

Question? Oh, that was just a bluff to see how he'd react.

I raise my voice. "I don't have a question. I have advice. Come out now before this becomes a kidnapping case."

Denise is standing at the bathroom door, looking confused. But, like Rhonda, she keeps her cool and doesn't say anything.

"Kidnapping?" asks Cameron.

"That's what you'll be charged with when the police come here with a search warrant for that room. Assuming they find who I think is in there." I point at the closed bedroom door.

"That's ridiculous!"

I raise my voice even louder. "Maybe. But that will be the charge and how the media present it. Once they find out what really happened, then it will be worse . . . for *them*."

Cameron stares at the bedroom door but says nothing. The kidnapping charge has paralyzed him.

"Come on out, ladies. I'll even give you the chance to come forward yourselves and have your attorney spin it however you want. Five . . . four . . . three . . ."

I have no idea what happens at "one," but I don't have to figure it out because the bedroom door opens and Pauline and Charlene step into the living room in their pajamas.

"He's not a fucking kidnapper," says Charlene.

"We haven't done anything wrong," adds Pauline.

"No. Draining ten pints of blood from you over several weeks to make it look like you were murdered is a perfectly normal thing to do. I'm sure your parents will understand."

"Yeah, well, you can talk to our lawyer," says Pauline.

I hold out my phone. "How about you call your parents first and tell them you're alive, you dimwits? Then call your lawyer, who I'm sure is a very real person and not someone you just made up."

"Are there reporters out there?" asks Charlene, looking at the door.

"In the world? Yes. In the parking lot, waiting to take your photo? No."

"Damn," says Charlene. "What happened to the ones we saw on the news?"

Jesus. While Charlene's mother was worrying herself to death watching cable television, her sociopath daughter was watching the same program, hoping they used her best Instagram photos.

"Unbelievable," I mutter. "Rhonda, call the sheriff. Cameron, put some clothes on. You don't want to get arrested dressed like that."

"I'm getting arrested?" He seems shocked.

"What did you expect? An invitation to join the Paw Patrol?"

"What about them?" he asks, pointing to Charlene and Pauline.

"They're minors and stupid. It's up to the sheriff to decide how he wants to handle 'em."

Twenty minutes later, I'm standing in the parking lot for the apartment complex as deputies interview the girls inside the apartment and talk to a handcuffed Cameron in a squad car.

"How did you know?" asks Denise.

"The photo of the bathroom. The toilet seat was down, and it looked too clean for a guy like him. And watching those videos, I realized they were putting on a performance. Two crazy girls go into the woods and mysteriously vanish—becoming instant celebrities."

"Yeah, but what was their endgame?" asks Rhonda.

"I don't know if they had one. I don't think they thought this through all the way. The blood seemed clever, but it was a bad touch. It makes it hard to spin that they "got lost." Although they may have some dumb explanation for how they expected it to go down."

"All this to be famous," says Rhonda.

"Don't they know they'll be the bad guys when this gets retold?" asks Denise.

"I don't think they care." I check my watch. "Let's get some sleep, then head back to Quantico. I've got to make sure my boyfriend isn't about to get murdered by a UFO cult."

CHAPTER SEVENTEEN
COSMIC AGENCY

When I first met Gerald, he had his nose down in his laptop in Robert Ailes's room of misfit toys, which I'd just been added to. With hair like a Muppet's and the face of a fifteen-year-old, Gerald was hard to imagine ten years later as the mature grown-up sitting in front of me now, going over my case file as my supervisor.

Gerald is understanding and has a mind for details that amazes me. He advanced quickly and should be running the FBI, if you ask me, but his greatest weakness holds him back.

He's not a political animal. Gerald, like our mentor, Ailes, wants to get things done the right way and doesn't like cutting corners or paying favors.

"How did Parry and Elliott do?" he asks.

"Excellent. I think they're going to be fine agents wherever they end up."

"Okay . . . tell me really," he says, sensing my hesitation.

"They're smart. Real smart. They're just not street-smart yet," I explain.

"Neither was I."

"No, you weren't. It took a bullet for you to understand the stakes. But I watched you change before my eyes. I don't want those two to have to go through that."

"Most cops never do," replies Gerald.

"I know. I'm just saying they still don't know how ugly the world can be. Maybe they never have to learn. I hope they don't have to. I just don't know how to teach that."

"Understood. Maybe after more time with you, they will."

"More time? They're done with the academy. Now they're looking for permanent assignments."

"I know. We'll see," says Gerald.

Clearly there are gears turning in his mind. I get the feeling that the Tree Man assignment wasn't a one-time thing but a test run for something else.

I know enough to not shoot him down before he's had time to present his master plan. I'll just have to wait.

"I need a week or so off," I say.

"Sure."

"This is the part where the supervisor asks why," I remind him.

"This is the part where I point out you have about two years of unused vacation time and I have the discretion to put you on sabbatical whenever I want. You need the time, you have the time."

"You really do make it hard for me," I say, leaving out the rest of the sentence: . . . *to leave the FBI.*

"I know your value. Trust me. You could get away with a lot more than I'll ever let you know."

"I'll start showing up in my pajamas and test that."

"Even I have my limits," he says quickly.

"See, there's one thing that I can do to get you to fire me."

"I'd do worse than fire you. I'd promote you and make you do *my* job."

"Okay, okay. Understood."

"During this time off . . . do you need anything?"

"Actually, there might be one thing . . . I'd like to do some research and check our files about something," I reply.

Gerald nods. "May I ask what kind of something?"

"Something personal. It involves Theo."

"Ah. Has Dr. Cray stumbled onto something new?"

Gerald gets along with Theo quite well, although the same can't be said for others at the FBI. From a distance, Theo is a suspicious person. Heck, even up close he's still suspicious.

"Possibly. That's why I need to do the research."

Another nod. "We have a new serial killer lab that would love to work with him."

"As a suspect or an adviser?"

Gerald smiles at that. "The latter, I think. Unless there's something else about Dr. Cray the FBI should know?"

Should is an interesting word. "Nope. Actually, he's not on a serial killer case. At least I hope not. It involves a research station in New Mexico backed by a group called the Cosmic Agency."

"That doesn't sound much like a federal agency, although we have a Space Force now, so I shouldn't be one to judge," quips Gerald.

"It's a private foundation backed by Thomas T. Theismann. I can't find out more than that. I think it's just a shell organization."

Gerald looks up. "Theismann? What do they do?"

"They fund research. Mainly involving the search for extraterrestrial intelligence."

"Thomas T. Theismann? The investor?"

"Yes. Apparently, he has a secret hobby and has spent tens of millions of dollars on it."

"Huh. He seemed like a very . . . rational man. This is like finding out that Warren Buffett likes to bet on professional wrestling."

I knew next to nothing about Theismann when I looked him up, but Gerald's reaction doesn't surprise me based upon the little reading I've done.

"What's Dr. Cray's involvement?" asks Gerald.

"I can't say specifically. But I have concerns."

"About Theismann? He must be ninety by now."

"Not necessarily about him. Just the whole thing. I'm not sure what Theo has walked into," I say, as if Theo were a curious cat who got lost in another neighborhood.

The analogy fits, the more I think about it.

"I'm sure he's . . . well, he's Theo Cray," replies Gerald as he thinks about what he's saying. "Should I call our SWAT team now or put them on standby?" he jokes. Almost.

It's probably nothing and I'm being an overprotective girlfriend. Girlfriend . . . that's a role I've rarely identified myself as playing.

"I just want your permission to do a little digging. I'm sure it's nothing," I say, trying to convince myself more than Gerald.

"Yeah . . . right. If both of you have tingling Spidey sense, I wouldn't treat it lightly. Do what you think is appropriate. I'll leave it at that. Fair enough? But remember: I don't have the kind of pull that Ailes did to get us out of trouble."

"Understood. Just remember that blackmail is always an option," I reply.

"True. Do I dare ask what's next?"

"I'm going to Philadelphia. A scientist named David Ikeda blew his brains out in a hotel room under suspicious circumstances during a science conference there five months ago," I tell him.

"That's horrible. What was his field?" asks Gerald.

"Computational biology," I say matter-of-factly.

"That's Theo's field," he says, putting it together. "And who did he work for?"

"An organization funded by the Cosmic Agency."

"Good lord, Jessica. What has Theo gotten himself into?"

"Hopefully, a coincidence."

"Uh-huh. Well, Theo has a habit of uncovering the fact that not all coincidences are coincidences."

And that's precisely why I'm worried.

CHAPTER EIGHTEEN
BRAINSCAN

Detective Richard Esparch uses his laser pointer to illuminate the floor and the wall of the hotel room of the Silver Spire Suites where Dr. David Ikeda was found dead after hotel staff responded to the sound of a gunshot.

While the room has been put back into service and all evidence of what happened is long gone, it's been listed as only available for booking if the hotel has no other vacancies—lest a guest find out what happened and complain to management.

People die in hotels all the time, and operators are under no obligation to tell you. But it still makes sense to avoid renting out such rooms unless you need to.

"Blood spatter was found here and here," says Esparch in a slight Philly accent that makes him sound like a movie cop. "Not a pretty sight."

He's in his late forties, has a bit of a gut, and dark hair that shows no sign of receding. Esparch is also exceptionally polite and is eager to explain the case to me.

"He was on the bed here with the gun in his right hand."

I flip through the file. "It says that the gun was unregistered. How common is that for a suicide?"

"Not common. Now, he lived in New Mexico. Bringing a gun on a plane in checked baggage is possible but a hassle. And if he didn't make up his mind until he got here? Well, I'm sorry to say it isn't hard to get an unmarked gun in this town."

"I understand. But how would a man like Ikeda go about it? He doesn't strike me as the type that has a lot of knowledge of the criminal underworld."

"True, but go into any pawnshop a few blocks from here and ask for a gun and someone behind the counter will give you a number to call. We try to clean that up, but they have photos of our undercover guys on file. We have to use informants to do those kinds of gun buys or else get the ATF involved, and that brings its own hassles," he explains.

"His wife said that he'd been depressed recently, but not so much that he'd take his own life," I reply, commenting on the file.

"Yeah. It's hard. I had a friend that did it a few years ago. Quiet guy. I knew he'd been dealing with some issues, but I thought he was on a turnaround. Next thing you know, I'm at his funeral telling his children their dad loved them. Now I coach their baseball games," Esparch says with a deep sigh.

"Was there anything about this that stood out to you?" I ask.

"Not really. It felt like a lot of other suicides. An hour before, he sent his wife a text saying that he loved her. Then a minute or so before he pulled the trigger, he texted saying sorry."

"What about people at the conference? Did they say anything?"

Esparch shakes his head. "Nothing specific. Ikeda had gone to his room after the last session. He didn't socialize with anyone. People said he seemed distant. Which, as you know, fits the profile."

"Yes, it certainly does. Nothing else?"

"I checked the security camera footage. There's one at either end of the corridor, watching the door and the stairwell. You can actually see Ikeda's door from the elevator landing cameras. The man walked in and a few hours later was carried away on a stretcher."

Either side of the hotel room has doors that can connect to the adjoining rooms when both are unlocked. "And the people in the other rooms? Did they notice anything?"

Esparch is patient and doesn't mind the fact that I'm basically going over every point of his case. "The man in 604 was out to dinner. 608 was booked but had a last-minute cancellation. The name of the man in 604 is in there. Riembau, if I remember. From Quebec."

"And 608?"

"Like I said, empty. He couldn't make it to the conference. We even checked with his university. He was teaching class at the time."

"Is his name in here?"

"Yeah." Esparch thinks for a moment. "Leonard Minyala, I believe."

"Did you speak to Ikeda's wife?" I ask.

"Over the phone. His company picked up his belongings."

"The Cosmic Agency?"

"The what? No. It was something like South West Data Science. It should be in there."

I flip through the notes and find that Ikeda was listed as an employee of an Albuquerque technology company by that name and not anything visibly associated with the Cosmic Agency. It could have a weird corporate structure, but I should look into it further.

"Do you have any doubts?" asks Esparch, curious if he missed anything.

"Not really. You're very thorough," I say sincerely.

"I gotta run and pick my friend's kids up from school. Call me if you need anything. Hold on to the file as long as you like. There's DVDs in the back—of the security footage."

"Did you ever get any footage of him from a pawnshop?" I ask.

"No," Esparch replies. "For that, we'd need a warrant."

❦

After he leaves, I sit at the hotel room desk and go through the case file thoroughly. The autopsy illustrations concur with what Esparch described, and a gunpowder residue kit confirmed that Ikeda's hand had held a gun that fired.

Suicide, it seems. But there are a lot of tiny clues that can indicate otherwise. If someone is found with a bullet wound in their head and a gun in their hand, it's not always an open-and-shut case.

Police know more about what a staged suicide looks like than most people who would consider trying to pull one off. For starters, the lack of gunpowder residue on the hands would be a giant red flag. If you ever look at a time-lapse film of a gun firing, you see how much material gets sprayed out of and away from the weapon.

If you've ever fired a gun and smelled your hands afterward, the odor's hard to miss. Forensic kits pick up even microscopic amounts. They can also tell you when the residue is suspicious. If you find residue but it's also on the palms, then that indicates a gun was fired near their hands but they weren't holding it.

Not all forensic exams get into these kinds of specifics. In Ikeda's case, they simply wiped his entire hand and detected enough residue to show his hand was near, but not necessarily holding, the gun.

Powder burns on the face show how close the gun was to the victim's head. In Ikeda's case, it was almost directly on his right temple.

I take a seat on the edge of the bed where Ikeda was found and put my finger to my head like a gun.

What was he thinking?

I notice that the mirror is to my left and the window to my right. In front of me is a wall with a sad painting of a sunset over a mountain. Would I want this to be the last thing I saw before I died?

I hope I never have to find out.

I pick up the folder and flip through the pages, hoping something will jump out at me. Sadly, nothing does.

Ikeda sounds like a quiet man who was dealing with some kind of internal turmoil and decided one day to end it. But what was the turmoil?

According to the report, his wife said he'd been stressed, but that was it. There's no mention of what he'd been stressed about. Did she even know? Did she know more than she told the police?

What if their last conversation had been an argument and they said ugly things to one another? Would she tell the police? Would *I*?

No. I'd let my guilt tear me to pieces, but I wouldn't let anyone else pass judgment.

The interview with the man in room 604, Riembau, was short because he wasn't in the hotel at the time. But I wonder if he heard something before? Maybe an argument between Ikeda and his wife? An argument between Ikeda and someone else?

I take out my phone and call the number on the report to hear his side.

"Hello," answers a man with midwestern accent.

"Dr. Riembau?" I ask.

"Sorry, wrong number," he replies.

I check the number again and ask if it is correct.

"Yes. But that's not me. I have to get ready for a class," he says curtly.

Class?

I check the notes.

"Excuse me. Are you Dr. Minyala?" I ask.

"Yes . . . ?"

The numbers somehow got switched.

"I'm sorry. My name is Jessica Blackwood. I'm an agent with the FBI." I'm about to apologize and hang up but decide to see where this goes. "I have a question about your reservation for the BrainScan conference."

He sighs. "As I said before, I never went to the conference. I never even signed up for it. I told the people at the foundation I didn't have time and they could give it to someone else."

"I'm sorry, the foundation?" I ask.

"Yeah, the World Science Exchange people. But they ignored me. Now I'm dealing with *this*."

"So you never signed up for the conference and you never reserved the room?"

"God, you guys are slow," he groans. "Yes, that's correct. They said I won a grant, but I never applied for it. Okay?"

"That does sound fishy," I say by way of encouragement. "Could you email me everything they sent you?"

"Are you serious?"

"I'm sitting in a hotel room where a man's body was found, and your name is on the registration for the room next door. You can either forward it to me or someone from your local FBI field office will want to interview you."

"You people are a pain," he grumbles.

"Yes, we are. God forbid that something happens to someone you love; if it did, you'd want me to be just as much of a pain in the ass."

He takes a moment to respond. "Yeah, you're right. I'll send you the email."

CHAPTER NINETEEN
Grantee

I'm back in my office at Quantico in a building that once stored physical inventory of car tire prints, fabric samples, and a million other random items that could sometimes be used to solve a crime. Now the rooms that stored those items are mostly empty. The FBI lab that occupied this building is in a newer state-of-the-art facility with rows of computer servers and advanced genetics tools instead of binders filled with carpet swatches and clay impressions of teeth marks.

The dirty secret in forensics is that evidence is often used to make a suspect fit a crime instead of to find the suspect. Theo once went through an academy forensic textbook with a yellow highlighter and stack of Post-it notes and pointed out every place that mentioned a research study that had since been contradicted.

"They reference a study that supports something like a legal argument," he'd said as he dropped the book on the kitchen table. "All they care about is that one paper supports a claim and not that all the other ones that came after refuted it."

To get some idea of Theo's sense of integrity, he still sends out annual emails to former students with the subject line "What I got wrong (maybe)" and a list of all papers that conflict with things he taught in his classes as a professor.

"You know, education normally doesn't come with a warrantee" was my response.

"It should," he replied.

If Theo could do a factory recall and gather all his students to explain how much things have changed, I'm sure he would.

If Theo were where I am right now, he'd break the Ikeda situation down into some simple questions and attack each one.

1. Did David Ikeda kill himself?
2. If not, who wanted him dead?
3. Why?

I can't answer question #1 from the case file. The second question's just as hard, and the third is impossible to know without an answer to the other questions.

Okay . . . maybe I can tackle this from a different point of view. A motive, à la Theo, is an intent held either by an individual or a group acting with a degree of coordination.

Ford Motors doesn't actually want anything, but the system that makes up Ford wants to sell you a car in the same way a car salesperson does. While there's a CEO and a board of directors, there's no magical homunculus sitting in the middle of it all making the decisions. Well, not since Henry Ford died.

The point is, you can sometimes find the cause by looking at the systems. How did this car end up in my driveway? Maybe it started with a commercial that got my attention.

How did David Ikeda end up dead in his hotel room? Maybe it started with an idea in his head or somebody else's head. Maybe it began when he interfered with a system.

I take some note cards from my drawer and scribble a few thoughts, then pin them to a corkboard:

David Ikeda
Leonard Minyala
Detective Richard Esparch
Alfonso Riembau
Silver Spire Suites
South West Data Science

I add three more items to the board on the other side of a piece of blue tape:

Theo Cray
Cosmic Agency
Thomas T. Theismann

The Cray approach would be to start making connections between the different points, treating them like vectors. The Blackwood approach would be to follow my intuition and hop on a plane to talk to or stick my nose into whatever person or situation smells the fishiest.

Let's try a hybrid approach: the Blackcray method.

South West Data Science was a surprise, because I expected Ikeda to work for the Cosmic Agency.

Hmm. Let's do a search . . .

The FBI database doesn't have much on South West Data Science other than some security clearances for working with government-controlled computer systems.

However, when I use Theo's database, it does something called a "nearest neighbor" search and finds similar companies. This might be because they share employees, addresses, governance boards, clients, or other factors.

His software spits out a cluster of bubbles showing that the Cosmic Agency shares directors with South West Data Science. Basically, SWDS is a subsidiary.

That would explain the confusion. This arrangement is unusual in technology. You can have a nonprofit that owns a for-profit. The advantages are that the for-profit can pay employees stock options and participation benefits. Even the United States government "owns" companies like this. The Aerospace Corporation is, for all intents and purposes, an extension of the United States Air Force. Because the federal government has salary caps, it can't compete with technology companies for talent. By creating a company to serve as a contractor, they can pay higher salaries.

So, Ikeda actually worked for the Cosmic Agency, which is also the group that Theo is currently entangled with. And the Cosmic Agency is secretly funded by Thomas T. Theismann.

What other connections are there?

Oh!

I add World Science Exchange to the corkboard.

Let's look 'em up . . .

According to their website, the World Science Exchange is supported by a generous grant from the Foundation for Excellence in Science Research.

Let's put *them* into Theo's nearest-neighbor system . . .

The Cosmic Agency and the Thomas T. Theismann Trust appear as giant related bubbles.

I play back the hotel security camera footage and scrub through all the people coming and going through the floor's hallway. I see Riembau enter and exit his suite two hours before Ikeda was shot. Nobody ever enters 608, the room registered to Leonard Minyala, who claims he never asked for or wanted the room or the registration.

I scroll back further, to when the cleaning personnel are making their rounds, seeing whether anyone used that as a distraction to sneak into Ikeda's room.

Nothing.

There're several people who walked through the floor before and after Ikeda's death. I grab screenshots of their faces for future reference.

I still don't have anyone going into or next to his room. On a whim, I call the Silver Spire Suites and get the manager.

"Hello, this is Agent Blackwood with the FBI. I believe we spoke earlier today? This is Mary-Beth?"

"Yes, Agent Blackwood. How may I help you?"

"Can you look up some reservations for me around the BrainScan conference?"

"Of course. Do you have room numbers?"

"Yes. 604, 606, and 608."

"One second . . . 604 was registered to Alfonso Riembau. 606 was registered to South West Data Science, and 608 was registered to World Science Exchange," she replies.

"Okay. What was occupancy like?"

"We were at full. I remember calling one of the organizations to ask if they could release a block of rooms that nobody had checked into, but they wouldn't. They said their guests were coming, but they ended up being no-shows," says Mary-Beth.

"What rooms?"

"Let me check. World Science Exchange had rooms 608, 610, and 612. I believe 612 is the only one that ended up being occupied, and that was only for one night. We could have used the others," she explains.

"One more thing: Can you give me the name of the occupant of 612?"

"Yes. Hold on. Sean Griffman. Everything was put on the World Science Exchange credit card, so that's all I have on him."

"Thank you very much," I reply, then hang up.

So the mysterious World Science Exchange booked three rooms next to room 606 and only one was used—but it wasn't next door to Ikeda's.

Is this all a coincidence?

I'm reminded of a magic trick my grandfather created on a bet with my dad and my uncle . . .

CHAPTER TWENTY
THE REALITY BOX

My grandfather once got into an argument with my father and my uncle Darius over an illusion—basically, any large prop used to do something magical with a human being, like sawing them in half or making them levitate.

Darius and my dad had built a contraption the size of a telephone booth designed to hide a person. Darius had thought of the method of concealment, and my father had constructed it. They demonstrated it to my grandfather in the driveway of our run-down mansion in Bel Air.

Grandfather smoked away at his cigar and replied, "Too obvious," after I appeared in the box.

To his point, I was ten and could have folded myself into a carry-on suitcase, but his argument was that the method wouldn't fool anyone.

"The walls are thicker than they should be," he pointed out.

"They're only three inches on the front," protested Darius as he used a tape measure to prove his point.

"I don't need a goddamn measuring stick to tell me if it works or not. Are you going to go up to everyone after the show and use your logic to batter them into wonderment?" Grandfather pointed a well-manicured finger at his temple. "Magic is up here. Not in all your tools and plywood," he said as he gestured toward the garage workshop.

"Good luck making magic happen without them," replied Darius.

"Oh really?"

My grandfather loved three things more than anything: the word "goddamn," a good cigar, and some fool telling him a thing can't be done.

"I tell you what. Why don't you rip all that out and make me a simple plywood box with a door and we'll see about that."

"Like an outhouse?" asked Darius.

"Minus the shitter. We'll call it the Chinese Telephone Booth or something. But don't go making it look like a pagoda. Just a simple wooden box. We'll test it tomorrow at the El Rey."

For anyone sensitive to the concept of cultural appropriation, I advise them to never, ever look at an old magic catalog filled with gaudily stenciled faux-exotic items with names like "Jap box." While the argument could be made that this was done out of reverence for the rich Asian tradition of stage magic, the bucktoothed caricatures straight out of wartime propaganda posters complicate things.

"Tomorrow?" asked Dad.

We were putting on a show at a Los Angeles theater the next day. It wasn't a high-paying gig, but it was local, so Grandfather could test out new things. The audiences were more blue-collar than the kind we'd perform for in other places, but honestly? They were the best.

"We'll put it onstage before I do the card manipulation act so you two clowns can stand at the back of the hall and decide," Grandfather told them.

"You got it, boss," said Darius.

"Are you sure?" asked my father.

"Getting cold feet?"

"One box coming up" was Dad's response.

"We didn't settle on a wager," noted Darius.

"My humiliation isn't enough? Okay, the two losers have to act as chauffeur for the distinguished-gentleman winner. Or vice versa should rapture happen and the age of miracles truly begin."

"Deal," said Darius.

"Why do I feel like he's going to go find some tree to dance around and say his name like Rumpelstiltskin," muttered Dad.

"As it would happen, I need your firstborn to show me how to work the infernal machine," replied Grandfather, referring to our iMac. "Come along, Jessica, let's leave these two apes to their grunting and find out what happened to my actual sons, whom I'm certain the hospital misplaced."

As I followed Grandfather inside, I heard Darius taunt my father, "Is she your child or his?"

(Later on, that would take on a deeper meaning when I found out my mother may have been involved with more than one member of my family. That kind of thing can mess with you.)

The next night, I stood on the side of the stage in my tuxedo tails and hot pants—too unaware to be awkward about what I was wearing and slightly cognizant of the fact that every other little girl in the auditorium was looking at me with a mix of admiration and jealousy.

Grandfather let the last card appear from his hand and flutter into the top hat I was holding, then walked to center stage to address the audience after the applause died down.

"You've probably noticed a rather large box behind me. No, it's not a coffin filled with dirt where I sleep at night. I never sleep," he added.

Grandfather had a rhythm and an impish delivery that could make something sound like a joke even though it wasn't. He said he learned it by listening to fast-talking Yiddish comedians who performed in the Catskills, where half the audience couldn't understand the jokes.

"I need several volunteers to come up here. My granddaughter, the elfin beauty over here, will hand out black ribbons to people. When you get one, come up onstage and gather around the box."

I walked through the crowd, and a sea of outstretched hands reached out from people desperate to be part of the mystery. I handed out the ribbons—actually thick pieces of black cloth—and took my place at Grandfather's side.

"I was explaining to Jessica Plato's Allegory of the Cave a few weeks ago when we visited the ruins of Greece as the guests of the royal family. She said she didn't understand how the blind men chained to the wall looking at shadows couldn't understand the true nature of reality. 'Grandfather, can't they realize that the inconsistencies in the silhouettes were best explained by some deeper structure in reality?'"

He looked down at me and shook his head. "I know, she's a simple child. Thankfully she has her looks."

The first time he made this joke, I kicked him in the shin and it brought the house down. I was seven before I realized the joke was actually a backhanded sarcastic compliment.

Once he made this joke and realized he'd forgotten a prop and walked offstage to get it, I said to the audience, "I know he's a simple old man, but at least he has his looks . . . sort of."

The audience roared in approval. My dad had a horrified look on his face offstage. Rule number one was never, ever upstage Peter Blackstar.

Grandfather came running onstage, and I was genuinely afraid he was going to insult me in front of a thousand people.

Instead, he bellowed, "If anyone is interested in adopting a miserable child, please see me after the show."

I held up my hands like I was begging for a volunteer parent.

Grandfather pointed me offstage, letting me know our comedy duo schtick was done for the night. Dad pulled me into a protective hug and whispered, "If he yells at you, just know it's his way of telling you that you're amazing."

Maybe so, but I wish my grandfather had yelled a little less and my dad stood up for me a little more while growing up . . .

Anyway, after the show, Grandfather was all smiles. There was no yelling. "Runt, that was good. Real good. Just know when and how to end it before you give me the death blow. They still have to respect me after."

The next time we were working in concert, I took his joke and crossed my arms like I was angry. This was funnier than an eye roll, which alienates the other person. Crossed arms escalated the joke playfully.

"I propose an experiment with these volunteers so we can educate my granddaughter. If you would all be so kind as to tie those ribbons over your eyes like blindfolds, cutting off one sense, we'll test your grasp on reality."

The volunteers blindfolded themselves, and Grandfather inspected them and gathered them into a spot behind the tall crate my dad and Darius had made. He opened the door so that the interior faced the back of the stage and the blindfolded people. The audience was looking at the back of the box.

"Now, if I tell you this box is empty, you have only my word to go by, as charming and sincere as I am. I hardly expect you to take the word of our volunteers here, because they can't see their own noses, let alone the interior of the object of our attention. So let's allow them to explore the box with their other senses, chiefly their hands.

"If you would feel inclined to do so, please hold your hands out-right and step forward and inspect the entire interior of the box."

The volunteers all stumbled around until they found the box and began to run their hands around it and walk inside while bumping into each other.

"No trapdoors? Secret compartments? Why don't you all move back and one at a time step inside the box to inspect it for yourself? Jessica will tap each one of you when it's your turn."

I moved through the volunteers and guided one, then another, into and out of the cabinet.

"All right, I believe our committee has had a chance to inspect the box. Who was the last person to do so?"

A man raised his hand.

"Okay. You will be the foreman. Do me a favor and close the door to the box. You'll notice a padlock with your hands. Please secure that over the latch."

The man shut the door and locked it as instructed.

"Would all of you take off your blindfolds and rotate the box one hundred eighty degrees? Then stand over on the line by the edge of the stage."

They spun the box and did as instructed.

"Foreman, please walk over to the microphone and answer my questions as truthfully and honestly as you can. Did you notice any trapdoors?"

"No," replied the man.

"Hidden compartments? They'd feel hollow," explained Grandfather.

"I did not."

"Did you stand in the center of the box?"

The man nodded.

"Was there anyone else in there?"

"Absolutely not. I touched all the walls. There was nobody there," said the man.

"I'll give ten thousand dollars to anyone who can prove this man or the people standing here have been asked to lie by me. Did any of you feel anything unusual or out of place inside the box?" asked Grandfather.

They all shook their heads no.

"Foreman. Would you be so kind as to use this key to unlock the door? But do not open it just yet."

The man took the key and unlocked the padlock.

"Now take the flashlight from Jessica and pry open the door an inch or so and take a peek."

The man flipped on the light, opened the door wide enough to put his face into the crack, and let out a loud scream, jumping back and dropping the flashlight. He put his hands on his knees and started laughing hysterically.

"Yes or no. Is the box empty?" asked Grandfather.

"Hell no!" said the man, his face still white.

"Would you say your perception of reality wasn't what you expected?"

"Yes. Oh, yes."

"So you see, Jessica, I think I've proven my point. With their sight sense limited, they weren't able to get an accurate view of reality," lectured Grandfather.

"Yes, Grandfather, but what's in the box?" I asked, speaking on behalf of the audience.

"It's immaterial to the discussion. Please stay focused. As I was saying . . ."

"What's in the box?" I whined, not realizing that I was echoing the plot twist to the movie *Seven*. This drew a big laugh.

"It's *not* relevant."

"Fine." I walked toward the box.

"Jessica, darling. I don't think you're prepared for reality. Let's talk about something else. Step away."

I grabbed the edge of the door, ready to open it, then thought twice and stepped away.

After a long pause, Grandfather said, "It's better that way."

The audience was murmuring more loudly now, on the edges of their seats.

A moment later, a man in a convincing gorilla suit burst through the door and let out a loud roar, scaring the hell out of the audience. Children shrieked, and a man jumped out of his chair with an expletive.

The gorilla ran around the stage, then lunged at me. I jumped into the aisle and ran toward the back, screaming. The gorilla chased me back up to the stage and through the wings, then back down the aisles to the middle of the audience, where I finally stopped and held out my hands, pleading for it to leave me alone.

The gorilla stopped, stood upright, and took off the mask. It was Grandfather.

I wasn't expecting this part. Apparently, I more than stage-whispered, "Holy shit."

I looked to where he'd been standing and, obviously, he wasn't there. I don't know when he switched himself for the actor or who had been the original gorilla in the box, but it must have been when we were running offstage, before returning to the aisles.

Dad and Darius were at the back of the theater, shaking their heads in disbelief.

They immediately knew how the illusion was performed, but they couldn't deny the fact that it had utterly devastated the audience.

Grandfather made a motion of putting an imaginary chauffeur cap on and grinned at them.

Darius flipped him off. Dad looked depressed. He put Grandfather on an impossibly high pedestal, and this illusion had only made it taller.

While the Reality Box, as it ended up being called, doesn't directly correlate to how David Ikeda ended up dead, it does point in a direction I should explore.

I scan through footage and make a map of the hotel room. I'm like the volunteer foreman in the Reality Box. I think I see everything I need to, but I don't.

I call the manager of the Silver Spire Suites again.

"Sorry to bother you, but I have a dumb question: I don't know if I've seen this, but are all those rooms capable of adjoining?"

"Not dumb at all. Yes. All the rooms on that floor can be adjoined if they're unlocked."

"Thank you."

I look down at my sketch of the hotel floor. If someone wanted to kill David Ikeda and not be seen by the hotel cameras, he could do it by progressively going through doors between the adjoining rooms.

For a professional, and this guy had to have been one, the locks wouldn't pose much of a challenge. In fact, with prior access and some putty and a magnet placed beforehand, it would have been ridiculously easy.

I make a phone call to one other person, then dial Detective Esparch's number.

"What's up?" he asks.

"Can you get a technician to get some prints from the Silver Spire Suites?"

"We got the door handles and the sinks. Nobody went in or out of the room," he reminds me.

"Not through the front door. But the next three rooms were all reserved to one party," I explain. "All adjoining . . ."

"Yeah, but isn't that a bit of a reach?"

"Is it? You can get a master key for those locks on eBay. It'll take you all of twenty seconds to go from one end to the other. Not to be a jerk about this, but these doors are just mental constructs—not immutable laws of physics," I reply.

"You'd be the expert on that. Okay, I buy it."

"Here's the other thing: I looked up the name of the one man who occupied the fourth room. His name is Sean Griffman."

"Who is he?"

"I wish I knew. The conference has no record of his registration. He doesn't even exist on Google. It's a made-up name."

"Damn. I'll get right on it."

"Please do so."

I realize my hands are shaking as I click off the call.

Theo could be in even more trouble than I realized.

PART THREE

EXPLORER

CHAPTER TWENTY-ONE
MIST

Our airplane flies low enough over the jungle that Trevor and I can look out the windows and occasionally see through the breaks in the tree cover made by spot clearings and logging roads.

Trevor is less anxious about the airplane flight than he was about the helicopter. He explains the history of the area as we fly in this chartered plane from the Guatemala City airport, where Research Station Alpha's jet landed, to a regional airport close to where the secondary signal was detected.

We're accompanied by two staff members: Ronald Urbina, the man who interrogated me in my interview, and Teresa Bilton, who works directly for Fiona Joss.

Trevor points out the jungle that stretches into the horizon under a cool mist. "They did an extensive mapping with LIDAR—you know, lasers—a few years ago of the northern section of this region. They found thousands . . . *thousands* of stone structures and parts of cities that had been concealed for almost a half a millennium.

"We suspect the Mayan civilization was larger than historians estimated, but this would indicate ten million or more people at its height. That's twice the population of medieval England. Who knows what else is down there?"

"What *is* down there?" I ask over our headsets.

"You mean where we're headed? I don't know. The infrared just shows a shape. It could be a complex, a temple, or the ruins of a granary. Anything. You can't think of the Mayans as stuck in time. Their first cities were founded at the same time as Rome. Harvard College had been around for sixty years by the time the last Mayan city fell to the Spaniards. That's quite a reign and a hell of a lot of history. Who knows if they had their own version of Confucius or Aristotle? The Spanish Inquisition destroyed most of their written history. We'll never know what we lost."

"What about the signal? Why here?" I ask.

"Are you asking me if I think the Mayans talked to aliens? That's a silly question. Ancient astronaut pseudoscience is about as insulting to me as intelligent design probably is to you. Every day I hear from a moron that watched a cable show and decided to write me his theory but can't be bothered to read a book by someone who actually knows what they were talking about. It's also insulting and racist to suggest these people needed help to build their civilization while northern Europeans did it on their own," Trevor goes on.

"Yeah. Hard to believe they needed aliens to show them how to cut out a living human heart or decapitate the loser of a ball game," I reply.

"Those are exaggerations."

"Which part?"

"Well, it wasn't always like that. And it's not like there weren't traditions like that in Europe. We have entire churches constructed of bones," he replies, I think referring to the Santa Maria della Concezione dei Cappuccini.

"True, but they died naturally and got turned into IKEA furniture later," I point out.

I'm not really trying to argue these points with him. My goal is to off-balance him a little. I've been trying to decide whose side he's on.

Is he working with Joss and Research Station Alpha, or is he a genuine independent thinker?

"Why are you out here?" I ask.

"What?" says Trevor, still hopped up from our discussion.

"If you don't think aliens, then why take the trip or even work with Research Station Alpha?"

"Not every unusual explanation is aliens or alien contact. Do you know what happened when ancient civilizations found meteors they witnessed falling from the sky?"

"Spears or religious relics," I reply. There were entire Indian tribes that spent generations in one spot because of the abundance of meteoric iron.

"Exactly. What would an ancient culture do with a part of a spacecraft or some advanced device they couldn't work with their tools? They'd probably treat it like a gift from the gods and bury it in a temple so their enemies couldn't find it."

"So you're not looking for alien astronauts?"

"No. I think it's far more likely a civilization much more advanced than ours would send out millions of probes to distant planets, and some of them may have found themselves on planets with intelligent species. Given the number of potentially inhabitable planets in our galaxy, it's possible that more than one civilization has done this. I consider the possibility of a probe making it to Earth nonzero. Maybe many of them," he replies.

"So, no ancient aliens."

"No, Dr. Cray. I'm looking for black boxes."

When we land, there are two rented Jeeps and a man named Horatio waiting for us. He serves as a guide for a botanical research project; the research station was able to borrow his services on short notice.

"Hello! So, who's the man with the plan?" he asks in almost perfect American English as we throw our gear into the back of the vehicles.

"Dr. Barker has the directions," says Urbina, indicating Trevor.

Trevor lays the printouts on the hood of the first Jeep. "We want to go here. It's about thirty kilometers northeast. It appears there's a small road that comes within three kilometers of the spot."

"There?" asks Horatio. "There isn't anything there."

"Don't you work for botanists?" I ask.

"Yes. Why?"

"When they point to a plant, do you say, 'Hey, there's nothing there'?"

Horatio lets out a loud laugh. "If I knew you wanted plants and trees, then that's a different matter."

"Actually we're—" Trevor starts to say but gets cut off by Urbina.

"Just here to take some plant photographs for a survey."

Bilton whispers to me, "They can be very touchy about exploring ruins without a permit."

"Somebody should have told Trevor that," I reply.

"He should know better."

Thirty minutes later, we're taking a road through the low-lying hills deep into the jungle with Horatio in the lead and Rolando, another driver, following behind. I'm in the lead Jeep with Trevor and Urbina while Bilton is in the second one by herself.

Trevor is up front, asking Horatio questions, while I sit in back and listen along with Urbina.

The road winds through the jungle with the trees and vegetation looming overhead like we're in a green tunnel that goes on forever.

This main road is nearly a hundred miles long from end to end. Looking out the window, it's not hard to imagine a lost civilization or two could just be a few hundred yards from the side of the highway.

I get Trevor's sense of excitement about what could be out there. When I was in the Burmese jungle, I saw carved rocks that dated to the Early Bagan Kingdom. I could only wonder what had been there before them.

"Cray, what's the craziest thing you believe?" asks Trevor.

"Neanderthal and Denisovan extinction may have happened more recently than our fossil record presently shows," I reply.

"You mean the wild men stories?"

He's referring to the stories of wild men that almost every culture has. The descriptions of them sound a lot like what you'd see in an exhibit at a natural science museum of the different hominids that have walked the Earth.

We know that the path from proto-chimpanzee to human wasn't a straight line. For most of *Homo sapiens*'s history we've shared the planet with other species of upright-walking apes. Some used tools and maybe language. The remnants of our closest relatives, the Neanderthals and the Denisovans, can be found in our DNA. Not the DNA we share from common ancestry with those hominids, but the mutations we inherited from our ancestors who interbred with them later on.

"I think those stories are mostly describing other tribes who are shier. Maybe some kind of racial memory. But what I suspect is that our fossil record is hampered by the fact that a good portion of the record of human habitation has been underwater since the last interglacial—and that some of the best places to live are horrible at leaving fossils.

"Twenty years ago, you could fit every chimpanzee fossil ever found into a shoebox," I say. "If some really ambitious Denisovans made their way here during the start of the Wisconsin glaciation and kept to the coastline, we might never know it. They could have walked all the way down here, set up shop somewhere beyond this highway, and left no trace after the jungle dissolved their bones, like it does everything else," I point out.

"A hypothesis that can't be tested," notes Urbina.

"Trevor asked for crazy," I reply with a shrug.

I decide to spare them my lecture on simulation theory and how there's a strong argument that it's not only highly likely we're all living inside some kind of computer program but we're also probably no more important than an animated screensaver application.

"Would you entertain the possibility that at some point an advanced civilization might have made some kind of contact to influence our cultural development?" asks Urbina.

"It's possible, but I don't know what it explains," I reply.

"Angels, demons. Stories of beings more advanced than us."

"To what end?" I ask.

"To guide us," Urbina says in a way that I think means he takes this very seriously.

"Why not land in a flying saucer in the middle of the Roman Colosseum and say, 'Cut out this slavery bullshit'? That would probably have been a good way to guide us."

"Maybe it's more subtle than that."

"If it's so subtle that it has the same effect as not existing at all, it seems logical to assume it doesn't exist."

"Maybe for some. Maybe for others it's as obvious as the sun," answers Urbina. "Maybe that UFO did land in the Colosseum and you just didn't realize it," he replies.

"I'd think Caesar would have mentioned it in his memoirs. It would have made a great opening chapter."

"What if Christianity was the flying saucer?" he asks.

I catch Trevor's eye in the rearview mirror, along with his slight smirk.

I feel like I got invited on an all-expense paid vacation and my host just shoved a pen into my hand so I could write a check for a down payment on a time-share.

"Um . . . I'm open to the idea that many things are possible. Want to hear my ideas on simulation theory?"

"Perhaps another time. I'm just curious what it would take for you to believe your worldview isn't what you believe it is."

"You're making an assumption that I have a view of the world that centers on a specific truth. I don't. I have a collection of opinions with varying degrees of probability. I'm willing to discount any one of them if there's sufficient evidence."

I realize that everyone I've met on this crazy adventure fits into one of two categories: open-minded scientists willing to entertain even crazy ideas or believers who embrace Theismann's hypotheses with religious zeal.

"This is where the road ends," says Horatio. "We'll have to go by foot from here."

"I'm excited to see what we find," replies Urbina.

I'm a little scared of what we might find.

CHAPTER TWENTY-TWO
PASSAGE

We follow a path that was made by either people or wild boars. Horatio uses his machete like an artist, carving a path through the stray branches while barely breaking a sweat or slowing his pace.

Trevor follows behind him, noting our route on GPS to make sure we don't get lost. We're looking for the source of the transmission with the full understanding that the original coordinates are only an approximation. I used some algorithms to try to get a more precise fix, but I only narrowed it down to a few hundred meters.

Out here, ten meters can be the difference between you and a lost temple you'll never know about.

I have a pretty good sense of direction, but even I don't want to test it out here. This part of the jungle is flat, making it hard to spot landmarks.

Birds jump around in the trees as we invade their territory, and hoofed mammals scurry along as they hear our approach.

Howler monkeys let out calls to warn their friends of our approach, and I occasionally get a glimpse of one watching us from the trees.

We're probably the first humans they've ever seen. What do they make of us?

I glance behind me and see Urbina and Bilton talking at a distance. Their voices are hushed, and Urbina's nodding. As the sunlight breaks through the canopy and casts them in a golden glow, I have an image of a monk and a nun carrying on a theological discussion.

I notice the hacking sound from Horatio's machete has stopped. I look ahead to see if he needs to take a break; instead, he's studying the trail.

I make my way to the front and stand next to him. His eyes are focused on the distance where the foliage blends into an opaque organic wall.

The birds have grown quiet, and the only sound is the distant cry of a howler monkey warning his tribe.

This section of the path has already been cleared. Branches with freshly cut ends litter the ground, and another path merges with ours from the left.

In Guatemala, drug dealers grow opium in the mountains and mainly marijuana in the forests. We may have accidentally intruded into narco territory.

"We should probably go back," says Horatio.

"Have you dealt with these people before?" I ask.

"Yes. You can bribe the watchmen, but not the foreman. If they see too many gringos, they get nervous. It's best to avoid it altogether before we're seen."

"I suspect we've already been spotted. I don't know if retreating is a good idea. We could be walking into an ambush," I tell him.

"What's going on?" asks Urbina.

I hold up my hand to silence him.

"I'd rather take the chance and walk out of here than walk into something," says Horatio.

"They could be doing something else. I have an alternative option." I set down my backpack and start to unlace my boots.

Horatio looks at me like I've gone insane. "Getting undressed?"

"Not quite. But almost." I pull off my shirt so I'm wearing only my hiking pants. With less clothing to catch on vines, I'll be able to move through the jungle more easily and quietly.

"Wait twenty minutes. If you hear two howler monkey calls four seconds apart, it's dangerous. Three and it's safe," I explain.

"You have got to be kidding." Horatio turns to ask the others where they picked up the mental patient, but I've already slipped into the trees.

I move quickly, keeping my footing on fresh logs and damp ground. In the jungle, sounds travel differently than you might expect. Similar to how crunching on something in your mouth feels like it should rattle the windows.

Dry brush makes noise that can travel far, brushing past leaves and ferns less so. An easy way to observe this is to look at what the wind moves and what it doesn't.

Another method is to align your path so there are trees between you and where you're trying to avoid being observed from. They not only block you visually, they also cause the sound you make to bounce away from where you're headed.

Holding a leafy branch in front of you can work as improvised camouflage. It has the same effect as more sophisticated tactical patterns in that it breaks up lines that indicate a person is there. We're legally blind outside a very small spot in the center of our vision. We don't recognize this because our eyes are always moving around our environment and filling in details for our brain. What we think of as vision is actually our memory getting frequent updates about points of interest. This is why glowing alarm clocks appear to bounce at night and simple optical illusions fool us.

While our peripheral vision is bad at details, it is highly tuned for motion and brightness changes. That's why you want to move slowly. Your chance of being observed depends on how much the person you're trying to avoid being seen by is moving their eyes around their environment. If they move a lot, you can move more quickly. If they're fixed on a spot near you, then you have to move at a glacial pace.

My path is parallel to the new trail we discovered. I stay ten meters away from it, which is as close as I feel comfortable. I've spent time with indigenous hunters who could move along a trail just a few feet away from you and remain unseen if you didn't know you were being shadowed.

So far I haven't seen any other people, which may be a good or a bad thing. I want to see them before they see me.

Sunlight glows from a bright clearing ahead. The blue fabric of a tent is visible, alongside folding chairs.

I reach the edge of the campsite and wait. There's no sound of people speaking or walking around. It appears empty, but the coals in the fire are still smoldering, and two metal coffee cups are sitting on the rocks surrounding it along with a very dirty toothbrush next to a box of toothpicks.

These could be watchmen for a drug field, campers, treasure hunters, documentary film producers, or a thousand other things.

I move into the campsite and spot something gleaming on the ground near the edge of the tent: a rifle bullet.

This was dropped in a hurry. Not a good sign.

I grab a large white rock from the ground and head down the trail that connects to ours, going fast while still trying to keep quiet.

I spot the backs of two men dressed in dirty shorts and T-shirts. One is in his twenties, the other his forties. The older man has a rifle pointed at my team.

"We're just tourists," says Bilton.

"I suggest you tour somewhere else," says the younger man in mildly accented English.

"We only want to go a little farther," Trevor pleads in Spanish.

"This is as far as you go," replies the younger man.

"Could you just put down the rifle?" asks Horatio.

The younger man steps to the older man's side. "The rifle stays put."

I'm behind the two of them in a split second. Horatio looks terrified when he sees the rock in my hand.

"We can be civil about this," I say behind the older man.

He spins around as I expected, but I'm already in too close for him and grab the rifle's stock with my right hand, knee him in the chest, pushing him backward, then catch my balance as I take the other end of the gun from him while he stumbles back.

I immediately hold the rifle high over my head in a surrender motion. "Let's just talk for a moment."

"Give us the gun back, asshole!" says the younger man as he lunges toward me.

I lower it, yank back the bolt, pull it free, then toss him the now-useless gun.

"Here. We can negotiate for the rest of it later," I reply.

The younger man starts to walk toward me, but the older man holds him back. We make eye contact, and he scrutinizes me.

I hold out my right hand. "Dr. Theo Cray. And you are?"

"Eduardo," he says, shaking my hand hesitantly. "Are you all scientists?"

"Most of us," I reply.

He eyes us suspiciously.

I hold up the toothbrush. "We're not here to take your discovery or interfere with your archaeological site. We're just very, very curious about what's out there."

"This is trespassing. We'll call the government," says the younger man.

"Alfonso, please," says Eduardo.

"What university and what department?" asks Bilton.

"We're with the UMAC foundation. Look it up," says Eduardo.

"I will. And how about if we make a ten-thousand-dollar donation right now?" Bilton proposes.

"We're not here to take credit for anything," I add quickly. "We just want to see."

"Why here? Why now?" asks Eduardo.

"Long story."

CHAPTER TWENTY-THREE
THE LYING GAME

We're all gathered at the campsite sitting on logs and chairs as I explain to Eduardo and Alfonso a version of events that's not a lie but not the entire truth. Urbina and Bilton have realized that I'm probably better at handling this kind of situation. But it's not like I'm giving them a choice. If we'd wandered into a narco growing operation and that pair handled things, I'm not sure we'd be alive right now.

"We're with a research group that's using satellite imagery and a new method to spot interesting archaeological locations," I explain.

"What kind of method?" asks Alfonso.

When he's not threatened, he's a bright and capable graduate student, so he's still quite suspicious of us.

"Basically, we look for some other outlying feature or collection of features that makes a location interesting. Hypothetically, this could be where two or more trade routes met. In an industrialized location, it would be a place where there's a lot of communication with other regions," I answer.

"And how would you tell this from a satellite image?" asks Eduardo.

He's not buying this. That or there's something else going on.

"It's different in each case. It could be geographic features, proximity to resources and water. Anything."

"Okay, but why here?" Eduardo is persistent. "Why this location?"

Bilton looks like she wants to say something, but I glance in her direction, indicating she shouldn't. Trevor already understands why. His reaction to alien astronauts was probably muted compared to how Eduardo would respond if I told him that we're here because of a signal from space.

"The infrared images looked interesting. We thought this region was unexplored. All we wanted to do was conduct a surface survey and take some photographs. If we found something worthwhile, we'd contact the government and work with a local organization—and provide funding," I reply.

"Who are you again?" he asks, motioning at all of us.

"We're from a group of different research organizations funded by Thomas T. Theismann," says Bilton. "You can look us up."

"And you just came down here on the spur of the moment?" He studies me closely. "There's something familiar about you."

Mentioning serial killers doesn't feel like a prudent move. "Perhaps we met at a conference."

"We can go get the permits if you like," says Bilton.

"We have the permit for this location," responds Alfonso.

"Yes, but maybe we can talk the government into a joint arrangement if we're able to show that we can bring real value." The subtext of what she's saying is that we can buy our way into here whether they like it or not.

Eduardo lets out a sigh. "No need. I'll show you the excavation. It's not terribly exciting, but if this is what you came all this way for, fine. It's about a forty-minute hike from here. Alfonso and I were about to leave, but I'll take you there while he packs up our camp."

We follow Eduardo on a barely perceptible path that leads into thick jungle and goes over rough terrain. Trevor asks him questions about the region while I hold to the rear of our group alongside Horatio.

"You had me scared when you appeared behind that guy with the rock. I thought you were going to kill him," Horatio says so only I can hear.

"I just wanted the element of surprise," I whisper back.

"You looked crazy. I almost didn't recognize you. What do you think of these guys?" he asks.

"I think we make them nervous."

"Me too. You think they were out here tomb raiding and we surprised them? I know some people from the university will make money on the side selling things. As long as it's small, the government doesn't care too much."

"He doesn't strike me as a crook," I tell Horatio, looking ahead at Eduardo, who's in an animated discussion with Trevor.

Bilton and Urbina are keeping close together, conferring with each other. The idea of the nun and the monk in a deep philosophical conversation continues to stick in my mind.

"Just a little farther," says Eduardo from the top of a hill as he checks the GPS.

"Why is your camp so far away?" asks Bilton.

"It's easier to get equipment there and use it as a staging area," he replies.

"For two people?" questions Urbina.

"Oh, that? I have a much bigger team. This is their week off. It's just been Alfonso and me for the last several days."

"I still don't trust the guy," whispers Horatio. "I feel like he's walking us into a trap. You know the scientists I work with have told me that they know people who make deals with the narcos to do research."

"That seems rather unusual," I reply, realizing it's maybe not so weird.

The cartels that own the poppy and marijuana fields aren't outcasts living in the hills. They have nice houses, send their children to school, and interact socially with other people in the community. It wouldn't be that out of line for a researcher who wants to understand something about the local wildlife to get permission from someone acting as a go-between—possibly even a person in the government.

"Here we are," says Eduardo at the top of another hill.

I join the rest and peer down into a small clearing where a flat hill appears to have a set of stone steps leading to the top.

The terrace is elevated about eight feet and is made of carved stones that have shifted over the years and been invaded by weeds and vines.

Urbina and Bilton jog down the hill and toward the steps. Trevor takes out his camera and starts snapping photographs. Eduardo seems unbothered by any of this.

"We think it may have been a ceremonial site. This area was agrarian and didn't have the resources for larger monuments and structures you see elsewhere. But I like the potential because I think it more accurately represents what an average Mayan community was like," he explains.

"When have you dated it to?" asks Trevor.

"We think this was in continuous use until about nine hundred years ago. It was probably abandoned during a famine period."

Bilton and Urbina climb up the steps to the small terrace and survey the area. I'm not sure what they were expecting. Stonehenge?

These seem like perfectly fine ruins. Nothing fancy, but nice and ruined, as promised. Eduardo graciously steps out of the way so Trevor can take more photographs.

Rolando, our other driver, is clearly bored by this. He confides to me, "If you want real ruins, we can take you to good ones. We can even go to Tik'al, where they shot *Star Wars*."

"Perhaps," I reply, then start walking around the location, my eyes on the ground.

The grass and weeds are fairly thick. Occasionally I see bits of broken stone embedded in the dirt. There're no statues or monuments with Mayan glyphs carved into them.

It's what Eduardo said, a totally average Mayan ruin. No rock calendars. No temples for human sacrifice. Not even a ball court.

Bilton and Urbina are on the terrace in deep conversation. From their hand gestures, it looks like they're talking about doing their own excavation—which reminds me of something . . .

I walk around the site one more time to confirm a hunch that started the moment Eduardo agreed to give us the tour.

He spots me off to the side and follows me. "Is everything fine?"

I point to Urbina and Bilton. "You see them?"

"Yes? They seem very interested in this location. I hope they're happy with what they've found."

"You don't understand. They think they've found something. Right now, they're discussing how much it's going to cost to pull the entire permit from you and do their own dig," I explain.

"Well, that's their choice. I've been more than polite," he replies.

I look him in the eye. "You still don't understand. I don't mean for just here. I mean all your permits. Including the location you didn't want us to see."

"This *is* the location," he protests.

I hold up the dirty toothbrush from the campsite. "This is alluvium. It came from an old riverbed, or near one. This site is too high and dry. Your actual site is only a few hundred yards from your camp, isn't it? Alfonso is back there trying to cover everything up this moment. It's pointless. Those people may not find what they want, but their bungling will make your work here hell. Look, no one is trying to steal credit. I'll make sure of that."

He furiously shakes his head. "This is something I don't want credit for. This could ruin my reputation. I sent everyone home because of it."

"Because of what?"

He says nothing, only shaking his head.

"We'll keep it a secret. Trust me, we're very good at that." Until they decide to tell the world.

"I don't even understand what we found. Or how it happened. I just know it doesn't make any sense."

"Tell me."

"Fine. Fine. Then it'll be your problem."

CHAPTER TWENTY-FOUR
THE FIND

Water swirls under the board below my feet as a small tributary from the river feeds the pool at the mouth of the cave entrance Eduardo has led us to.

The side of the hill is muddy and covered with foliage, except for this section, which resembles a dark gray spearpoint with a gash down the middle.

Boulders that had concealed the cave entrance are piled up on either side. Pickaxes and shovels poke out from under a tarp that Alfonso didn't have enough time to conceal from us. The younger man is now standing to the side of the entrance, possibly trying to decide if he should be angry or relieved that he doesn't have to maintain the lie.

"About seven months ago, someone brought me some interesting samples of pottery," says Eduardo. "They were kayaking the stream and found them on the bank. They led all the way up to the mouth here, but the opening was partially covered. If you look closely at the stones, you can see that some of them have carvings.

"They describe the entrance to the underworld. Part of the mythology. We've only found a few chambers like this . . . or like this at first glance."

"Why isn't it boarded up to prevent grave robbers?" asks Trevor.

"I'm in the process of doing that. I sent some of my students for supplies to seal this up until we decide what to do. I'm supposed to notify my supervisor about what we've found, but I only told her of the other location," Eduardo admits.

"Seal it up?" asks Bilton. "Why?"

"It's a significant find. We need more researchers here, but . . . it's complicated."

"Complicated?"

"Things aren't what they should be."

Eduardo can't know that this statement will have Bilton and Urbina practically drooling. God knows what they're expecting, but something that makes Eduardo nervous is bound to thrill them.

"It's easier if I just show you." Eduardo takes a flashlight from Alfonso and leads us into the cave. "Please don't touch anything, and walk on the boards. It can get slippery."

Trevor follows him, with Bilton and Urbina behind. I take up the rear with Horatio. Rolando waits outside with Alfonso, as per my whispered request to keep an eye on him.

The light bounces off the slick rock walls and outlines the bodies of everyone ahead of me. Our footsteps make a metallic echo as the vibrations bounce around the slanted passage. It's wide enough for me to touch either side with my arms but too tall to touch the top. The ground begins an incline and goes above the water table.

"There are other passages here we haven't explored, but this is the main one. Watch your step in a moment. There's a small carved staircase. Please stay on the boards. We still haven't done an inventory of the ground. There could be important fragments."

Eduardo reaches the top of the steps and turns to face us. The passage grows wider behind him but is concealed by his shadow. "Again, I ask that you keep this a secret. What we found initially was a remarkable discovery. There's nothing like it. We think that the area above this cavern was part of a much larger complex, and we've only begun to explore it. However, what we found in here . . . ? Well, I don't know what any of this means."

He points his flashlight at a dozen large stone blocks on either side of the proscenium where he's standing.

"We had to move these first. They were blocking the entrance. The carvings on them have been worn a bit by age, but it's what we found behind them that is so . . . unusual."

Eduardo steps aside and uses his flashlight to illuminate a large stone sarcophagus in the middle of the chamber.

Trevor rushes forward and uses his flashlight to illuminate the carving on the surface.

"You never find a tomb like this in a cave. They're always in temples," says Trevor as he stares in awe.

Bilton and Urbina rush over and look at the cover.

Urbina whispers one word: "Pakal."

Trevor shakes his head. "Similar, but not quite. This headdress is different."

Eduardo glances at me. "Do you know what they're talking about?"

I nod. K'inich Janaab' Pakal was a Mayan lord in the seventh century whose tomb was found in the Temple of the Inscriptions, a large pyramid structure in Mexico.

Viewers of pseudohistorical documentaries know him as *the* proto–ancient astronaut. The lid of his sarcophagus depicts a Mayan-style illustration of a deity intertwined with the world tree.

To those uneducated in Mayan artistic styles, which is basically everyone, it looks a lot like a man sitting in a recliner adjusting mechanical knobs and levers.

This one image has done more than any other to fuel the idea that we were visited by aliens. Its gross misinterpretation is the bane of Trevor's and Eduardo's life work.

Every dinner conversation where it's brought up probably leads the men into a half-hour discussion about how Pakal was actually quite an interesting and well-documented monarch who had one of the longest reigns of any leader in either the Americas or Europe and why that inscription doesn't look like what people think it does.

Part of the misunderstanding is that people don't pay that much attention to dates in history. We tend to compress everything before a certain point back to the time of the Egyptian pharaohs.

In reality, when the builders of the largest pyramid in the world, the Great Pyramid of Cholula in Mexico, were completing their finishing touches, the Catholic Church was already eight hundred years old and the University of Oxford had just started teaching classes. A hotel in Japan was founded a century before that and is still in operation to this day—although I hear their rates have gone up.

The line between present, past, and ancient history is a messy one. Amateurs too excited to do actual learning jumping in with insane theories only complicates things.

"Have you been able to date this?" asks Trevor.

"Only approximately. Seventh to eleventh century," says Eduardo. "Well, this part."

"This part?" replies Trevor.

"It's not the cover that bothers me so much. It's what's inside. I want to keep it shut until I can talk to the authorities . . . but I don't know what difference that will make now. Move the sawhorses over so we can slide the lid open."

I help Trevor place several sawhorses and boards next to the sarcophagus so the lid can be slid to the side without crashing to the ground.

Eduardo places his hands on top of the lid. "Please understand that when we found this, there was a seal all the way around the lid. I've examined the fragments, and that's where we got the dating from. Also, there were calcium deposits that had built up over time. I'll show you the videos if you like. You should want to see them. I need you to understand I did everything as I should. And I swear to you that there's no way this lid had been opened in the last one thousand years."

Trevor and I grab the edge of the lid and give it a heave toward the boards on the sawhorses. Eduardo supervises, making sure it doesn't fall.

Before the lid is even halfway open, I hear Urbina exclaim, "My god."

Trevor glances over my shoulder and adds, "Holy shit."

Urbina and Bilton are pale. Eduardo is shaking his head. Trevor leans over the sarcophagus to try to process it all.

"That ain't right," says Horatio.

I forgot he was standing behind us, watching everything. But he's summed it up perfectly.

No, it's not right.

We didn't find an ancient astronaut.

We found an ancient *cosmonaut*.

CHAPTER TWENTY-FIVE
ELECTRICAL STORM

The flight suit and helmet are unmistakable, the faded red letters spelling CCCP still visible, although the fabric of the suit has eroded away, revealing the rubberized pressure undergarment and the metal bands holding everything together.

Both the suit and the man inside it don't look a day over a thousand years old.

"Who would do such a thing?" asks Eduardo.

"What do you mean?" replies Bilton, who acts like she was just given permission to dry her hands on the Shroud of Turin.

"Make a hoax like this," he says as he points to the cosmonaut.

"Why do you say this is a hoax? You said you inspected the seal," asks Urbina.

"Because I'm not an imbecile. This makes no sense. I'd have an easier time believing an alien, but a man from the 1960s? This . . . this is just cruel."

I understand how he feels. This would be like me looking at bacteria in my microscope and seeing a "Made by Apple in California" logo.

Urbina whispers something to Bilton. I don't have to hear them at this point to know the words: Theismann Hypothesis.

"Wait, are you gonna tell me that Theismann predicted *this*?" I ask.

"Look closer at the man's flight suit. He's actually an airman. Probably a pilot of experimental high-altitude aircraft," says Urbina.

"Oh. Thank goodness. I thought this was something weird. I'm glad you cleared that up." I shake my head.

It's my voice, but Jessica's words are coming out of my mouth. Was I always this sarcastic?

"Trevor, would you explain to Dr. Cray that part of the hypothesis?" asks Urbina.

"Physics isn't my strong suit, but Theismann thought that advanced civilizations could use shortcuts in the space-time continuum . . ." the archaeologist begins.

"Like wormholes in the show *Stargate*," says Horatio.

"No. These are different."

"Okay. But how?" asks Horatio.

Trevor throws his hands in the air. "The math is different. You'd have to talk to Dr. Sexton."

"With enough energy it might be possible to pull apart the fabric of space and slide from one place to another," says Urbina.

"Ah," says Horatio. "You mean like the show *Sliders*."

Urbina ignores him and continues his explanation. "If you had a sizable lightning strike or electrical activity, that might cause it. But it has to be higher up in the atmosphere. In fact, some theories support the idea that lightning starts much higher up and is triggered by cosmic events. We have people studying it."

"I can't wait to see what they have to say. So how does that explain a man from the twentieth century in a tenth-century sarcophagus?" I ask.

"Time travel," mutters Trevor.

"I'm sorry?"

"Time travel," he says a little louder.

"That's in the Theismann Hypothesis, too?" I exclaim. *What isn't?* "And when can I read it?"

"When Mr. Theismann decides you can," says Bilton.

"I'm very curious to hear what you all have to say, but let's take this conversation back to camp. It's getting dark," suggests Eduardo.

I use my phone to take photos of the cosmonaut and the sarcophagus, then help Trevor slide the lid back into place.

Back at Eduardo and Alfonso's camp, the group is sitting around the fire discussing Sergei the Time-Traveling Cosmonaut. Bilton has been on and off her satellite phone at the far end, talking to her colleagues back at the research station. Occasionally she asks Trevor to come over and explain something or corroborate a detail.

I can tell he's troubled by the discovery. Jessica once described this kind of situation in magic as the "too-perfect" trick.

Basically, if a magician asks someone in the audience to think of a number and says the number the person is thinking, the audience is left with only one conclusion: the volunteer is a stooge. While that may not be how the effect was done, the audience has little reason to believe otherwise.

A stronger magic trick would first establish the credibility of the audience member in a way that his being a stooge would seem very unlikely and leave the crowd with no explanation.

If you find a cosmonaut in an ancient tomb, someone planted a cosmonaut in an ancient tomb. He didn't travel through time. Or at least that's the assumption under too-perfect theory.

Of course, that leaves the question of how the cosmonaut ended up in the tomb. Eduardo is adamant about the seal never having been opened. The sarcophagus was carved into the rock of the cave, which rules out the idea that it was transported and put in place.

This is even more of a sealed-room mystery than the robot-assault case I looked into. A challenge like this would be fun if I understood the motives of everyone around me.

Urbina and Bilton are suspicious, but they seemed genuinely surprised by it. Urbina has been doing a lot of pacing and is less talkative than before. He seems like a man who thought he wanted a profound religious experience but is now having second thoughts.

Bilton tends to play everything cool. However, even from where I'm sitting, I can hear the excited tone in her voice. It could be an act, but she doesn't strike me as that convincing.

Eduardo takes a seat next to me and asks, "What do you make of all this?"

"I don't know. I'm kind of just watching things unfold," I reply.

"Can you tell me what brought you here in the first place?"

I look over and see that Urbina and Bilton are having a joint conversation with someone on the sat phone.

"Sure. Let's go for a walk."

Once we're out of earshot, I give him a little more detail. "We detected a transmission from this region. A strange radio burst. I can't go into why, but that's why we're here."

"Do you think that's connected to the astronaut?" he asks.

"I think we're supposed to *believe* it is. Beyond that, I don't know."

"All this talk of wormholes and rips in the fabric of space has got me confused," he admits.

"I understand."

He grabs me by the elbow. "I don't know that you do. You see, after we opened the tomb four days ago, things got very weird. My students said they heard things and saw strange objects in the sky. I sent them home because they were acting like scared children. At first, I thought it was just their nerves. Now, I don't know."

"Do you think any of them will tell people what you found?" I ask.

"I don't know. Maybe to friends. I told them someone was playing a prank on us. Someone from a different university. In fact, I thought maybe you were the ones who did this."

"I wasn't any part of this," I reply.

"What do I do now?"

Eduardo is desperate. He seems like a sincere person who wants only to focus on his work and avoid anything sensational or potentially scandalous.

"I wish Jessica were here," I say out loud.

"Who?"

"A friend. This is right up her alley. Tell you what. After everyone has gone to sleep, let's go take a look at the tomb again."

CHAPTER TWENTY-SIX
MYSTERY BOX

I use my flashlight and hand to explore the surface and area around the sarcophagus. I can't find any places where there might have been a seam that could have been used to lift the lid without disturbing the seal around it.

I pour some water from my canteen to see if it seeps into a crack, but the stream trickles down the stone and pools on the floor. It's not the most scientific test, but it tells me that if there is some invisible seam, it was made with expert precision.

"Do you think they were able to lift the lid without disturbing the seal?" asks Eduardo.

"That's my working hypothesis. Although I wouldn't rule out the idea that they were able to fake the seal chemically. I'd love to get into my lab and try that."

My current "lab" is a card table in the spare bedroom of Jessica's apartment. She tolerates this as long as nothing smells.

Eduardo kneels to watch me work. "What about the stones that covered the entrance to this tomb?"

"One mystery at a time. First I have to notice what doesn't fit."

"Like an astronaut in a thousand-year-old tomb."

"Well, yes. Did you do any testing on the body?"

The corpse looks sufficiently aged. I wonder if someone pulled it from a cemetery in Russia to make DNA testing even more confusing.

"I've sent some fragments that had fallen off. But I haven't got any results back. I want to wait for a proper exhumation," he tells me.

Good science takes time. It's also why a lot of the lab work in criminal-court cases is rushed and shoddy. No prosecutor would ever ask for a second opinion if their lab confirmed what they wanted to hear. It'd be the moral thing to do, but not the practical thing.

There's still the little matter of what or who sent the signal that Sexton's secretive intelligence contractors discovered. It certainly wasn't old Sergei the Time-Traveling Cosmonaut from inside his crypt.

"Tell me about what your students saw in the sky."

"Some of them have very vivid imaginations. I don't know what to make of it all," he replies.

"Okay. Tell me about the ones with the less-vivid imaginations. What did they see?"

"A dark shape flying over the jungle in a circle. Only for a few minutes. There were no lights. There was intermittent fog on that night, and you could only see this shape when it flew by and made the stars disappear."

"It sounds like you saw it, too."

Eduardo nods hesitantly.

"When was the last time you saw it?"

"It was last night. I sent the students home this morning," he replies.

"Around 3:00 a.m.?"

"Yes. How did you know?"

"A hunch."

Okay, we have a dark shape flying around the sky at 3:00 a.m., seen only by some horny and/or intoxicated college students at the exact same moment that some nearby entity sent a signal to our mysterious space probe.

If this is a hoax, it seems like having some very dubious witnesses observe it wasn't the goal. The UAP could have been incidental—a mistaken observation of something entirely mundane.

"Do you ever see DEA or Guatemalan Air Force planes fly over the jungle looking for drug farms?"

"I have seen some airplanes circle in the daytime," he replies.

It's a poorly kept secret that the US government has entire fleets of aircraft registered to fictitious companies that they use to combat terrorism and narco-trafficking. The CIA has secret planes. The FBI has secret planes. Even county sheriffs' offices in Florida have planes under fictitious registration that they use for surveillance.

The names of many of these made-up companies were revealed when some online journalists decided to take all the flight logs from the United States over a three-month period and use a machine-learning algorithm called Random Forest to see which of those flight plans were consistent with surveillance activity—i.e., flying in circles or making sweeping patterns over a region.

Some of the suspect planes were actually private aircraft used for skydiving and doing commercial aerial photography, but it turned out there were way more government planes than expected.

It's no different in countries that have partnered with the US to battle drugs and terror—basically, all of them.

The dark shape Eduardo's students saw plausibly could have been a blacked-out drug-detection plane with surveillance equipment—or even a former government plane with jamming equipment that could be used to send a signal.

It's just a theory, but it better explains what happened than wormholes, cosmic lightning, and rips in the fabric of space-time.

That still leaves the mystery of how Sergei got into the crypt—let alone *why.*

Impossible objects in impossible situations are Jessica's thing. Once again, I wish she were here. Unfortunately, I didn't bring a satellite phone on this trip.

Although there is the one Bilton has . . . Maybe I could ask to use it? But that would make her and Urbina even more suspicious of me than they already are.

"Where's the nearest place I can get a cell signal?"

"Out here? Nowhere," says Eduardo. "I just use WhatsApp."

"WhatsApp? Out here? How?"

"On my Wi-Fi. We have a Starlink antenna. Alfonso mounted it on a pole attached to a tree. You can get a signal from outside the cave if you're high enough," he explains.

"Nice," I tell him. "What's the Wi-Fi password?"

"Theo? Where the hell are you?" asks Jessica as she answers her phone.

"In the middle of the jungle, standing on top of an ancient burial tomb that may or may not be the gateway to the underworld. You?" I reply.

"Trying to find out what happened to David Ikeda. It's not good. They found him in a hotel room a few months ago with an apparent self-inflicted gunshot wound."

"That's not good."

"No, Theo, it's not. It gets worse. Several doors down from his room another man was registered under a false name. And all the rooms were reserved to organizations connected with the same people you're with right now," she replies. "*Adjoining* rooms . . ."

"That's really not good."

"You need to be extremely careful. I don't know what they're up to, but someone connected to them almost surely killed Ikeda."

"I'm trying to figure out the *what*. Without breaking my NDA . . ."

"Screw the NDA," she snaps.

"I have to assume they're sincere until proven otherwise," I reply.

"And coded messages don't break the NDA?" she shoots back, referring to our recent communications.

"I said that under their surveillance. It's part of having plausible deniability. I've been through this before legally. I know what kinds of questions an attorney will ask and how to respond without breaking an oath."

"You're ridiculous. If they go after you for divulging their little secret, it won't be with a lawsuit. It'll be with a bullet."

I think this over, envisioning David Ikeda dead in his hotel room. "Fair point. So let's say we found something inside a tomb that shouldn't be there. How could it have gotten there?"

"Somebody put it there. Any other dumb questions?"

"Okay . . . let's say the lid to the tomb was sealed, and the researchers who opened it say the lid hadn't been disturbed for a thousand years. How then?"

"They put it there one thousand years ago," she replies.

"Well, the thing in the tomb didn't exist one thousand years ago."

"Like an iPhone?" she asks.

"Yes. If you opened an Egyptian tomb and found a sealed sarcophagus with an iPhone inside, what would be your explanation?"

"What model iPhone?"

"How is that even relevant?"

"Some are thinner than others. Maybe they slipped it in between the cracks," she speculates.

"There are no cracks, and it's too big to fit that way," I explain.

"How big?"

"Human size." I don't mention that it's a human wearing a space suit.

"Okay. Think about this in reverse. This is how my grandfather invented magic tricks sometimes. And also, strangely, it's how I think Ikeda may have been killed."

"In reverse?" I reply.

"Yes. Follow me. What if right now you placed something into the crypt, sealed it securely, and then waited a thousand years. Yes, I know you'd be dead, but this is your uploaded consciousness in some nerd robot you made that waits the full thousand years . . ."

"I'll allow it," I reply.

"So, you unseal the tomb, which has never been tampered with, by the way, and the thing is gone. What would your explanation be?"

"It evaporated."

"You didn't bury dry ice, Theo! This thing doesn't evaporate. It's gone. As in not there. How?"

"And the seal hasn't been tampered with?"

"Nope. Theotron 2.0 is even better at this than you. He declares that it's impossible . . . excuse me . . . that it's effectively zero probability. What's your explanation then?"

"Oh. Then it's obvious! I was thinking about the too-perfect theory, but in the wrong way," I realize out loud.

"So . . . the answer is?"

"They didn't go through the seal or the sarcophagus. They went *under* it. Didn't the Warlock pull something like that?"

"Yep. Same wine, different bottle. I think somebody's been paying attention to his methods."

The Warlock is a terrorist and serial killer that Jessica put behind bars, only to watch him manipulate a legal way out. This time we're confident that he's locked away for life. He's also under intense surveillance by people who were embarrassed by him in the past and would just as soon see him dead.

"So, what should I look for?" I ask.

"If you don't want to disturb the body looking for a trapdoor, somewhere near the site you might find piles of rocks and dirt. If they had to do a lot of excavating to create the tunnel, there should be evidence."

"Anything else I should look for?"

"Yes. How do you know the seal and everything else is what they say it is? There's an easier way to do all this, and that's by getting someone to lie."

"I trust the man who told me. He faces a huge professional loss if this gets out."

"All right. But do you trust everyone that he trusts?"

"I'm not sure that I do."

Jessica doesn't respond. I check my Wi-Fi signal and realize that it's dead.

"Dr. Cray?" says a voice behind me.

I turn around and see Alfonso standing a few feet away from me, holding the rifle. I pat my pocket and remember that I gave him back the rifle's bolt earlier tonight.

"Yes?"

"I need you to help me find Professor Eduardo. I think he's lost."

"He was in the cave the last time I spoke to him."

"I checked. I think he wandered off. Would you come with me? Please." He points the tip of the gun at my torso.

"Have you ever killed someone before, Alfonso?"

"We just need to take a walk," the young man insists.

"Did you check to make sure I didn't damage the bolt?" I ask.

He hesitates and glances down. I hurl my iPhone at the bridge of his nose between his eyes, and it makes a loud crack.

Alfonso stumbles backward and a hand flies to his face, loosening his grip on the rifle. I'm on him by the time his hand touches his nose.

I yank the rifle away, kick him in the balls, and slap the rifle butt against the side of his head, sending him stumbling backward until he falls over the edge of the ridge we're standing on and slides down a muddy hill.

I take the longer path down, assuming that he's knocked cold, but he's gone by the time I reach the spot where he fell.

Returning to the site of our standoff, I find my phone. The glass is cracked but the screen still glows. I pick it up and put it in my pocket.

"What was that noise?" asks Eduardo as he steps out of the entrance to the cave, noting the rifle in my hands.

"Alfonso stumbled," I reply.

There's a small chance Alfonso was being sincere that he couldn't find Eduardo, that the rifle was only a nervous precaution. But I don't stay alive by waiting to see the outcomes of those situations without taking action.

If Alfonso makes his way back to camp, I'm going to have some apologizing to do. If he doesn't, I'm going to need to have a difficult conversation with Eduardo about who he hires for research.

I spin around when I hear gravel and rocks sliding and the splash of water.

Urbina stands nearby, staring at the rifle I have pointed at his chest. His hands fly up. "It's just me!"

I lower the gun. "Is that a good thing?"

"We have to head back to the research station!" he says excitedly.

"What's going on?"

"We got another signal!"

PART FOUR

CRIMINOLOGIST

CHAPTER TWENTY-SEVEN
MISSING PERSONS

Jane Ikeda meets me at a coffee shop in a Santa Fe strip mall. It's a sparsely decorated place without all the distractions of a Starbucks. Maisie, the older woman working behind the counter, is friendly and knows everyone by name. She gave Jane a warm greeting as we entered and started her order without asking.

I get a double shot of espresso to make up for my lack of sleep. I'd arrived in Santa Fe a few hours before Theo called me, because something told me that things were about to get interesting here. Call it intuition or paranoia.

Jane looks around the shop and sighs. "I started coming here a lot after David passed away. Journaling, reading, searching the internet. Anything to not think about what happened, but of course it's all I could think about."

"I can't imagine what that must have been like," I reply.

In my line of work, you find yourself saying those words a lot. I also have a pretty good idea what books she read, what blogs she visited, and the rest of the road map for her grieving journey.

Sometimes I talk to family members right after their loss, and they're still trying to process everything. Those people often appear in a daze, as if in a dream they expect to wake up from.

Jane is past that point, I think. She's now realized that the heavy burden and looming shadow doesn't go away. This grief will always be there. Even if she's able to move on, she'll be forever saddled with the nagging thought that she did something wrong.

"The funny thing is that we didn't get to see each other that often. David spent so much time at the institute. But we had fun together. Did you know he volunteered to tutor my students who were struggling?"

Jane is a math teacher at the community college. According to Rate My Professors, she's well loved. I also saw a couple mentions of David and was curious about that.

"That's very kind of him."

"He'd go sit in the library and help anyone who asked. David loved explaining things. I think it's also because the work at the institute was so secretive."

Her voice trembles as she thinks about the moments that made her late husband special. When they're alive, it's easy to see the flaws. When they're gone, you tend to notice only the hole in the Earth that they left.

"I had a former student email me a few days ago. She's now at Stanford. She wanted to know if she could talk to David on the phone because she was feeling so much pressure." Tears stream down her cheek. "I wish David had someone he could have spoken to."

I reach out and hold her hand. Jane clasps my fingers with hers.

"I'm sorry," she says. "I shouldn't be unloading on a complete stranger. I've been good about this for a while."

Maisie walks by our table and places extra napkins for Jane, who wipes at the corner of her eye. "Hah. That's our routine. I cry and scare away the customers. She gives me tissues."

Maisie gives her a hug. "I ain't here because I like the smell of coffee."

As Maisie walks away, Jane confides, "Between her and talking to Elena, I've managed to get through this."

"Elena? Is she your therapist?"

"Elena? No. She's Edward's wife. Or rather, widow. Although I hate that word," she adds.

"I'm sorry. Who is Edward?"

"Oh, I forgot. Edward was a friend of David's. He died accidentally a week after David. At least we think it was an accident. I worry that what happened to David may have affected him. But I don't want Elena to go through what I'm feeling."

"Did he work with David?"

"No. They studied together. Edward lived in California. He worked for some other foundation."

"What's the name of the foundation?"

She thinks for a moment. "The Center for Data Science?"

I type the name into my phone and get the name of the parent organization: World Science Exchange. A chill runs down my spine.

"Did David tell you what he was working on?"

"Computer modeling. He also studied alternative computational systems."

"Like different kinds of programming languages?"

"Sort of. But more like, how would a Roman computer have worked, given their number system? Or the ancient Chinese. How different could your mathematics be and still do useful work? Would some systems actually be more helpful?"

I nod my understanding.

"He once explained that a more primitive system might have struggled with advanced mathematics but excelled at artificial intelligence because they'd have to embrace fuzzier computation. He even built an electronic abacus for a research conference. That kind of thing. David and Edward would get on a call and go late into the night, discussing alternative computational systems." She shrugs. "I guess there are worse hobbies your husband could have. I preferred to leave the math on the blackboard and come home and do something else."

So we have two computer scientists with the same obscure interest working for the same network of companies who died within a week of one another.

Suspicious much?

"What do you know about how Edward died?" I ask.

"It was off the Pacific Coast Highway. They found his car and some empty whiskey bottles by a cliff. He was spotted at a bar drinking earlier that day, and they think he got drunk and fell."

"Into the ocean?"

"Mm-hmm. They found his iPhone washed up on a beach a few miles south. I guess they tracked it."

"Was he a heavy drinker?"

"I never noticed. Elena says that he'd started getting bad about it. I guess from stress and, well . . . David."

"Do you know if the two talked before David's death?"

"Probably. They were off at some retreat a few weeks before David died."

"A retreat?"

"I don't know too much about it. It was supposed to be some kind of conference and meditation thing. It sounded very New Agey. David thought it was silly, but he went because the institute asked him to."

"And Edward?"

"I don't know why he was there. David didn't tell me much about it. But for a meditation conference, he didn't come back very relaxed. In fact, I'd say it stressed him out."

"What about the BrainScan conference? Was he eager to go to that?"

"No. We were going to take a trip elsewhere, but the institute told him he needed to go. I don't want to play the blame game, but sometimes I feel like they worked him to death," she says.

Quite literally, I'm beginning to think.

"What else do you know about the retreat?"

"Nothing. It was at some place in Arizona. I looked up the address, and it belonged to an organization called the Messengers."

"Did David say much about it when he got back?"

"No. I think he used the phrase 'bullshit built upon a lie.' He wasn't into yoga or meditation, to be honest. The way he described the people at the conference, it sounded a bit cultlike."

Cult. Here we go.

"Could you dig up the address and any other information you have about it? Also, Elena's contact info?"

"Okay. But I think Elena is done talking to the police. She's gone through quite a lot."

"I understand," I reply.

I understand that I will not let her feelings get in the way of me making sure Theo isn't in any danger.

CHAPTER TWENTY-EIGHT
HOUSE CALL

Elena Chang does not look happy to see me sitting on her doorstep as she pulls her BMW into her driveway.

I don't know if it's my very presence or the fact that I still haven't gotten much sleep since I spoke to Theo the night before. I managed a one-hour nap on the connecting flight from Santa Fe to San Jose, which hopefully gave my deathly complexion a slightly warmer look.

"Can I help you?" she says in a less-than-helpful way as she gets out of her car.

"My name is Agent Blackwood. I left you several messages," I reply as I stand.

"I'm sorry, Ms. Blackwood, but I don't have time for this. You can speak to our attorney if you have any questions."

"It will only take a few minutes."

She has her house keys in her hands. "I'm past this now. I really don't want to go through this again. I've said everything I know. Now, please leave."

"I don't want to ask you about Edward's passing. I'm curious about David Ikeda's," I tell her.

She pauses. "What about David?"

"Can we go inside and talk?"

"No. But there's a park at the end of the block. Let's go there."

Ikeda's death piqued her interest, but she's so guarded. I don't know if she doesn't want me in the house or is simply trying to maintain a barrier.

We walk to the end of the block where there's a small neighborhood park and an unoccupied picnic table. I take a seat opposite her and wait a moment before speaking so I don't barrage her with questions and run into a wall.

"This is a nice spot," I remark.

"It's one of the reasons we bought here. But let's not talk about real estate. Why are you here?"

The woman is blunt, I'll give her that.

"I don't think David Ikeda killed himself. In fact, I think the organization he and your husband worked for is highly suspicious."

"They didn't work for the same organization," she tells me.

"Not on paper. But they did. Doing what? I have no idea."

"Is this an active case with the FBI?"

"I can't talk about that. I'm just here to get some details about what happened to David."

"Then I don't think I have much I can say."

She's holding back and she wants me to know that. *What's going on?*

"What can you tell me about the Messengers?"

Her eyes lock on mine. "Nothing. I've never heard of them."

We both know she's lying. For some reason she's decided to put up her wall.

"Doesn't Jane deserve to know if David was killed?"

"I guess you should find out, shouldn't you?"

She's squeezing her hands into fists and her knuckles are turning white. I can't tell if this is anger or fear.

"Does it bother you that people think your husband is a drunk who fell off a cliff?" I ask, taking a battering ram to her wall.

"People can think what they want. I know the truth," she replies.

"And what is the truth?"

"Edward loved me more than anything. I'd have done anything for him. And he would've done anything for me," she snaps.

"So don't you care that his death may not have been accidental?"

"Are you saying he killed himself?" She laughs. "Edward was happy."

"But the drinking? Was that a sign of happiness?"

"It wasn't *that* bad."

"I'd say getting drunk and falling off the PCH is about as bad as it gets. Wouldn't you?" I'm being mean to her for a purpose.

She gets up and shoves a finger in my face. "You're a bitch. A flat-out coldhearted bitch. You know that?"

"So I've been told. But at least I'd want to know if my lover had been murdered instead of letting people think he was a borderline suicidal alcoholic. Maybe that's just me."

Elena drops back onto the bench. "Edward wasn't murdered and he wasn't suicidal. Can we just drop it?"

"How would you know?"

"I know he'd never take his own life."

"I mean how would you know he wasn't murdered? Wouldn't you *want* to know?"

"That case is closed. I've moved on. Let him rest in peace."

She's scared. But of what? I go into full bitch mode. "I would let him rest in peace, but we don't know where the body is, do we? Convenient if he *was* killed, isn't it?"

She stares at me with her jaw clenched. "Let. It. Go."

"I can't."

"You have to," she insists.

"Someone I love may be next."

Her jaws unclench as she scrutinizes my face, trying to tell if I'm lying.

"His name is Theo," I explain. "I care for him very much. And I'm not going to let anything get in my way."

"Theo Cray? The scientist?"

"Yeah, the one with the crappy television movie," I reply.

"You had a bad one, too, if I remember."

"A couple. So, you know I'm serious. If there's something you need me to know, tell me."

She shakes her head. "I'm sorry. That's it." With that, she turns and walks away.

I don't chase after her. I've already done enough damage for one day.

I'm sitting upright in bed on my laptop at a Days Inn hotel near San Jose Airport when a small knock comes at my door. I set the laptop aside and walk over and undo the latch.

A woman in a business suit with a hotel name tag is holding a small package.

"Ms. Blackwood?"

"Yes?"

She hands me the package. "This was left for you at the front desk."

"By who?"

"I don't know. It was literally just left at the front desk."

"One second." I take the package by a corner and set it down, then grab my badge. I show it to her. "Check the lobby security camera footage and bring me a clip of who sent this. Understand?"

She nods. "Should I call the police?"

"No. Just get me the footage."

I close the door and take out my travel kit. First, I put on a pair of rubber gloves to avoid adding more fingerprints. Then I swab the package for any trace of explosive using a chemical reagent.

It comes back negative, which only means that a sloppy bomb maker didn't send the package.

Next, I use a high-power laser Theo gave me to illuminate the package from the other side.

There are no wires or suspicious parts.

I pass a small metal detector over the package, and it doesn't detect anything metallic.

I decide that it's reasonably safe to open, but I do it inside my briefcase with the opening facing away from me. This way if there's a bomb, it might spare the important parts of the profile photo for my online dating account.

I cut a slit into the side of the package and pull the contents free, watching the reflection in the hotel mirror so I don't have to stick my face over the edge of my case.

I pull a paperback book from the package. I give the pages a flip and find only paper. No hidden compartments. No white powder. No plastic explosives.

I'm sure Theo could explain how the pages could have been impregnated with a compound that would explode on contact with air, but he's not here to chastise me.

I'm pretty sure it's just a book.

Why would anyone send me a book?

I close the briefcase and set the book on top of it.

It's an old paperback. It smells like it's been sitting on a shelf since the 1970s.

The cover depicts a man looking at the stars with symbols and equations floating over his head.

The subtitle reads: *A Journey into the World to Come.*

The title is *The Messengers*.

I guess I know what I'll be reading tonight.

CHAPTER TWENTY-NINE
DREAM CHASER

The Messengers by Anthony Masters does not exist on Amazon. You cannot find it on eBay. It's not in any public library catalog I've searched.

Yet the book is professionally produced. It has an ISBN number, and the publisher, Charon Publishing, lists several other books on the back page that are still available to purchase to this day, albeit used. *The Messengers* was the last book they published, in 1975.

Outside of the copy sitting on my nightstand, it's as if this book never existed.

The author, Anthony Masters, also doesn't appear to exist. His name is likely a pseudonym. The biography in the back describes an obviously fictional character.

> *Anthony Masters travels the world in his eighty-foot sailing yacht, The Dream Chaser, searching for clues about the origin and destination of mankind. An accomplished private pilot and astronomer, he hand-built the most remote telescope in the world on a mountain peak in Katmandu.*

If the biography is wish fulfillment writ small, the rest of the book is wish fulfillment writ the size of Jupiter.

The Messengers is a novel split into five acts about a young man named Terrence Powers. When we first meet Terrence, he's a college student at MIT on a scholarship he earned because of his scientific brilliance. This, despite being an orphan (obviously) from a rough background.

At MIT, his professors have difficulty accepting his ideas or his rock-and-roll lifestyle. Did I mention he plays the electric guitar?

He writes a "brilliant" research paper on using Fourier transforms—first to determine what the perfect frequencies are for great music, then later as a method to detect trends in world events.

His professors are too stupid to recognize his brilliance. His paper is rejected and his scholarship is revoked.

While strumming his guitar on a rooftop with one of the interchangeable women in his life that he "loves deeply and truly but owes it to them and the world to move on," he sees a bright star in the sky and he gets an inspiration.

In the second part of the book, we watch as Terrence goes cross-country in his custom van, selling his specially designed guitar amplifiers in rock-concert parking lots and bedding many women. His amps become successful after a band that sounds a lot like Led Zeppelin starts using them, and soon he's the CEO of a technology company.

Terrence moves into stereos, robotics, and mainframe computers. But his real passion is the stars.

He builds a facility in the desert and spends his time in a sensory deprivation tank that's wired to radio telescopes pointed at the stars.

The book, which up until this point took an omniscient point of view—describing everything from his Harmonic Hypothesis to how the breasts of a redheaded girl he met at a concert tasted—takes an odd turn:

> *When Terrence finally emerged from the chamber, nobody knew what he'd experienced and he would never tell, but the look on his face was that of a man who gazed into the eyes of God and saw his own reflection.*

Terrence becomes a man on a mission and sells all his earthly belongings to fund "quantum photovoltaics," which would have solved the energy crisis except that a trusted friend sold the technology to oil sheiks, who promptly destroyed it. Despite that setback, Terrence travels the world in his solar-powered van, teaching people how his Harmonic Hypothesis could unite us all, solve our problems, and bring us into the Cosmic Order. His followers become known as the Messengers . . .

And the Cosmic Order? It seems while Terrence was gazing into the eyes of God (or his own), he was shown a vast, multispecies, universe-spanning civilization. For mankind to join it, we simply had to embrace the Harmonic Hypothesis and all it implied.

Through his charismatic efforts, Terrence attracts a following (and beds even more beautiful women) but also attracts critics and enemies.

In the final act, he's arrested and charged with treason on what sounds like flimsy legal arguments and watches as a spurned lover tells the court that Terrence was planning to use his Messengers to take over the world.

He's given a death sentence, even when the lover recants. On the moment of his execution, which is televised on all channels, Terrence reaches the final frequency and vanishes in a rainbow of light that stretches all the way into the stars. (Apparently it was an outdoor execution.)

The world weeps over the loss of Terrence, but little do they know that in the epilogue, Terrence opens his eyes to see the face of the most beautiful woman he's ever beheld. She kisses him and tells him that his work has only begun.

The novel ends with a promise to readers: Terrence Powers will return in *The Man from the Stars*.

I'm not sure which ripped-off party should feel more offended, the James Bond producers or the estate of Robert Heinlein.

The novel's derivative nature aside, why was it sent to me? Is someone trying to tell me that conference-organizing Messengers are connected to the Messengers in the book? By someone, I mean Elena Chang.

Is this just a casual coincidence, or does she know something else? It wouldn't surprise me if the founder of the retreat Ikeda and Chang were at took some inspiration from the book. In fact, the only thing that would surprise me is if they made it all the way through the novel.

There's a weird historical link between cults and science fiction. Not only do science-fiction writers create cults, sometimes cult leaders become obsessed with science fiction.

The Japanese cult that used nerve gas in the Tokyo subway attack were avid fans of Isaac Asimov's Foundation series. Strangely enough, some claim that Osama bin Laden may have been influenced by the books as well. Beyond thematic connections, *foundation* translates into Arabic as "Al Qaeda." It's probably a stretch, but maybe not something to be discounted.

Of course, science-fiction authors bear no more responsibility for what readers do than the Beatles do for writing "Helter Skelter."

Assuming this meditation retreat was inspired by Masters's pulp novel, what of it? Is the implication that Terrence Powers is Thomas T. Theismann? Did Theismann read the book at one point and decide that, although he lost his chance at cruising the country in a custom van and bedding rock-and-roll groupies, he could still try to communicate with aliens and have a Christlike death and resurrection?

Did he buy up all the copies so nobody else could steal the idea?

One way to find out is to talk to the publisher. If they're still around, they should be able to explain why the book ceased to exist.

CHAPTER THIRTY
LIMITED EDITION

Daniel Shadwell, the publisher of Charon Publishing, answers the phone with a gravelly voice that hints at years of tobacco use.

"This is Dan. What's up?"

"Hello, I'm calling about a book that's no longer in print," I reply.

"I don't handle the catalog anymore, and I don't keep any copies. Your best bet is the internet," he says brusquely.

"I'm calling about *The Messengers*."

"Oh, that!" His booming voice takes on a friendly tone. "I was wondering when you guys were going to call. Are you the new accountant?"

Let's see where this goes . . .

"I'm new at all of this. Explain to me how it works?"

"The agreement is that you send me eight hundred dollars a month. I didn't get it the last two months, and I've been calling the number, but nobody picks up," he complains.

This is interesting. I need to keep him talking without getting suspicious.

"We have new software. I need you to give me some details to put into the different sections. Could we start with when the first payment was made?" I ask innocently.

"Oh, um, August or June, I think. I asked for a lump sum, but this was the arrangement." He sighs.

"That would be this year?"

"Hah, what? They sure didn't tell you anything. No. 1975. That's when they bought the rights. Not that it did them much good. It's almost fifty years and nothing has happened with the title. Don't tell your bosses I said that."

"Don't worry. Again, I'm sorry, could you tell me what rights they bought?"

"The book rights, obviously. They also had that silly nondisclosure agreement. I can't remember how they phrased it. Hold on. I got the original contract here. One second."

I hear the sound of heavy breathing and the screech of a metal drawer that hasn't been opened since the Carter administration.

"Here we are. World rights to publish, plus a confidentiality agreement not to disclose the existence or current status of said property. At the time, they were worried Kubrick or Spielberg would to try to steal this concept. I asked them why they didn't simply go talk to Bob and get the film rights to *Stranger in a Strange Land*. His was a much better book. But these people didn't get the business. East Coast types. They wouldn't know talent if it hit them between the eyes."

"Let me just add that here . . . one second . . . hmm. Okay, this is dumb. I have a drop-down menu of several different companies. Which one am I supposed to use?" I ask, imagining a screen in front of me.

"I hate all that electronic garbage. Remember when a filing cabinet was a physical thing? Nah, you're too young. Once upon a time, all those buttons on your iPhone used to represent real things," he grumbles.

I'd lecture him about the vast filing system in my grandfather's basement filled with newspaper clippings, magic routines, and contracts that he threatened I'd inherit one day, but I need to continue my charade of Jessica the dimwit accountant.

"Studio Films International," says Dan.

I'm about to blurt out that I never heard of them but realize that might blow my cover. I'm also aware it could be a trap. "Huh. That's weird. It's not on my drop-down list."

"Oh really? Maybe I have the wrong contract. What names are on there?"

I think Dan is a little suspicious.

"I have the World Science Exchange and some other companies we handle the accounting for, but nothing film related." I need to call his bluff of my bluff. "I can email my boss and see what he says when he gets back from vacation."

"Oh wait. I found it," says Dan, pretending to shuffle some papers around. "Here we go: New Science Studios."

"Okay. Let me see if my system checks that out." I pretend to type on an invisible keyboard. "Okay. It didn't reject that. Can you give me the address?"

"Sure, it's 4821 Cattlecreek Road in Miller, Arizona. I think that's near Tucson. I'll give you the phone number, too."

I add up how much Dan has been paid to not publish the book over the years. *Yikes.*

"This all seems so odd. They've paid you more than half a million over the years. Why didn't they just pay you the lump sum you requested?" I ask, assuming this is a good accounting question.

"Good question. I would have taken five grand at the time. It's not like the book was going to be a bestseller. But that was the arrangement. It worked out pretty well for me," he says smugly.

I wonder if they did this to keep the book a secret? It would be hard to enforce the secrecy agreement after the fact if Dan talked about the book. They could sue him, but the horses would be out of the barn.

"Makes you wonder how the author made out," he muses.

"You mean Anthony Masters?"

"Yeah. The legendary explorer 'Anthony Masters' and his magical yacht," he says with a laugh.

"Have you ever met him?"

"Met him? Never. They handled all that," he replies.

"They?"

"Your people. Or rather, New Science Studios. They're the ones that paid me to publish the book. I'm surprised he isn't in your list of payees. Maybe they bought him outright. Lucky bastard."

Paid Dan to publish the book, eh? "And you say you've never even talked to him?"

"No. Not that I know of," he adds after a moment.

"What do you mean?"

"I could have met him at a science-fiction convention. A number of named authors do ghostwriting on the side. The novel doesn't read like someone with real talent, though. I had to clean up a lot of it. You should have seen the original manuscript. Every woman's breast tasted like strawberries. Sorry. I'm not very politically correct or, what is it? Woke?" he offers apologetically.

"No need to apologize. Who originally contacted you about this book?"

"Cecil Preston. He was old when I met him, so I doubt you've heard of him. He arranged the publishing and the *un*publishing of the novel."

"That's so odd. Why do you think they did that?"

"I have two theories. Either they decided that they had such a hit concept that they legitimately feared Hollywood would steal it—which is laughable—or they were embarrassed by the reaction to it and decided to pretend it never existed."

"Reaction?" I ask.

"At their request, I sent early copies to a couple reviewers at science-fiction magazines. They tore it to shreds. Vicious. Hilarious, too. When I told Preston this book was going to be eviscerated, he pulled all the copies from the warehouse. Although half had already been sent to bookstores . . . He then wrote to the reviewers and bought the publishing rights to their reviews, effectively shutting them up for all time."

"Did Preston ever explain how they found the author?"

"Yeah. He said something about how they ran a publishing contest to find new and talented writers. Masters was supposed to have been the winner. He may have been new, but he wasn't talented. Actually, my pet theory is that Cecil Preston was the actual author. Or he hired someone to ghostwrite the book. It happens a lot. Sometimes a producer gets an idea for a story and they pay some novelist who needs the money to write it. Either way, the world never got to find out what happened to Terrence Powers after *The Messengers*. And I was really hoping to find out what alien breasts tasted like . . . Sorry. No offense."

"None taken. I'm sure we all want to know the answer to that question. I'll update the information here," I assure him.

"Thanks. It's getting harder to pay rent and all the medical bills," says Dan.

Oh, great. Now he's expecting that check and I got his hopes up. I feel like the worst person in the world.

"Mr. Shadwell, between you and me—if this payment doesn't go through, I think the rights to the novel revert back to you."

"What good would that do me?" he asks.

"Confidentially, there may be more interest developing in this book than anybody realizes."

"Hah. I've heard that one before. Let's just make sure the payment goes through."

CHAPTER THIRTY-ONE
Book Club

"That's one heck of a story," Theo says to me over FaceTime while his charter jet gets refueled and a crew change at an airport near Monterrey, Mexico.

"The novel or the story behind it?" I ask.

"The novel sounds bad, but you know my literary tastes aren't very sophisticated."

"Theo, you don't have literary tastes. You just process information. And yes, it is bad."

"Is it weird that I really want to read it?"

I'd given him a short description plus the details Shadwell had shared with me. I didn't go into all the specifics.

"Weirdly, you might like it. The Harmonic Hypothesis is right up your alley."

"The what?"

"Oh, I didn't tell you. When the protagonist isn't slaying chicks, he's developing his grand unified theory of everything called the Harmonic Hypothesis. It applies to everything from the stock market to alien contact. By the way, how is the alien part going?"

"Someone may have tried to murder me after we spoke in Guatemala. But it's not important. Tell me more about this Harmonic Hypothesis."

"What?"

"Some research student. I think he got paid to look the other way with the cosmonaut hoax," says Theo.

"Cosmonaut?" I ask.

"Yes, that's what was in the crypt. Anyway, we'll be back in New Mexico soon. Tell me more about this book."

"No. Tell me about that." Sometimes you have to be blunt with Theo. Most times.

"After we spoke, one of the people who worked on the dig approached me with a rifle. He didn't say he was going to kill me. But I didn't want to explore the possibility too much. So I took his gun."

"And?"

"And he disappeared into the forest. End of story. His professor said he came from a rough background and his family was having money troubles. Things may have escalated. That's all I know. Anyway, tell me about this Harmonic Hypothesis."

"You're a very difficult man. Fine. Let me read you a passage . . ."

> Terrence Powers listened to the pulsing sounds of the rock band onstage while the lead singer whipped his hair with a frenzy and the crowd bounced up and down. The massive array of speakers blasted them with wave after wave of sonic booms, and their bodies moved in what first looked like random patterns, but on deeper examination he saw the gyrating hips of the men and the supple heaving breasts of the young women and realized there was an order to it all.
>
> The concept of a "concert" took on new meaning to him, and he visualized the interweaving patterns of sound and motion until he could separate them in his mind, splitting apart each frequency like a fingerprint and seeing how one influenced the other. From the bulging crotch of the bassist to the erect nipples visible through the white T-shirt of the sumptuous redhead standing so

close to him he could smell her, he saw the Harmonic Hypothesis in all its dimensions.

He understood.

He took the crumpled paper from his pocket that contained his professor's dismissal of his ideas and tore it to pieces and threw them into the air. He then laughed and admired the way the shreds vibrated as they fell—their seemingly chaotic cascade violated by a rhythm that could not be denied.

He'd show them. He'd prove to them the reality of the Harmonic Hypothesis using the very medium that revealed it to him.

Glancing at the primitive amplifiers onstage and the crude pedals under the feet of the guitarists, Powers grinned. He'd show them all. But first he'd find out the name of the cute redhead and ask her if she wanted to see his custom van.

"Good lord," says Theo.

"Bad, I know."

"What? Um, yeah. But I think I want to be Terrence Powers," he replies.

"It's adolescent wish fulfillment."

"With a very vivid description of how a Fourier transform could work in infinite-dimensional function spaces. I mean I get why his professor dismissed the paper. He'd need to explain why some frequencies would still be present despite the Riemann–Lebesgue lemma."

"Theo! Listen to me. You don't get to be Terrence Powers. No one gets to. He's not real," I explain to a grown man.

"Of course he's real," replies Theo.

"Excuse me?" *Did he lose his mind in the jungle? Again?*

"Don't you see it? Terrence Powers, or rather Anthony Masters, *is* Thomas T. Theismann. MIT dropout with a brilliant theory nobody understands. Becomes wealthy from his vision. Searches for aliens . . ."

"This book was published in 1975," I reply.

"Right after Theismann made his first millions. He clearly decided he had a very bright future in front of himself," says Theo.

"So he wrote a book about it?"

"And then got cold feet when he realized how it might affect his investors. Steve Jobs was still walking around barefoot on the nightshift at Atari at this point. The financial world didn't accept eccentrics like they do now."

"So he buried the book."

"But not the dream. He held on to that."

The more I think about it, the more it makes sense. Dan Shadwell thought Cecil Preston was the author. It now makes sense that Preston was merely an attorney Theismann hired to be his go-between.

"I sent you something. Take a look," says Theo.

I click on the message and I'm taken to a web page for a US patent for a guitar amplifier. The assignee is none other than Thomas T. Theismann.

"Jesus. Does he drive around the country in a custom van solving complex math problems while hunting for groupies to bang?" I ask.

"Doubtful. But I'm sure he wanted to. Hell, *I* want to. Terrence Powers is my new life model."

"Don't let me stop you," I reply curtly.

"I meant the custom van and the math problems."

"Uh-huh. Can you get me the contact information for the kid who almost killed you? I might have a few pointers for next time."

Theo ignores my joke and changes the subject. "The people at the institute talk a lot about the Theismann Hypothesis. It is a series of predictions and equations that are supposed to describe a number of things, including alien contact."

"Have you read the Theismann Hypothesis?" I ask.

"You have to be invited by the man himself. It's never been published. Which isn't very scientific."

"But is very cultlike. Which is why I'm suspicious about the retreat David Ikeda and Edward Chang went to. The phone number of the company that was sending the publisher checks also matches a phone number connected to a place called the Colony. It's an old ranch I think Theismann may have purchased originally to turn into a film studio," I explain.

"And now it's a meditation retreat?" asks Theo.

"Yes. Different owners, too. It was purchased in 1982," I reply.

"By another Theismann entity?"

"No. This is actually a nonprofit called the Institute for Humanity. Although it was sold for one dollar. Which sounds a lot like a donation."

There's a knock at my door.

"One second, Theo. Someone's here."

"Please let it be a delivery person with the sequel to *The Messengers*."

It's the hotel clerk I spoke to several hours ago.

"I got the surveillance footage and made you a printout of the person who left the package," she explains.

"Thank you."

I take the printout, shut the door, and take a seat on the bed.

"Well?" asks Theo, having overheard the conversation.

"Patience."

I pull out the photograph and stare at it for a moment. It's not what I was expecting. Not at all.

"And?" says Theo impatiently.

"Shut up. Sorry. Give me a minute."

I do a search on my laptop. Things that I overlooked before start to make sense. Now one part of the puzzle is a little clearer to me.

"We know who gave me the copy of the book," I tell Theo.

"Mrs. Chang?"

"No." I look at the photo from the lobby and shake my head. "Mr. Chang."

"Edward Chang? Isn't he . . ."

"Dead? He's supposed to be. But they never found a body. I thought it was because the murderer didn't want the body found, but I should've known better. Now I realize it's because Chang wanted to hide himself."

I sigh loudly. "See, his wife slipped up a couple times, but I overlooked it. She said 'our attorney' and spoke hesitantly when talking about her husband in the past tense. I thought it was just the grieving process. Now I realize she's helping him hide."

"Why?" asks Theo. "Is Theismann behind it?"

"Maybe. Definitely someone connected to him. I just can't understand why," I reply.

"I felt the same looking at the body of the cosmonaut in the Mayan tomb. *Why?* Who would take this seriously?"

"Are you kidding? We have scientists and government officials looking at blurry footage from military aircraft using equipment they don't understand and screaming 'aliens.' The richest man in the world is building a space fleet to invade Mars. What does it even mean to stretch the imagination now? Maybe there's some weird angle . . . Would a time-traveling astronaut or an alien signal affect the stock market? Is that it? So, for a day, Theismann could make an extra billion or so?"

"I don't know. It would be a very long con," says Theo.

"Maybe. But who knows how Theismann thinks? I mean, if you read his book, you'll realize he thinks a lot about breasts. But you get what I'm saying."

"Possibly. But I think there's an angle that we're not seeing. Theismann is brilliant. He's not a pretender. He's also incredibly wealthy. I don't think he wants more money. He wants something else."

"Yes. We covered that. He wants to cruise around in his van for hot chicks," I reply.

"More than that. He wants to talk to aliens."

"Alien babes, hon. You need to read the book. But yes. Maybe this is a ploy to get us all to believe so we support this endeavor. Either way, I want to visit the Colony and speak to these Messengers."

"Is that wise?" asks Theo.

"You of all people don't get to ask me that."

CHAPTER THIRTY-TWO
RACHEL

"It's so nice to meet you. I'm Sally," says the gray-haired woman dressed in white who meets me at the front gate to the Colony. "Can I see your driver's license to check our records?"

"Of course!" I say as my Uber drives off. I take the license from my purse and hand it to the woman.

She snaps a photo of it using an app on her phone. "This will only take a moment. Oh, here we go. Welcome to the Colony, Rachel!"

Today I'm Rachel Banks. A recently divorced woman of some means with short red hair and a longing to belong somewhere. My long brunette locks are in a wastebasket back at the hotel in Santa Fe.

I learned to cut and dye my own hair when I was thirteen. That was helpful when I wanted to hang out with my friend's friends without them realizing right away that I was the girl magician who sawed Jay Leno in half on *The Tonight Show*.

When we could afford it, I went to a fancy private school in Beverly Hills along with the brats of famous actors and a few child stars. Those kids wanted people to know who they were. I wanted anonymity.

Working high-profile cases for the FBI also gave me access to fake identities that would pass a basic background search. This turned out to be crucial when I applied for a job opening at the Colony.

While doing background research, I came across an online ad for a job in Tucson that got me suspicious:

> Meditation retreat is looking for full-time employees who want to help others pursue a life of peace, tranquility and exploration. This is not a high-paying job but the rewards are immeasurable. Room and board is provided. We welcome you to be a part of our loving community. Couples are welcome.

If that's not a cult-recruitment ad, I don't know what is. *Come work for free in our compound!*

For the phone interview, I presented myself as the perfect recruit: a vulnerable woman who found out her husband was cheating on her—with another man. Financially well off and still young.

When I told them I was going to be in Tucson later today to visit some art galleries, they extended the offer to stay a few days and interview.

The Colony is outside Tucson, in the foothills of the mountains. On Google Maps, it's one of the lusher pieces of real estate in the area due to the natural well the property happens to be located on.

Driving out to it, I found the Colony was hard to miss. It looked like an oasis in the middle of parched desert scrub.

Google Maps showed a man-made lake with a dozen buildings scattered around it, including a solar panel farm and what appeared to be large warehouses—possibly for the film studio that never got made.

Sally leads me up a stone path that runs alongside an artificial brook. It has a pleasing sound, and the smell of water is potent in the dry air.

The well-watered trees have produced shade coverage, and the temperature feels ten degrees cooler inside the gated compound.

Wind chimes sway in the breeze, and I'm immediately taken back to the gardens I liked to stroll through when I performed in Japan.

Whoever designed this place knew what they were doing. The path winds around small hills covered with shrubbery, and each turn reveals a new landscape, making every acre feel like ten.

A rabbit jumps across our path in lazy bounds, not worried about our presence.

"There's one of our staff members," says Sally.

"I see clothing is optional."

She laughs. "I guess we do make exceptions from time to time. When the guests aren't here, some of our staff members have been known to test that exception at night in our pond."

"That sounds fun," I reply. I want to let her know that I'm adventurous.

"It is. Of course it was a bit more . . . um, wild when there were more men around," she replies.

"More men? What do you mean?"

"Oh, we have another colony project. Some of our members are off building it. This is just a prototype, really."

"Where is it?" I ask.

"We haven't announced yet." She leans in and whispers, "Somewhere more tropical."

"Intriguing. So, when does the interview start?"

"Darling, this is the interview," she replies. "Would you be more comfortable in a stuffy office with a desk between us?"

"Hah, no. So what do you want to know?" I ask.

"Me? I already read your Facebook and looked at your photos. I think I know a lot about you."

Did I mention the bureau's undercover-identity work goes deep? One press of a button and we can generate a thousand photos and an entire social media presence.

"Oh, I hope there wasn't anything too embarrassing." *And that you won't ask me anything I can't remember from the profile.*

"Not at all. This is your interview, as in you get to interview us. You had the job the moment you decided to call. Now it's up to you to decide if you want to stick around with this crazy group."

"What are you saying?" I ask.

But I already know the answer: this is advanced cult mind-manipulation. I have to choose them and rationalize why. She'll then tell me how hard it is, and I'll tell her I still want it. She'll tell me they aren't perfect, and I'll tell her I accept that.

"Ask me anything you want, and if you're happy with the answers, your shift starts. Deal?"

Sally takes me on a different path, this one leading around the lake. I get a sweeping view of the buildings and notice a tall circular structure with a dome.

"Is that an observatory?" I ask.

"Yes."

"I love those."

"Why is that?"

"I love looking at the stars. I love thinking about all the possibilities. When I was a little girl, I used to wonder if there was a little girl on some other planet looking down at me." This is true.

"I wondered the same thing. We all do here. We're explorers," she explains.

I decide to be a little more direct. At least as much as "Rachel" would be. "Okay, what's this all about? I get that this is a meditation center, but I couldn't find out much about you."

She gives me a broad smile. "I guess you could say we're a cult, dear."

I acted appropriately shocked. "A cult?"

"Yes. I think that's the honest way to describe it. We're a small group with a belief that's outside the mainstream. We tend to dress alike and share some of the same views. I think 'cult' is the right word. Of course, Pythagoras and his followers were a kind of cult. Same as Jesus and his apostles. The founders of the Declaration of Independence. The first abolitionists. I could go on. But you get my point. 'Cult' doesn't have to be a bad word," she explains.

I smile and nod, trying to keep my memory of discovering an entire suicide cult that had hung itself out of mind. But it's not working. I still see the small feet twisting in the air. The sound of the lone survivor hiding in the dark, wanting to know when his mother was coming back.

"Rachel? Are you okay? Was this a little too much, too soon?" Sally asks worriedly.

"No. I'm fine." I realize that I'd stopped walking and was no longer the nervously smiling Rachel. I make an attempt at a laugh. "So, what is this crazy belief?"

"We believe that we're not alone in the universe and that we have to become better as a species for the rest of the universe to accept us. It's not that radical of a belief if you accept the idea that we're not alone," she points out.

"No, I guess not. But your website didn't say anything about it."

"That's so we can avoid attracting the wrong type of person. Which I don't think you are."

"That's fascinating. It's a lot to take in. I'm surprised nobody has mentioned this." Really surprised.

"We don't tell everyone. And those we do? We just ask them not to tell it to the world. Which I'm asking you now. Can you promise me that?"

"Yes. Of course. But what if I was a journalist?" I ask.

"Then you'd have a very boring story. We're not much different than any group that believes God, in all his majesty, didn't reserve the miracle of life for one planet," she explains.

"So you're religious?"

"Yes." She takes a cross out from under her collar. "I'm a Catholic. I go to Saint Peter's in Tucson and help out with the charity drives. Some of our members are Jewish. We have a few atheists. But the Colony doesn't have a religion. If there was one, it would be science. A more helpful way to think about us is like an open-ended university. We have libraries and classes. We're on a lifelong journey of learning."

"But . . . aliens?" I ask.

She puts a finger to her lips. "Maybe not aliens. But something. Anyway, your shift is about to begin. I'm afraid there are some dishes in the kitchen and then some dirty linens in the laundry." She smiles. "Now's your chance to escape, honey. Or tomorrow. Or the next day . . ."

CHAPTER THIRTY-THREE
Colonist

Daphine, a woman with braids who appears to be close to my age, is helping me fold the sheets that just came out of the large industrial dryer. The laundry room, like everything else I've seen so far in the last few hours, is high quality and what I'd expect at a top resort.

"So what do you think so far?" asks Daphine.

"Everyone is very nice here."

"Did Sally give you the whole 'we're a cult' speech?" Daphine asks as she takes the end of a sheet from me.

"Yeah. That was a lot on the first day. But I appreciated the honesty."

"That's our way of giving people a chance to run for the hills. It's not too late," she says with a grin.

"I don't think I'd run from that. I mean, I really appreciate it." At least in the way that Rachel would. After all, she ended up here because her ex-husband had been harboring a secret his entire life.

I'm beginning to get a sense of the game in this place. While I washed dishes, I talked to Kathy and Colin (an older man and one of the few I've seen). They were quite talkative, telling me about the latest gossip, which was about as tawdry as what you'd expect at a librarian luncheon.

It seems Catherine (not Kathy) had made a veggie macaroni but had to substitute actual cheese at the last moment and forgot to tell Ginnifer, who has gone vegan but secretly isn't able to give up her Saturday-morning McDonald's milkshake habit.

There was no talk about levels, secret powers, or the insatiable sexual appetite of the founder. In fact, my subtle prying couldn't find out any details about who actually runs the Colony. It clearly can't be the self-organizing collective that it appears to be.

I suspect the hierarchy is a little more invisible. While I thought Sally was running the show because she'd greeted me first, she had to dart off to tend to a delivery and mentioned something about making sure Janine wasn't upset. But then I overheard Janine was frustrated by the task board this week because it conflicted with her plans.

I now have two theories that are not quite contradictory. The first is that the ultimate leader isn't here. He's more like a visiting CEO. The other theory is that the acting leader is somebody who I've already met and may actually be my workmate Daphine.

She's perceptive but working hard to seem disarming with girl talk.

"You don't like secrets?" she asks.

"I think some are important. But not when they affect other people," I reply.

"Hmm. Sounds like this comes from personal experience," she says, pretending that Sally didn't tell her of my oversharing phone call about my husband's infidelity.

"A lifetime of personal experience, I guess. I hope I've learned," I reply.

"Men are the enemy?"

This is a tricky probe. She might be trying to find out if I'm just here to rebound for a few weeks or am ready to make a true life change.

"I don't know. Maybe some men. Marriage was interesting, and I'm not ruling it out again. I just felt like I was missing out on something. At first, I thought it was children, but really it was . . . I don't know."

"Doing other people's laundry?" she jokes.

I look down at the pillowcases I'm folding. "I could do this all day. It's weirdly relaxing. You know?"

The pile of laundry in my bedroom back home screams otherwise . . .

"Well, stick around and you're going to get plenty of tasks like this," Daphine warns.

"Is it weird that I'm kind of looking forward to that?"

"A little. But we're all a bit weird. The men in town stay clear," she says.

This is an interesting direction she's taken the conversation. "I noticed there aren't a lot here."

"Sadly, we have them working on a construction project," she replies.

"How long has it been?"

"A while," she says. "You ready to get back into the dating pool?"

"I can think of one aspect of dating that sounds appealing. The last couple of years with Frank were a bit . . . boring," I confide.

Daphine leans in and whispers, "Just because the men aren't around doesn't mean there won't be men around." She hands me a stack of sheets. "Put those on the cart and we'll take 'em to the guest cabins."

There's no more talk of men as Daphine and I make beds in the cabins. Even though there are no guests this week, it's routine to make the beds every day and do a spot-cleaning of the rooms.

The cabins are contemporary in design and resemble detached hotel rooms grouped in clusters of four.

As we make the beds in the second cabin, I try more idle conversation with Daphine.

"So, who are the guests?"

"We mainly do corporate retreats for a small group of clients."

"By clients, do you mean people or businesses?"

"A select few companies we've worked with over the years. It helps pay the rent, so to speak," she explains.

"Are there trainers for these events?"

Daphine tucks the corner of a sheet under the mattress with precision. "Some of us teach. For the important ones, Mike comes and runs the sessions."

"Who is Mike?" I ask.

Daphine smiles. "Who is Mike? That's a great question. Everyone here has a different answer."

"What's yours?"

She shakes her head and grins at a thought. "Mike is the funniest motherfucker you've ever met. Also the greatest dancer. That boy can move better than fools half his age."

"Is Mike the leader?"

Daphine lets out a loud laugh. "Whatever a leader is, Mike's the opposite."

"A follower?"

"More like a stray cat that wanders in from time to time. You'll understand when you meet him. Hard to miss on his big old Harley. You can hear him coming for miles. All the girls here start running to their bunks to check their makeup." Daphine studies my face and shakes her head. "No. It's not like that. We're not going to dress you up in a white robe and present you to him under a full moon. He doesn't mingle with the staff, if that's what you're worried about."

"I wasn't thinking about that," I lie.

"You might when you meet him. When God was giving out charisma, Mike said, 'I'll take yours.'"

All right, I think my cult bingo card is full now that I've identified the charismatic leader who openly professes to not want the burden of leadership while clearly being the boss of this group.

His hands-off policy, whether real or perceived, only makes him more interesting. It also means this group can attract men that aren't worried about being made a cuckold by the leader who declares *droit du seigneur*.

"What did Mike do before this?" I ask.

"Before the Colony? What didn't he do? He sailed around the world on his sailboat. Flew planes. Built observatories." She points out the window. "Including that one out there."

Who does this sound like? Is Mike actually Anthony Masters, a.k.a. Theismann?

"Did he ever write?"

"Write? Mike? Not that I know about. Maybe back in his school days at MIT," she replies.

"Do you have any photos of him?"

She shakes her head. "He hates to be photographed."

"Oh. Oops."

"But I took one with him anyway."

Daphine pulls out her phone and shows me the lock screen. She's kissing the cheek of a handsome man with a gray goatee who resembles Josh Brolin.

Definitely not Thomas T. Theismann. But possibly Thanos.

"I see what you mean. He's cute."

"That's enough," she says, playfully pulling away the phone.

I need to look him up.

"What's Mike's last name?"

"I never asked," she replies. "He's just Mike. Anyway, I've got to go get dinner ready. Feel free to walk around. If there's not a lock on the door, make yourself at home. Just be careful of the greenhouse and the storage sheds. Their roofs need repair and aren't safe. You should check out the library. We're very proud of it."

"Sounds good," I reply, fully determined to look inside the warehouses she called "sheds."

CHAPTER THIRTY-FOUR
EXPLORER

I spend the several hours before dinner wandering the grounds and investigating the library. To my great disappointment I can't find a copy of *The Messengers*, let alone, heart be still, its elusive sequel, *The Man from the Stars*.

There is a vast section of books on astronomy and quite a lot also on pseudohistory. This is a place where one can read Carl Sagan and Erich von Däniken in one sitting and not realize the contradiction.

The other members are super friendly and amazingly talented at small talk. For a cult population, it's quite extraordinary.

I had an entire half-hour conversation with one woman about all the things she liked to add honey to. It was neither boring nor enthralling. There were also lots of conversations about family members, what their nieces and nephews were up to, and even two women with children who go to school in town.

Despite Sally's talk of this being a cult, to the locals this place is a resort with a live-in staff that's maybe a bit eccentric but not secretive.

They are embedded into the community in plain sight. Even the all-white uniforms don't seem much more unusual in Tucson than nurse uniforms or maid outfits.

The Colony has mastered the ability to fit in. They did this by telling everyone up-front they were a little weird, then proceeded to show up at the church picnics like every other upstanding member of the community.

Some of what Daphine told me still has me thinking. There was the subtle implication that members of the Colony do more than fluff the sheets of the guests—at least in certain situations.

I can't tell if that means this is secretly some kind of brothel or a place like any other resort, where sometimes horny guests and horny staff hook up. I could throw a rock in any direction in Palm Springs and hit a resort like that.

I also still haven't determined the connection between the Colony and what happened to David Ikeda or Edward Chang.

Did someone attempt to blackmail them? Was Ikeda treated as a "special" guest and recorded without his knowledge?

Was it something else? Did "Mike" talk to him?

I have a feeling the elusive Mike's charisma could run both ways. He could be the type that makes you feel like the most important person in the world or reduce you to the dust beneath your feet. My grandfather was like that. In some ways, I think he lifted me up and ground my father down.

After helping clean up the dinner dishes in the group dining hall, I join a few others at the observatory for tonight's show.

Upon entering, I realize this is the real center of the cult and the closest thing they have to a church.

A medium-size telescope is mounted on a platform, reachable via a winding staircase. But the real show is below, where a large HD projector displays on a screen what the telescope is looking at.

People sit around on beanbag chairs, looking at the screen, listening to chill-out music, and carrying on conversations while someone gives a little star show, describing the feature attraction of the night.

There are only eight people here, not the full forty I counted during the day. But still a good turnout for what appears to have been a daily event for forty years.

"Fomalhaut is interesting because it's a very young star. Somewhere between one hundred and two hundred million years old, it was forming as mammals began to appear on Earth along with flowering plants. It still has a large debris disk around it and what could be an early planet," says an older man's voice on a speaker.

I look around and can't see who is talking. The voice continues in almost hypnotic tones, describing other features in the night sky as the telescope tracks them.

The lecture's so soporific that I find myself dozing off . . .

I wake up and I'm alone in the observatory.

Damn it! I fell asleep.

The projector is still showing images of the stars. The voice is no longer there, but the chill-out music plays in the background.

I check my watch and see it's past 3:00 a.m. I guess nobody wanted to wake me.

I get up and walk out of the observatory, feeling like a guilty teenager who fell asleep at a basement party.

I follow the path from the observatory around the large pond and notice the outline of one of the warehouses above the tree line. Somewhere in the back of my head, James Bond music begins to play and I decide that it's time for 008, my age at the time I became obsessed with being a spy, to have a look at what's inside.

Although they said I couldn't go into any locked buildings, to a born escape artist, locks are mental constructs, not actual things.

Of course, Daphine also warned me to stay away because of the failing roof, but that's only a risk if the roof falls on me and I get killed.

I take my time walking around the pond, making sure that I'm not being observed by anyone. Although I can't know whether I'm being watched on a security camera.

I decide the worst-case scenario is I get caught and they ask me to leave. If I detect the slightest indication of violence, I'll explain that I'm an FBI agent and that my supervisor knows I'm here.

Unless they're nearing completion of some world-domination plot, I think it unlikely they'll kill me.

Unlikely, but not nonzero, as Theo likes to say.

I make a yawing motion to check behind me, then take the path to the first warehouse. Far from looking decrepit, it seems brand-new and has a van and a pickup parked in front of its roll-up door.

At the back end there's a doorway. I stroll by, checking that I'm not being watched, and take out my lockpicks in case the "no locked doors" policy is more metaphor than reality.

Before I open the door, I put my ear to it and hear the whirring sound of an air-conditioning unit that's either mounted on the side of the building or on the roof that's supposed to be unsafe.

It takes me five seconds to pick the lock. I'm rusty. I'm inside two seconds later with the door shut as silently as possible.

I wait a long minute for my eyes to adjust and start to make out the details of the room from the illumination of the exit sign over my head.

There's a rack of jumpsuits to my right with rubber boots below them.

To my left is a wall of locked cabinets. Ahead of me is another door. There's no lock on it, only a handle.

I push it and step into space.

Literally into space.

There are stars stretching from floor to ceiling and what looks like a mountain range in the distance.

I move farther into whatever room I'm in and find the ground is dirt.

Up in the sky, there's a tiny blue star.

Blue star?

Wait a second.

I know where I am.

I'm on Mars.

Okay, I'm not literally on Mars. At least I don't think I am. I can make out the seams in the ceiling where the projection meets the side walls. And the sound dynamics in here are what I'd expect in a room this size.

Also, I'm not nuts. I didn't snooze in the observatory until we invented teleportation.

This is some kind of Mars simulation.

As my eyes adjust, I realize what I thought was another mountain range at the other end of the warehouse is actually a building. More correctly, a habitat, much like what you see in artists' conceptions of what it will look like to colonize Mars.

Okay, this is beyond nuts.

I walk across the Martian landscape, stepping across small crates, and get close enough to see a porthole on the side of the habitat.

I do a double take when I see a rocket ship in the distance with vapor steaming off the side. It's merely part of the projection but looks quite convincing.

I move closer to the porthole and press my nose up against the glass.

My eyes are still adjusting, but I can make out details from the glow of equipment inside. I see space suits, computers, an air lock, a bunk.

And someone staring at me.

Oh damn!

I instinctively do what Agent 008 was trained to do.

I run.

CHAPTER THIRTY-FIVE
MARS BASE

I wake up a few hours later as my roommate Kathy (not Catherine) starts her morning routine. Our room is basically a small dorm room in one wing of the staff quarters with a communal bathroom at the end of the hall.

She was sound asleep when I got back from Mars. I spent the next half hour pretending to sleep while keeping an eye open for henchmen bursting into the room at any moment.

They never appeared. Despite whoever was inside that Mars habitat clearly seeing me.

Maybe they thought I was a dream? Or a Martian?

I could only wonder about that mystery for so long; finally, I fell asleep.

"How did you sleep?" asks Kathy.

"You mean here or in the observatory?" I reply.

"Both, I guess. I've gone to sleep there a few times myself. I love astronomy, but for some reason it's . . . hypnotic," she says, using the same word I'd thought of to describe the experience. "Are you going to stay with us today?"

Am I going to get kicked out? "I think so. If you guys will still let me."

"As long as the task board has tasks, we're going to need taskers," she says.

My first task of the day is to go help serve breakfast. So I put on my sweats and make my way to the kitchen in the next building. By that time, Kathy (not Catherine) is already there, getting ingredients out of the refrigerator.

※

The rest of the morning involved making breakfast, eating breakfast, and then cleaning up after breakfast. It wasn't backbreaking, but it wasn't as exciting as poring over a cold case in search of something that was ignored.

I think I'd rather be in the woods hunting down the Tree Man than cleaning dirty dishes and making sure there'll be enough tea for lunch.

Rachel, on the other hand, loved this kind of work. A slightly spoiled only child who lived with a husband who never gave her enough affection, she craved approval and some feeling of value. Even if gaining value meant counting the boxes of Grape-Nuts.

When I arrived in the laundry, Daphine wasn't there. Instead, my workmate is Colin, the older gentleman I'd spoken to yesterday.

"How's it going, Rachel? Ready for another day in this nuthouse?" he asks with a beaming smile.

"It doesn't seem all that nutty to me," I reply.

"Oh, you'll see," he says, either as a joke or a threat.

As we fold sheets, I make small talk while trying to pump Colin for more information. Like why the hell is there a Mars habitat at a meditation retreat? Some of the people here *have* to know what's going on in there.

"What did you do before you came to the Colony?" I ask him while we wait for the dryer to finish.

"Asking myself what I was doing with my life," he replies.

"Okay. A man of mystery."

"No. Just a joke. I was in the aerospace industry."

Do tell. "What did you do?"

"If I tell you it was classified, it's not because it was interesting or mysterious. It's because it was classified and painfully boring," he says.

"Which makes it even more mysterious," I reply.

"Which it's not."

"Okay. So, what did you study in school?" I ask.

"Electrical engineering. If you ask me what my graduate thesis was about, I'll have to have you killed," he jokes.

I think.

"I'm sure I wouldn't understand."

"Sadly, neither did any of the young women I tried to impress by telling them what I got my PhD in. Times are different now. Although I don't know if women have learned to appreciate the talent of an engineer," he says wistfully.

"I don't know. A lot of women think Elon Musk is cute."

He stares at me blankly. "Is he an actor?"

Wait . . . This man is an aerospace engineer and he doesn't know who Elon Musk is? Musk should be either his idol or personal devil.

"Not a very good one," I reply.

"Oh, then I'm not missing anything."

I am.

I remember a lecture by a former member of the Church of Scientology who had just come out of the secretive cult. He described being so immersed in internal matters that he had little awareness of the outside world. He said he knew who the president was at the time, but it felt like a distant fact unconnected to his own life. He wasn't prevented from knowing about the outside world; it simply wasn't relevant.

"You have any favorite YouTube videos?" I ask.

"That I *have* heard of. Kathy made me a DVD of some of them. They're hilarious. If you know of any good ones, please record them for me if you have the chance."

"Sure thing."

I've now decided the secret Mars habitat isn't the weirdest thing I've observed here. It's the electrical engineer who watches YouTube on DVDs.

I get the feeling that Colin is here for different reasons than everyone else . . . or is he? Maybe we're all trying to get away from something.

Poetic as that insight is, it still doesn't help me understand what happened to David Ikeda or Edward Chang.

❦

After I finish my afternoon chores, I return to the dorm to take a shower and change. And—time permitting—catch a short nap before I help with dinner.

The thought of sleeping is so powerful that I yawn as I open the door to my room.

"Up late?" asks an older man in a business suit sitting on my bed.

"Who the hell are you?" I blurt out.

"I'd ask you the same question, but I already know . . . Agent Blackwood." He looks at my face and hair. "You're one of those people who can change your looks fairly easily. That must be handy in your line of work."

"And you're one of those people that's about to get a broken arm if you don't explain why you're in my room."

"This is not your room. In fact, I'm here to tell you that it's time for you to leave," he explains.

"How do I know you're not some pervert who broke in here?"

He laughs. "I'm the conservator for this organization. I'll gladly produce the sheriff if you want corroboration on that. But I assume you don't want to complicate things with your superiors."

I stand firm. "Complicate things is all I do."

"And now you must complicate things elsewhere. I assume you've seen enough. These people are harmless. Perhaps a bit naive, falling for your well-crafted story."

"What's with the Mars base?" I ask.

"You mean the Mars simulation experiment that you trespassed into and interfered with? That has nothing to do with the Colony. It's just a shared space with a private research organization."

"You mean the Cosmic Agency? Or one of Theismann's other shells?"

His face freezes for a moment, telling me a lot about what he didn't want me to know. Somehow, either he didn't make the connection between me and Theo or has no idea that Theo is in the middle of another part of Theismann's operation.

"It's time for you to go," he tells me again.

"Fine. I'll pack my things. Could you just tell me what happened to David Ikeda while he was here? What messed him up? Did you send him to Fake Mars or something?"

His face freezes again. Interesting . . .

Sometimes cults use ostracization to enforce discipline. Rumor has it the wife of a leader of a very famous celebrity cult hasn't been seen since she went into isolation twenty years ago.

Did they do something like that to Ikeda?

The conservator gets up. "I'll leave you to collect your things. If you haven't left the premises in ten minutes, I will call the sheriff."

"And I will show him my badge. And I will talk to the Phoenix FBI office. And I will take the wonderful-smelling body soap and conditioner samples from the bathroom," I fire back, mocking him, but one hundred percent serious about the soap.

Part Five

Astronomer

CHAPTER THIRTY-SIX
NDA

I'm normally a paranoid man, so sometimes I have to stop and check myself to make sure that I'm not too paranoid. But I'm beginning to think that things have changed and my travel mates are watching me more closely.

On the flight back from Guatemala, Urbina and Bilton kept their distance. When we got back to the station, Joss acted even more distant than her distant self. I don't know what instigated this.

Urbina and Bilton are aware that I had an altercation with Alfonso. I spun the story slightly: he accidentally surprised me in the dark while I was taking a leak, and I punched him in the face.

For anyone who has ever been camping, it's a plausible story. Unfortunately, only Trevor seems to believe it.

Right now, we're in the main auditorium and Urbina is getting ready to make a presentation to the rest of the group—about what we found in the jungle, I presume. Interestingly, there's been no further mention of the new signal since we got back.

If I had to guess, they either haven't been able to decipher the signal or they didn't like what they got back. Since nobody is running around screaming, "It's a cookbook!" I'm going to go with the assumption they're still figuring it out.

Although I'm also entertaining the possibility that this is all real, and we're dealing with some cosmic jokers that just prank-called us.

Given the lack of news about the probe's second signal, the only new thing to discuss should be our Central American discovery.

In addition to us invited researchers, the full staff of the facility is here, and all the seats are filled. A younger man in his midtwenties is seated next to me wearing a many-pocketed vest. I think he's a technician who helps Patel with the radio telescopes.

Fiona Joss walks to the center of the stage. "Before Professor Urbina begins, I want to remind you of the NDAs you've signed. We treat those very seriously. Any violation of them and you will be ejected from this facility and have to deal with the legal consequences. Now, Professor Urbina would like to share with you what his group discovered in Guatemala."

She steps offstage and Urbina takes a pensive walk to center stage. After a long, dramatic pause, he starts:

"I don't know what to make of any of this. It's the kind of thing I hoped to see all my life, but now that I've seen it, I honestly don't know what to make of it. So I'll simply present the facts."

Urbina proceeds to provide what I would call an "evenhanded" description of what we saw. He's nowhere near as skeptical as I would be, but he at least tries to temper his obvious desire for it all to be true.

He knows it's absurd, but he also wants to share what could be a genuine discovery that would be earth-shattering if true.

I don't think he's in on it, because if he were, he'd never want to go near such a lie.

After his talk, my fellow guest researchers gather around the fire pit to discuss the time-traveling cosmonaut.

Sexton is predictably skeptical. He peppers Trevor and me with questions as if we were the ones claiming that it was all fact.

"And the stones hadn't been tampered with?" he asks.

For the hundredth time, I reply that I only know what Eduardo said, and I didn't see the tomb before it was opened.

Sexton paces around our chairs with his hands folded over his head. "It's too much. Too much."

My thoughts exactly. As Jessica says, it's gilding the lily.

"But still," Sexton says, "maybe this *is* the epoch? Maybe this is what happens. Weirder and weirder shit? Like what was it like for the Mayans when the conquistadors showed up? First, they see ships. Then men on creatures they've never seen before. Then rifles. They were probably thinking, *Shit can't get any weirder than this.*"

"And then it did," says Trevor. "Next thing you know, one of the longest-lasting civilizations ever collapses, and we're left with ruins and the ashes of a culture."

"That's dark," replies Sexton. "But . . . jeez? Is this happening?" He looks at me. "What's your take?"

"I don't have a take. I need more evidence."

He points at me. "How long is that going to be your answer? Eventually you have to get off the fence, Cray."

"Do I? I can see both sides from up here and maybe a little beyond," I tell him.

"Not every metaphor needs a quick comeback," Sexton grumbles.

"My apologies. I'm out of my element here. This isn't my area of expertise," I say in my best attempt at an apologetic tone.

"Bullshit. You know you think you're the smartest guy in the room. Hell, you probably think you're the smartest guy on the planet. Your fake humble 'I'm not an expert' act doesn't fool anyone."

"For heaven's sake, Sexton. Lay off Theo. Did he sleep with your wife?" says Anna.

"I'm single, Anna," replies the literal-minded Sexton. He takes a deep breath. "Sorry, Theo. I just expected you to be the guy to explain all this."

"I hate to disappoint you."

"No. We're good," he says as he pats me on the shoulder.

I can't tell if he's wound too tight or just did a line of cocaine.

We all call it a night and head back to our rooms.

❦

I'm dead tired but realize I should text Jessica with an update. My phone battery is dead from the facilities' weak Wi-Fi, so I reach into my laptop bag for the credit-card-size backup phone I keep for emergencies.

My fingers feel something unfamiliar, a USB-stick-size device with a built-in camera. I flip open a compartment and there's a slot for a microSD card.

I don't recall buying this. What good would it do to put a camera inside my bag?

I spot a tiny hole where a microphone could be located. Was it put here to listen?

I think back to whether I said anything to Jessica that wasn't coded. Nothing comes to mind. But my paranoia now seems justified.

There's a loud knock at my door.

"Dr. Cray, may we have a word with you?" asks Fiona Joss in a demanding voice.

"Just a minute," I reply as I try to decide what to do with the device.

I open the door a minute later with my shirt untucked, as if I were getting ready for bed.

She's flanked by Urbina and two armed security guards dressed in black polo shirts.

This can't be good.

"I apologize for the inconvenience, but we've had a security incident and need to search your room," she says.

"What kind of incident?" I ask, opening the door.

"Would you mind stepping outside your room?" asks the older guard.

I could protest, but I sense the outcome would be the same. Joss waits outside with me next to the open door while the guards and Urbina search my room.

"Can you explain the incident?" I ask Joss.

"Momentarily," she replies curtly.

"Are the other rooms being searched?"

Clearly the answer is no, because I would have heard the commotion. Joss stands there with her arms folded, watching me and looking over my shoulder into the open doorway.

The older guard, a man named Hendricks with a short salt-and-pepper beard and thick arms, emerges from the doorway. He holds up the small camera I found in my bag. He tosses it to me.

"Is this yours?" he asks.

"Not to my knowledge."

Joss takes the camera from my palm, then glares at me.

"Someone reported that you were acting suspiciously and suspected you may have had a recording device concealed on you during the presentation. Do you have anything to say?" she asks.

Sexton steps out of his room. "What's going on?"

"I wish I knew," I reply.

"Since this isn't yours, you won't mind if I take it to the security office and check the contents," says the guard.

"Maybe in the interest of transparency," I tell them, "we should all have a look right now. Glen, can you get your laptop?" I ask over my shoulder as I reenter my room.

"Fine," replies Joss.

Sexton retrieves his laptop and sets it on my desk. Joss pulls the SD card out and inserts it into an adapter. There's one time-stamped folder with today's date. She clicks on the movie file.

I study the faces around me to see who is the most surprised by what we see next . . .

The inside of the door to my room.

Have I mentioned how paranoid I am?

I don't like to stay somewhere without knowing who's coming into or going out of my space. Bringing an entire security system is impractical, so I built "the Device" as an alternative. It's a pocket-size radio that I set on my dresser or table facing the door. If I'm in my room when someone enters, it makes an alert sound. If they come while I'm away, it silently records video footage of my room.

It also records the MAC address of any wireless phones that come near it.

I've never had to use it before, although there have been plenty of instances in the past where it would have been helpful.

When I entered my room, I noticed the LCD display showed 103.8. Which isn't a radio station here. It tells me that someone entered the room while I was out.

Normally, it'll contain a video recording of housekeeping staff making my bed . . . but not this time.

The door to my room opens and the younger security guard, now standing to my left, enters, walks to the center of the room, looks around, sees my laptop bag, and slides something inside it—creating a dilemma for everyone watching.

The video's time stamp was made while I was at the fire pit with the others *after* the presentation.

Hendricks slams the lid of the laptop shut.

"Hey!" says Sexton.

Joss turns to Hendricks. "What was your man doing in this room?"

"I asked him to sweep the rooms," Hendricks says. "I didn't know our guests had installed their own illegal surveillance systems."

"I'm pretty sure you need to check the law on that one," I tell him.

"This is very complicated," says Joss.

"I'll uncomplicate it." I hold up the microSD card I switched out of the planted camera. "Your security personnel planted this device on me. I assume we'll find tonight's presentation on it. I suggest you compare the point of view of this camera with where I was sitting and you'll realize it was the young man in the suspicious-looking pocketed vest sitting next to me who recorded it. One of your staff, I believe."

Fiona turns to Hendricks. "Find out who that was."

"Yes, ma'am."

But before Hendricks leaves, Sexton lets out a loud laugh, saving me the trouble. "Hey, Ted Bundy, go clean up the crime scene."

Joss turns to him. "What are you saying?"

"You're not falling for this bullshit, are you?" Sexton asks her. "Clearly, Hendricks put his lackey up to it. Then there's the person who really recorded the presentation. And *then* there's whoever it was who put *him* up to it. I'm just a theoretical physicist, but that's, what, three to four people on your staff involved in all of this?"

"What the hell's going on?" asks Urbina, still trying to process everything.

"The calls are coming from inside the house," jokes Sexton, shaking his head.

"Wait outside," Fiona says to Hendricks and his lackey.

As soon as the men leave, Sexton says, "What do you want to bet they're not headed straight for their trucks and driving out of here?"

Good riddance.

Joss sighs. "Unfortunately, this leaves me very short-staffed in the security department."

"Well," I reply, "I can think of one particular person who might be helpful."

CHAPTER THIRTY-SEVEN
Hall Monitor

Jessica leans against the railing of the observation deck on the radio telescope and looks out across the array of dishes with their antennas pointing at the afternoon sky. A breeze catches a strand of her red-dyed hair, and she casually tucks it behind her ear.

In her black leather jacket and blue jeans, she looks like an A-list actress who stepped out onto Melrose Avenue only to get caught in a paparazzi barrage.

Her eyes are what you notice first, but it's the slightly mirthful quirk at the corner of her beautiful mouth that stops my heart. It's as if she's holding back a joke that she doesn't dare share with anyone, aware that every motion, every expression, every turn of her lithe neck is already being observed and judged. You can look at her, but her thoughts are her own.

"You're looking at me in a less than professional manner, Dr. Cray," she says, only briefly making contact out of the corner of her eye with a brilliant green flash that sends a shiver down my spine.

"I'm thinking less than professional things," I reply.

"Are you going to be a discipline problem?"

"Would you like me to be a discipline problem?"

"Later, maybe. When we know we're alone."

Although we appear to be by ourselves out here, I suspect the station's cameras can see us from multiple angles. It's not a secret that Jessica and I are involved, but while she's acting informally to help with their security, it's probably best if we keep things on a platonic level.

"Fiona Joss is an interesting piece of work," says Jessica.

"I haven't figured her out," I admit.

"Me neither. A bit of a queen bee. We spoke for over an hour in her office. I don't think she's terribly happy to have me here."

"Then why did she invite you?"

"Technically she didn't. I was asked by the lawyer, Martinez. He's a curious one himself. Under his nebbish exterior, I think he's Theismann's right-hand man. Someone has to navigate this rat's nest of intertwined corporate entities. There are nonprofits that own for-profits. For-profits that seem to exist solely to finance nonprofits. Holding companies that lease property to companies that then lease it back to other companies."

"Is it fraud?"

"I don't know. Gerald has a couple people looking into it. My gut says no. I think it's fifty years of corporate infrastructure that's become extremely complicated. Theismann's financials are solid. He has securities in blue-chip companies and doesn't seem to be overextended. It doesn't scream 'Ponzi scheme.' It may look suspicious, but I suspect that it's just really clever."

"I remember one of my professors explaining how Howard Hughes started his medical institute as a tax dodge and even had to fight the IRS over it. Now they fund almost a billion dollars of medical research per year," I tell her.

"Yes, but didn't he have to die for it to become legitimate?"

"That may have clarified their priorities a bit."

Jessica gestures toward the field and the radio antennas. "And what are Theismann's priorities?"

"Talking to aliens, clearly," I reply.

"Talking to them or faking talking to them?"

"I just don't get the angle. It's not like he's trying to con someone into funding his passion project."

"Are you sure, Theo? Is there a bigger picture?" Jessica watches me while I think about that.

"Like what? He fakes this so a slightly richer person will open up their wallets? Do you think Bill Gates and Jeff Bezos are going to take this seriously and start writing him blank checks?"

"Maybe it's not money that he wants. Not directly. Maybe he's trying to influence governments."

"How so?"

"Let's say this signal is announced and as far as anyone can tell, it's legitimate. Half the world will call bullshit. The other half will take it at face value. No matter what, people are going to start paying serious attention to space."

I nod. She has a good point.

"If the Chinese think there's a possibility it's real, they're going to be building a thousand facilities like this overnight and thinking about how to send rockets to the edge of the solar system. The US wouldn't be immune to the temptation, either. We'd probably start throwing even more money into space, building rockets and space probes. So maybe Theismann's hoping to kick-start the whole 'space' thing. Hell, even if it all turns out to be a hoax years later, humanity will still be well on its way to Alpha Centauri, and we might even have actual proof of aliens by then."

"Piltdown Man but with aliens," I muse.

"Which one was that?" asks Jessica.

"Piltdown Man was an alleged missing link between man and apes found in a quarry in England. Charles Dawson was a staunch believer in Darwin's theory of natural selection and wanted people to accept that we descended from apes. But the lack of fossil evidence at the time was frustrating to him and other people who wanted to replace a superstitious belief of origin with Darwin's rigorously scientific one. So instead of waiting for scientists to do the rigorous work, Dawson faked it.

"It caused quite a sensation and may have swayed some people, but the suspicion and then revelation of the hoax also gave more ammunition to those who wanted a reason to ignore science."

Jessica thinks this over. "So Theismann is hoping the ensuing real proof will overshadow his deception?"

"Maybe. I think if we actually end up talking to aliens, we won't be too focused on how we got to that point. Columbus may have lied to Queen Isabella about the circumference of the world because he knew she wouldn't accept the idea that there was an entire unexplored continent beyond the Atlantic. But she didn't exactly scream at him and call him a liar when he presented her with two whole continents to exploit."

"I saw the Erdapfel globe when I was a child visiting Europe. I remember staring at the globe and thinking how authentic and unquestioning it made the world look. There was Europe and Africa. There was Asia. And there was one big ocean between them. Nothing more. The certainty of it all." She shakes her head.

"If Columbus came back from his voyage today, Twitter and Facebook would still probably report his discovery as fake news," I joke.

"True. But the Native Americans might have fared better," she shoots back. "Okay, back to the problem at hand. Hypothesis one: Theismann is orchestrating this for reasons to be determined. Hypothesis two: Someone else is orchestrating this for reasons to be determined. Am I missing anything?"

"Well, yes. Hypothesis three," I reply.

"And what's that?"

"That it's real."

She studies my face for a long moment. "You really do take the 'non' in nonzero seriously, don't you?"

"I have to. 'Follow the science' doesn't mean step on the brakes whenever you come to a conclusion that disagrees with your point of view. It means follow and keep following. Science never ends. We even discover new things about simple things. There are entire journals about water. Water. Not the ocean, but just water. If we're still learning new things about that simple molecule, there's a hell of a lot more to learn about the universe."

"Okay, okay, I'll click 'like' on your YouTube channel. Now tell me what you really think about this signal."

"Well, bullshit with a nanometer-sized asterisk."

"And the ancient-astronaut miracle?"

"A femtometer-sized asterisk."

"That's smaller, right?" she asks.

"Considerably. It makes the alien-probe signal even more suspicious. It would be like a scientist holding a press conference and saying that they've discovered dark matter and, oh, by the way, ghosts are real, too."

"All right. Then here's our plan of attack. I'm going to probe around and try to get a sense of who the power players are around here. Who is pulling whose strings. You try to figure out how this could be faked."

"I've already been doing that."

She puts her hand on mine. "Theo, babe. I know, but I need you to do it differently."

"I'm listening . . ."

"If I know you, you've been walking around asking yourself how could they have faked this."

"I thought that's the point."

She shakes her head. "No. I need you to start asking yourself how *you* would fake this. You have an unconventional way of doing things. Butcher Creek ring a bell?"

"I can't say that it does," I lie.

So I bought a bunch of corpses from a body broker and staged an entire massacre in the middle of the woods to draw out a serial killer who was planning to release a pathogen that caused psychosis.

It seemed like the logical thing to do at the time.

Although it did ruin carving the Thanksgiving turkey for me.

Jessica's phone rings and she answers it.

"Hello? . . . I'll be right over," she says, then hangs up.

I follow her down the ladder into the equipment room under the satellite dish.

"How are you getting cell phone access?"

"I'm special. They have a cell phone booster for emergencies. You didn't know?"

"I didn't even think to ask. The whole radio telescope thing," I reply.

"That was Joss. The man who made the recording while he was sitting next to you has gone missing."

"Did he run?"

"Maybe. And Hendricks and Cunningham, the other security guard, have gone missing."

"Is 'missing' a metaphor for dead?"

"Maybe. Or hiding out like Edward Chang." She reaches for the door handle.

I grab her arm. "One second."

"What is it?" she asks, her green eyes focusing on me.

"Um, my timing is terrible, but there's never going to be an appropriate time for this. So, I'm not waiting."

I push her shoulders against the wall and press my lips against hers. Our tongues touch, and she grabs me by the hips and pulls me closer.

Her mouth touches my ear and she whispers, "Then we shouldn't wait."

CHAPTER THIRTY-EIGHT
DEEP SPACE

"How would you fake a signal from Neptune's orbit?" I ask myself as I pace the track that loops around the satellite arrays.

The sun is setting and the wind sweeping across the desert is getting colder, bracing my cheeks and bare arms. My jacket is still folded over my shoulder as I stubbornly refuse to wear it until absolutely necessary.

The first stars are starting to show on the eastern horizon. After the sun sets it should be a brilliant sky. The station is located in "Dark Sky" territory—places on the map with minimal light pollution.

If you look away from the buildings of the station, the Milky Way appears as a thick band stretching over the Earth. For most of human history, this was how we viewed our place in the universe. The stars and planets weren't distant scientific concepts, they were nightly parts of people's lives. It's easy to understand why our ancestors thought that their patterns and movements revealed truths about our world. Why else would the heavens exist?

With the artificial lighting that science brought to cities, the presence of the stars diminished, and they became a mute curiosity.

Nearly every culture believed that life existed somewhere out there. Either as the birthplace of the gods or a celestial sphere that contained beings that lived halfway between our reality and the next. Not to mention the idea that heaven is usually considered a place somewhere between the Earth and the outer reaches of space.

When we began to realize the lights in the sky were physical objects not that different from our planet and our sun, some of the mystery faded, but then we began to grasp the sheer size of the universe.

Not too long ago, we thought the universe was comprised of all the visible stars in our galaxy. Then we inspected the smudgy specks on photographic plates we thought were small stars and realized they were galaxies themselves—and there were more of 'em than we could count.

The most current estimate I've seen is two hundred *billion* galaxies. Our known universe didn't get slightly bigger since my grandfather was a boy. It became billions of times bigger.

I still don't think humans understand how to process that. I know I don't.

As someone who follows the evidence, I can't come up with a rational argument that can explain why none of those galaxies should have planets with life.

When I wrap my head around two hundred billion galaxies and the potential number of stars and planets contained within them, the chance of our solar system being the only one in 1,000,000,000,000,000,00 0,000,000,000 solar systems to develop life seems inconceivable to me.

I can't even think of a scenario in which the conditions were right only one time for intelligent life to develop. Plus, it seems like you'd have to have a heck of a lot of planets with not-so-intelligent life develop before one with clever toolmakers emerged.

So, yes, I essentially believe that other intelligent life lives somewhere in the universe.

But arriving in our own galaxy? Close enough to drop a probe on our doorstep? That's a bit of a leap.

Maybe I have the math wrong. Maybe I'm too much of a cynic. But it doesn't compute.

So how *would* I fake a signal from Neptune's orbit?

Perhaps that's the wrong question.

The fire pit discussions with Sexton and Rood have centered around ways a signal could be faked either on Earth or by using small cube sats—tiny satellites the size of a toaster.

The problem with that method is that it would be difficult to pull off without being detected.

Modern astronomy is built upon methods to determine how far away an object is from the Earth. The first challenge in faking a transmission from low earth orbit is that the satellite would be moving fast. In a low earth orbit, they can't stay fixed in place. Otherwise, they wouldn't overcome the pull of Earth's gravity. It would be easy to tell if something is two hundred miles up or more than twenty million based upon its movement over time. Stars and distant objects appear to stay in the same regions. Low-earth-orbit satellites whiz by.

A signal from a geosynchronous or a geostationary satellite would still be visible to ground-based observers. The former would move in a pattern like a figure eight in a small region of the sky, and the latter would be limited to an equatorial orbit.

Assuming for a moment you could keep a satellite perfectly fixed in the sky in the same area where radio telescopes are pointing, you run into the problem that a ground telescope a thousand miles from the satellite pointing at the same point in Neptune's orbit wouldn't be aimed at the satellite for the same reason that the person standing next to you has a slightly different view of your surroundings than you do.

Parallax is one of the most important tools in astronomy. Using data from two different telescopes at different locations or one telescope over a period of time allows us to tell if an object is moving farther away or closer in the same way you can tell the mountains are farther away than the roadside trees when you look out the window of your car.

This gets harder the farther out you look into space, but it works really well with nearby objects.

You might be able to fake the signal with multiple satellites designed to fool all the different radio telescopes that could end up pointing at the location of the "probe," but it gets to be an impractical solution with multiple points of failure.

Hmm. There's a flaw in my thinking . . . I'm assuming that a faked signal would have to be sent from an Earth orbit.

Given enough time and money, I'd just put a probe in Neptune's orbit and fake it from there.

Or . . .

❧

Sexton is sitting at the fire pit talking to Rood while Anna and Trevor listen in. I take an empty seat.

"Maybe the Chinese?" asks Sexton.

Anna leans in my direction and fills me in. "The current topic is who would want to fake the cosmonaut in the tomb."

"Why?" asks Trevor.

"To get us to waste a bunch of time and energy chasing wormholes and stupid theories," replies Sexton.

"Why not the CIA?" asks Trevor.

"The *CIA*?" scoffs Sexton.

"I'm not saying today's CIA. Maybe this was done forty years ago to mess with the Soviets," explains Trevor.

"What if it was part of a movie set? Didn't they film *Star Wars* near there?" asks Anna.

"One shot from a second-unit crew. And there were no cosmonauts in the movie," replies Trevor.

"Okay, nerd," Anna says.

"How many man-made objects have made it past Neptune's orbit?" I ask Sexton.

"New Horizons, Pioneer 10, Voyager 2, and Pioneer 11. In order of distance," says Sexton. "Those are the only objects. And yes, we already checked to see if they were in the path of the signal."

"Condescending much?" replies Anna.

"I'm sorry. It's just literally the first question people ask. No offense, Theo," says Sexton.

"Your answer is literally not accurate," Rood tells Sexton.

"Is there some secret probe I don't know about?" asks Sexton.

"You forgot to mention the propulsion stages—the motors that put rockets on their trajectories. Most of them have similar orbits," says Rood.

"Those don't count. We can't track them," Sexton objects.

"Theo's original question was about man-made objects beyond Neptune's orbit. There are at least twelve," Rood says.

"Are you counting extra stages?" asks Sexton.

"No. New Horizons had two spin weights on a solar-escape trajectory."

"Fine. But it still doesn't change the fact that going beyond the orbit of Neptune isn't the same as a Neptune orbit," replies Sexton.

"Since we don't know the precise paths of the propulsion stages, we can't say that. There's enough variability in their trajectory that Jupiter could have put them on a different path."

"The chances of that randomly happening are effectively zero," says Sexton.

"Could it be done intentionally?" asks Trevor.

"That would be absurd," Sexton scoffs.

"Not impossible. I've run some simulations that show scenarios where it could happen. I've been trying to cover all the bases," Rood tells us.

Sexton rolls his eyes. "Assuming that was possible, they don't have transmitters."

"That we know about."

"So you think someone snuck a transmitter aboard the booster stage of a space probe to fake an alien signal decades later?" mocks Sexton.

"I wouldn't so much say 'think' as much as 'fear.'"

Ever since the initial signal, Rood has probably been contemplating the impact this will have on his reputation, both positively and negatively, if it's a hoax. He'll never be able to live it down.

There are NASA scientists with blemishes on their career because they jumped the gun or made statements that didn't stand up to outside scrutiny. For Rood, this is the mother of all claims to make about the universe. Overlooking an important detail could be a career killer.

"What about some other satellite? One we don't know about?" I ask.

"You mean a secret space probe?" asks Sexton.

"Maybe a spy satellite."

"Out by Neptune? Who the hell are they spying on?"

"Maybe a repurposed satellite with engines for changing orbits. Could one have been put into a trajectory that would take it into a Neptunian orbit?" I ask.

Sexton shakes his head. "You'd need a really big propulsion stage. That kind of launch would be noticed."

"Maybe," interjects Rood. "Someone might be able to repurpose a smaller spy sat."

"It wouldn't have the fuel," Sexton points out.

"For a normal Jupiter slingshot? Maybe not. But there are other more complicated trajectories. I've seen some machine-learning models that show that some crazy paths don't require nearly as much fuel as you might think. Traveling-salesman kind of stuff that goes beyond the Interplanetary Transport Network."

"The what?" asks Anna.

"The Interplanetary Transport Network is a series of paths that can take you to different parts of the solar system using minimal amounts of fuel," Sexton explains. "Basically, you're using Lagrange points like a bus stop for the next planet to come along and move you to a new orbit. It just takes forever."

"So we have four potential objects and the possibility of a satellite being repurposed and put into a Neptunian orbit," I summarize for the group.

"Right. Because NASA has nothing better to do than hide antennas on their spacecraft to fake something like this," mocks Sexton.

"All you need to make a transmitter is a piece of metal and an electrical field," says Rood.

"What are you saying?" Sexton challenges.

Rood shrugs. "I have to consider everything."

"Not to mention that a number of older spy satellites might be incredibly vulnerable to hacking," I point out.

"I think that would cause an incident," says Sexton.

"Would it? If the Chinese or the Russians realized one of their satellites was drifting off into space, would they assume it was hacked or a malfunction?" I ask.

"That's really out there," Sexton murmurs.

"Which is easier for you to believe? Someone remotely hijacked a satellite or an alien probe is out there talking to us?"

"So we're now thinking Seeker isn't alien?" asks Anna.

"Hell if I know," mumbles Rood.

"May I take a look at the source code tomorrow?" I ask the older scientist.

"Which code?"

"All of it, if I can."

CHAPTER THIRTY-NINE
PATTERN SEEKER

At this moment, supercomputers around the world are sifting through countless images of healthy tissue, cancer, proteins, cells, and a thousand other complex structures, trying to find patterns.

Aside from the most basic maladies, we're past the point where your doctor pops your chest X-ray on a light panel and makes diagnoses based upon a cursory glance.

Agronomists use artificial intelligence to look for patterns in crops while biologists compare images of microscope slides to computer models to uncover what's taking place at a cellular level.

The last decade has seen a revolution in how artificial intelligence processes a variety of data, most notably images.

These days, it's facial-recognition systems overtrained on white faces to the point of creating biased systems that catch the headlines, whereas AIs doing more mundane work, like detecting blight on crops or determining how much forest cover was lost in Borneo, keep improving outside the media spotlight.

I've noticed an overreliance on some machine-thinking models in research where there's simply not enough data to get a meaningful answer and seeming ignorance about what those models could do when used properly.

My favorite example is a computer science student who was taking an introductory course on machine vision and wondered if software infected by a computer virus might look visually different than software that wasn't.

It turns out he was correct, and he had a million-dollar start-up before finishing the class.

When I hear stories like this, I wonder what else is out there waiting to be discovered. The answer is an infinite number of things.

Jessica jokes that my current situation in life is a side project of a side project and so forth, going back to the fifth grade, when I was asked to pick up a peanut butter and jelly sandwich from under my desk and instead discovered a colony of ants that had invaded our classroom.

I began mapping the patterns of the ants and all the colonies around my school and discovered a complex biological system. The school's guidance counselor diagnosed me as either autistic or schizophrenic when she saw my admittedly crazy-looking illustrations of the colonies.

Fortunately, my eighth-grade science teacher decided the appropriate treatment was to send me down the block after school every Thursday so I could hang out with the high school science club.

They adopted me as a mascot, and I got introduced to higher-level topics like genomics, Amiga computers, and the finer points of Monty Python at an earlier age than most science nerds.

As I sit at Rood's workstation and pull open the source code files for the different systems that run their array, the older man watches over my shoulder silently.

If he were to ask me what I was doing, I might absentmindedly mention something about chasing ants.

Computer programs—complex ones—are a lot like ant colonies. Every function performs a task in service of a specific function, like ants serving a queen.

This function over here might handle requests to a database like an ant might be sent out to forage for food in a known location. This other function makes sure that not too much memory is being used, the same way an ant makes sure the passageways of the colony are properly ventilated.

Sometimes it's harder than that. The ant chomping on my peanut butter sandwich had to be followed across the tile floor, up a cupboard, around a planter, through a crack in the weather seal around the window, down the side of the school, across a row of bricks, and to a small mound behind the basketball court. The total distance was nineteen feet.

When you follow the path of information through a computer program, it's a lot like following ants. Bits go in and out of functions, into different files, and get stored on the hard disk and copied and sorted in a thousand different directions.

Trying to find an exploit in code is tedious. Sometime it's in an extraneous file with a name like "TotallyLegitCode.py." Other times it's much more insidious. To make code more efficient, it's often compressed and can't be inspected unless the file is extracted.

There're also methods to get rid of all the white spaces and compact the code so it loads faster.

If you can't compare your machine's current code to the original programming, you have to go through it file by file, check the modification dates—even those can be faked—and look manually for something that stands out.

The clever student with the image-recognition virus detector realized that if you looked at the code in a line-by-line readout, a virus might leave certain patterns, like a series of short bits of code amid longer sequences.

Other methods include doing searches through the binary file for sequences like this:

```
01101000 01110100 01110100 01110000 00111010 00101111
00101111 01110011 01110110 01110010 00101110 01100111
01101111 01110110 00101110 01110010 01110101
```

That's the URL for the Russian intelligence service . . . in binary. Although it's probably not the URL a competent hacker would have his virus report back to.

My futile hope is that somewhere in all this source code I'll find something like that, or maybe a back door that got patched in, explaining why the station staff think they're talking to aliens.

After several hours of staring at screens, I have nothing. Rood has been patient while I checked his work and even offered helpful suggestions.

Sexton already went through all this before, going so far as to write special code to check each step of a signal's journey from the dish to the computer that makes a pinging noise when the signal's detected.

Inside, there's a military-grade microprocessor with signal amplifier algorithms that are hard-coded and can't be hacked with software—at least as far as I know. And military-grade, in this instance, doesn't mean cutting-edge. It refers to microchips built on dependable 1990s-level manufacturing techniques where you can see the circuit pathways under a desktop microscope.

"How is it going?" asks Sexton, who somehow mysteriously appeared next to the workstation.

"Beats me. There's nothing that screams hacked code," I reply.

"Then there's the fact that we have verification from a government-contracted facility. If they're hacked, then our entire defense system is fucked," says Sexton.

I hadn't even begun to think how that could be pulled off. If the station starts letting other organizations know about the signal and they verify it, I'm going to be at a loss for how they all got hacked.

"When do we get to know what's in the latest signal?" I ask Rood.

"We're still processing it," he replies.

"It's been almost two days," says Sexton. "We're starting to get suspicious. There've been two transmissions since we got here. Is there something else going on?"

"I can't say."

"You don't look happy about it," replies Sexton.

"I can't say," Rood says again, indicating that he is not thrilled with the way things are being handled.

"Rumor has it that the old man himself is handling communications now," Sexton probes.

"Who is that?" I ask.

"Theismann," says Sexton. "He's been following every step of this. I heard he's decided to take a more proactive role."

"I can't say," sighs Rood.

Interesting. So Theismann has decided he doesn't want to wait for his independent researchers to make their assessment?

"Dr. Cray, may I speak with you a moment?" asks Jessica from the control room entrance.

"Ooh. She just called you *doctor*. That can't be good," jokes Sexton.

No, it can't.

CHAPTER FORTY
FACTIONS

"Let's take a walk," says Jessica as she leads me to the path around the radio telescopes.

I haven't spoken to her all day, and I'm wondering what she's learned, in her security advisory role, about the missing people.

"How's it going?" I ask once we're out of earshot.

"I've had a very interesting few hours. Stuart Danegeld, the man who made the recording next to you, was apparently found dead in his car on the side of the road."

"Car accident?"

"Nope. Suicide. Bullet to the head. He sent a text message to Joss shortly before and apologized."

"We've heard this story before . . ."

"I was able to sit in while the sheriff's deputies spoke to his closest coworkers."

"Anything interesting come up?"

"Besides the fact that whoever killed David Ikeda is probably at this facility or has been here recently? No, they got nothing new. But I think I have a better understanding of how all of this is structured."

"The station?"

"This station. The others. Theismann's business portfolio. Everything. Well, almost. I think I see the shape of things. Maybe not the details." She glances over her shoulder to make sure that we're not being observed. "Everybody has their secrets. Everybody also has a little bit of gossip about everyone else."

"Any suspects?" I ask. "For the murder or my frame-up?"

"Everyone. I don't know who put the guards up to what they did. But Danegeld's apology didn't account for the camera in your room."

"Do you think Hendricks is the killer?"

"I checked into that. He was here when Ikeda was killed in Philly. There're security logs and witnesses. It could all be faked, but I don't think it was him. There are a lot of moving parts in this operation . . ."

"Such as?"

"As Theismann's wealth increased, he began to fund different organizations. Sometimes placing multiple bets. He funds three radio telescope arrays around the world. The other two are operated from this facility.

"Theismann also provides funding to different programs at academic institutions. Your friend Glen Sexton is a grant adviser on those. He has money going into meditation research, ancient languages, and artificial intelligence. Some of these organizations work together, others seem to compete with each other.

"In addition to that, it turns out that he actually owns a number of small defense-contracting companies," she explains.

"He's into everything."

"That's only the beginning. I tried to probe Martinez about what else Theismann was funding, but he would only tell me so much. I asked a friend in DC to go back through grant databases for the NSF and other agencies that aren't searchable online."

"Good thinking. What's our boy been up to?"

"In the early 1980s, he was spending a lot of money on UFO and psychic research. This was funded by shell companies within shell companies, but it was him. There was a lot of other weird stuff. I don't mean aliens. Payments and grants to organizations in other countries that have no paper trail."

"Was he funneling money for the CIA?" I ask.

"I don't think so. If he was into oil or minerals, I'd take a much closer look at that angle. These groups have names like Institute for Humanity or Pan-American Science Foundation.

"When I asked Martinez about some of these, he seemed genuinely surprised. I think the only person that has the entire map is Theismann. And he's nearly eighty years old. No children. Just two ex-wives and some nephews and nieces.

"Some of these organizations are investment funds that will probably outlive us all. But only Theismann has the whole picture. And from Martinez's body language, I get the impression that Theismann may be having trouble keeping it all straight."

"He is one of the richest men in the world," I observe.

"Yep. The other interesting fact is that people who work for Theismann tend to move from organization to organization.

"After I met Fiona Joss, I did some research on her. Before taking over this facility, she had an address in Tucson. Care to guess where?"

"The Colony?"

"Yep. Before that she worked as a product manager for a computer company in the 1980s. Owned by Theismann, of course."

"Please tell me you found Terrence Powers," I reply.

"Almost forgot to mention that. Back at the Colony, someone showed me a photo of their drop-in guru, Mike. Apparently, he and Masters share a biography."

"Wait. I thought Masters *was* Theismann? This is getting confusing."

"Maybe Mike helped Theismann write the book, or possibly he showed up Remington Steele–like and said that's who he was," says Jessica with a shrug.

"I don't think I get the reference," I reply.

"A TV show my grandfather was a consultant on. Pierce Brosnan played a man who showed up one day at a woman's detective agency and said he was the man whose name was on the agency shingle."

"Huh. Sounds suspicious."

"You just had to go with it. Television in the 1980s was like that. Anyway, it seems the more senior the people are in these organizations, the more they've moved around."

"Instead of children, he has all these organizations," I reply.

"I was thinking that, too. But there's another analogy that I think fits better. It's like a bunch of feudal lords in service to a king."

I think that over. "To what end? What's better than being king?"

"Being a god-king. To pull that off, you have to have a direct line to heaven."

Something clicks in my mind. "We still haven't been given any more info about the second signal. Rood seems frustrated. I think Theismann may have taken over communicating with the probe himself."

"Like a prophet having a private conversation with God? Interesting. I heard Bilton whisper something when she thought I was out of earshot," Jessica tells me.

"What was it?"

"Press conference."

I shake my head in disbelief. "The team will lose their minds. Everyone is expecting this to go out for independent verification before anything's said."

"Would you wait for an embargo before telling the world you talked to God? Especially if you were Theismann's age?"

"Why kill Ikeda and then let me stick around, though?" I ask.

"I don't know. Why did Nixon trust his inner circle? Why did he record himself, for that matter? It could be the king has devoted zealots who're acting without orders."

"Or something else."

"Or something else," she agrees. "Then there's another matter: I got an interesting text message sent from a burner."

Jessica shows me a screenshot:

If you liked the book I recommended, I think you'll find this very interesting:

0.2332569, −78.1104712

"Is that a coordinate?" I ask.

"It would seem so. Care to guess where?"

"It's almost exactly on the equator. My guess is Ecuador."

"Google Maps agrees. I checked it out. It's just jungle or at least looks that way. But here's the kicker. Guess who sponsors a large biological preserve there and has since the 1980s?"

"Terrence Powers?" I say half hopefully.

"You wish. On a lark, I asked Martinez if he knew anything about a property in Ecuador. His reaction told me he didn't. When I mentioned there might be a connection to all this there, he offered us a jet."

"Just like that?"

"Just like that," she replies. "If we head to the airport now, we can sleep on the plane and be there by early morning."

"And if it's a trap?"

"Theo. We're already in the trap. We need to find out who set it."

CHAPTER FORTY-ONE
PRIMER

I go back to my room to shove some clothes into my backpack while Jessica does the same at the other end of the guest apartment complex. Besides our impromptu trip to Ecuador, I'm presented with another surprise.

This one is a fat manila envelope with my name on it waiting in front of my door. I take it inside and set it on the bed while I gather my hiking boots and anything else I think I should bring on our little trip.

"You ready?" asks Jessica from my doorway.

"That was fast."

"I don't really ever unpack, in case you haven't noticed."

"I have. I still don't know how you don't look like you rolled out of bed."

"You have to know which fabrics to buy. The magic of modern textiles. What's that?" she asks as she sits on the bed.

"Someone left it for me."

I see a green flash in the mirror and turn around as Jessica uses the laser I gave her to candle the interior.

"Looks safe," she says before ripping it open.

"It could have—"

"An explosive activated by air. Polonium dust. The Avada Kedavra curse. Yeah, I get it. Huh. Looks like you have some reading material for the plane."

Jessica hands me a thick sheaf of unbound photocopies. On the cover is one sentence:

The Theismann Hypothesis

I start to flip through the pages and look at the equations and diagrams. They're professionally made, the kind you find in high-quality textbooks. It would surprise me if Theismann contracted with a publisher to help him produce this.

Jessica snaps her fingers. "Pack now. Read later."

I oblige, lest I invoke the wrath of a woman who can fieldstrip a pistol, make an MMA expert cry for mercy, and substitute my hot coffee for a frozen block of ice if I forget to take out the garbage.

"Yes, ma'am."

❦

Jessica falls asleep on my shoulder the moment the plane leaves the runway. We've both learned the art of catnapping, but I'm not in a sleeping mood, not with Theismann's masterwork sitting in my lap.

I read the introduction first, then the conclusion, and jump around before reading it in sequence.

Jessica once asked me why I didn't read books in the way God (or at least the author) intended. I explained I only do that with nonfiction (mostly) because the books are usually laid out in the way the author wants to tell a story and not necessarily the most convenient way to get the facts and make a critical evaluation.

Theismann's manuscript is quite the story. Although it doesn't have the custom vans or soul-rocking vibes of *The Messengers*, it's equally self-important. From the notes and references, it's clear that the book has been revised over and over again.

I'd compare it to Stephen Wolfram's *A New Kind of Science*, his attempt to make the argument that computation is its own branch of science in the same way that mathematics is. But Wolfram was trying to show how this approach could help understand how the universe worked using a different framework—a framework that some argued had already been created and had limitations when it came to its predictive capabilities.

Theismann isn't trying to describe a system that explains the world. He's claiming to have a way to make predictions about everything, including the connection between general relativity and quantum gravity. N-dimensional waves crossing a two-dimensional membrane or something like that. (I skimmed through that section pretty fast.)

The claims about alien life start in the section where he discusses how intelligence emerges. He discusses connections between brain waves and ideas spreading to create culture.

It feels a bit thin at times, but he has some interesting analogies. Like explaining why some ideas take hold. His description of how waves can either reinforce each other or cancel one another out could be applied to why some memes catch on and others don't. Effectively you can have infinite snowflake configurations in a snowstorm, but a single snowflake can only have one at a given time. Or something . . . I skimmed that part, too.

As the section on intelligence progresses, he talks about hyperintelligence—his term for a mind that's not only self-aware but also has complete mastery of its full computational capability.

In practical terms, we normal intelligent beings can't stop thinking about chocolate cake once the idea's in our heads. A hyperintelligent being would be able change the topic instantly and focus on world peace or nobler aims.

Theismann goes into some detail about the use of meditation and what he calls "alternative biological computational modalities," all of which borders on self-help, if you ask me.

One of his theories is that a race of hyperintelligent beings would eventually figure out the physical laws of the universe and femtotechnology (manipulating subatomic particles) and essentially alter the source code of reality.

It's not simulation theory—the idea that our universe is merely a high-tech simulation, a topic that I'll only expound upon when Jessica's having trouble sleeping.

Theismann proposes math predicting how long it would be before a hyperintelligent ET reached Earth. His estimate is that it's somewhere between nine and twelve billion years after the big bang. Although he has two appendixes to that. One explains that the big bang could actually have been the reformation of the universe. The second describes how a hyperintelligence could have arrived a few hundred thousand years after the big bang in a much hotter and more chaotic universe. He claims that if the conditions were right in certain spots, superfast chemical reactions could have triggered an accelerated evolution of complex systems. Although he doesn't put too much credence in that theory.

The conclusion of the book is that it's highly likely that hyperintelligence achieved the reformation we call the big bang, and rather than trying to study the specific physics involved, we should be looking for clues to their existence.

And thus the search for UFOs, alien astronauts, signals, probes, and a variety of other phenomena that Theismann judges could be glitches or intentional clues.

The book is a lot to take in. As far-fetched as Theismann can be, I honestly can't call his book pseudoscience.

He doesn't make a single concrete claim that conflicts with my understanding of reality. He has a whole ton of open-ended questions about ESP, supernatural phenomena, and other pseudoscientific topics, but he never claims that they are true or even that they have significant supporting evidence.

The book is really a series of "if this is true" and "if that is true" questions that lead to a . . . rather extreme conclusion.

I understand how someone like Rood or even Sexton could read it and say that there are interesting ideas to be explored. Theismann has a deep understanding of mathematics, and some of his ways of looking at problems could prove as practical as his world-changing economic models were.

I wouldn't call the man crazy at all. He is a very, very free thinker. Although there's an interesting subtext that disturbs me slightly.

In several places, he mentions the idea of "signals reinforcing one another so strongly that they create a pattern that causes reality to conform to it."

One interpretation of this is that you can force a result in the observer paradox in quantum mechanics simply by lying about which particle went through a slit. The universe would adapt to the inconsistency and rewrite its time line with a wave that travels backward in time. Or something.

I might be paranoid, but it reads a lot like, *If you tell a lie often enough . . .*

But in this case, you might actually rewrite the universe.

And that has me scared. A man who believes that a convincing lie can shape the cosmos in a way he sees fit may not have a problem erasing one or two inconvenient barriers in his path.

Obstacles that happen to be sitting in his private jet.

PART SIX

ENFORCER

CHAPTER FORTY-TWO
PSEUDOFACTUAL

Theo is still reading Theismann's manuscript when we land in Ecuador. While I negotiate the rental of a Jeep, he flips back and forth through the pages while waiting outside on a bench.

"You ready?" I ask, holding up the keys. "We can get some coffee and dessert at a roadside stand."

"Sounds good," Theo replies as he climbs into the passenger side.

I'm used to Theo's deep-thinking modes. His seeming absentmindedness can be annoying, but at least he doesn't pretend to pay attention.

After an hour on the road, he finally looks up from Theismann's manuscript and stares out the window at farms that are becoming less frequent as the jungle grows thicker.

"Well?" I finally ask.

"I'm trying to decide if Theismann is a good-hearted eccentric or a Bond villain set on dominating the universe," he replies.

"The book was that good?"

"It was certainly interesting. Want the CliffsNotes version?"

I glance at the thick stack with all its equations and formulas and wonder if I should have more coffee first.

"Sure . . ."

"Theismann starts with some interesting ideas about how complex systems work. He comes up with some useful analogies for understanding his take. Then he goes more into speculation mode about advanced artificial intelligence, his view of the singularity, and other science-fiction topics.

"I'd say the most disturbing element—and I may not be interpreting it correctly—is his concept of 'artificially stimulating a decontextualization of the structure of energy and matter in nonlinear space-time.' His analogy was a tuning fork operating at a more precise harmony, not only changing the sound of music played by a piano but actually rewriting the musical notes themselves," Theo explains.

"Okay. That's crazy," I reply.

"A little bit. He has some math that he thinks is quite convincing, but I'd have to spend more time examining it. He also makes a curious conjecture about what the existence of pseudorandom numbers implies."

I'm distracted for a moment by a police car several hundred feet behind us. It's following at normal speed. The road is deserted, and I've only seen three cars go the other way. I hope this is simply their stretch to patrol.

"Pseudorandom? Refresh my memory? Like in cryptography?" I ask.

"Exactly. Basically, you can use simple math to create numbers that are so complex there's no way to distinguish them from truly random numbers—at least with the computational power in our universe. There are some theories that suggest testing them with quantum computers could determine whether our reality is simulated or not.

"The irony, if that's the right word, is that Theismann made his wealth because all the other currency traders were using less precise mathematical models—i.e., operating in a less complex model of the real world.

"He suggests that maybe that *was* the real world . . . until he developed more precise algorithms. If you go back and average all the trades and decisions made before Theismann, you can't tell the difference between a pseudorandom and truly random system," Theo tries to explain.

"Babe. I understand the words but not the sentences. How much sleep have you had?"

Theo checks his watch. "Um, none. So, the super-compact version is that if you can have fake random numbers that reality accepts, you can also have fake events that reality treats as real."

"Like a lie everyone comes to accept," I translate.

"Yes! Exactly what I was thinking. That's the scary part. If he believes it."

I think it over for a moment. "Kind of like the Mandela effect."

"What's that?" asks Theo.

"It's a cultural memory that isn't accurate. Like the belief the Berenstain Bears family's name was spelled 'Berenstein.' That Fruit of the Loom's logo was a cornucopia or that Nelson Mandela died in the 1980s. That's where the phenomenon got its name. Which I never got because I met Mandela when I was a teenager. Incredibly nice, by the way."

Theo scratches his chin. "I can see why we'd think it was a cornucopia. It's probably a by-product of how we organize that information in our minds. Which is often designed to shortcut our thought process for maximum efficiency. We see fruit, we think cornucopia. The name Berenstain's unusual, so we replace it with a close correlative. I expect we probably have a lot more of these flawed shared memories."

"But Theismann is suggesting that it becomes truth," I reply.

"Yes. Basically, by collapsing our reality into one where that thing seems true. Then it effectively is. But you'd need more than just a bunch of people believing it. The pattern would have to appear in so many formats," he muses.

"Thank god Orson Welles didn't have access to the internet or we'd all be neck-deep in Martians right now."

"Yes. Kind of. But you get the point."

I'm reminded of a memory and have to laugh.

"What's so funny?" asks Theo.

"I have a very vivid memory of Orson Welles giving me a set of the Chinese linking rings for my birthday as a child and telling a story about finding them in a curio shop in Shanghai. I was super young, but I realize now that story was either manufactured or considerably embellished by my grandfather. He told audiences that story every time I performed the rings in our show." I shake my head and laugh. "I've been living a lie and telling it to other people."

"Well, Thomas T. Theismann would suggest that if nobody can contradict the story, then it's pseudoreal," offers Theo.

"Pseudoreal? Is that a real thing?"

"It pseudo-is . . ."

"I can pseudo-punch you from here without taking my eyes off the road," I tell him.

"It's a mathematical concept. Theismann uses it to describe something that's between real and not real. Instead of a binary, it has an integer value that's determined from an equation that measures the impact it has on the system around it," says Theo.

"Awesome. So he thinks if he fakes an alien signal and a bizarre ancient astronaut discovery, that makes it all true?"

"Kind of. It's more complicated. There would have to be other factors. And I'm still not sure if he thinks faking it would be enough. There's also the problem of the people who helped fake it knowing that it wasn't true. And to be honest, I don't see a sinister streak in the man."

"You don't have to be sinister to do sinister things, Theo. Trust me on that one."

The flashing blue lights of the police car behind us catch my eyes in the rearview mirror.

"We're about to be pulled over," I tell Theo. "You ever do anything illegal in Ecuador?"

"Does skinny-dipping in the Galápagos count?"

"Uh . . . you'd better let me do the talking."

A man with a name tag identifying him as Officer Serrano leans in and sees Theo through the open window. *"Americanos?"*

"Sí," I reply.

I can pass for native in many Spanish-speaking countries due to my ancestry on my mother's side. Theo, without his beard, appears Anglo and tends to stick out.

"Where are you headed?" asks Serrano in English.

"We're just sightseeing," I reply.

He studies us. "May I see your passports?"

"Of course. Is there some kind of problem?"

"No problem. We just like to know who's out here in case there are any problems, like your car breaks down."

That's not a very convincing explanation, but I hand over our passports anyway. If we were in Quito, I'd show him my FBI badge. Out here, I have no idea if he's a normal cop or also an informer who works for someone else who might not be thrilled to have an FBI agent lurking outside the established tourist areas.

Serrano holds up my passport, in which I have dark hair, and compares it to me. I forgot that I'd dyed my hair.

He seems satisfied that I'm merely going through some kind of life crisis; he uses his phone to take photos of our passports, then hands them back to me.

"Do you need directions?" he asks.

In most places, this is a genuine offer for assistance. In other parts of the world, it's a soft request for a bribe. The trick is to respond in a way that doesn't offend the police officer if he's *not* asking for a bribe.

Of course, in those countries where they'll come right out and ask you, it's impossible to offend them.

I was at a party at a friend's parents' vacation home in the Bahamas when the police showed up and demanded the music be turned down. When she offered them a bribe and they left, the other Americans were aghast.

She explained it succinctly: "In America, you have police. Here we have people that dress like police but are actually security guards who work for tips."

I pull out the map I bought at the rental car office and point to a location twenty kilometers ahead of where we are actually going.

"You would save us so much trouble if we didn't have to find a guide to tell me how to get here." I take a hundred-dollar bill from my pocket and set it on the map.

One key to successful bribing is to make sure that you don't insult them by forcing them to negotiate. Another is to never verbally offer a bribe. It's less risky for them to accept a bill that's offered nonverbally than to chance the transaction is being recorded.

Serrano hands the bill back to me without saying anything and takes the map. "You want to go here?"

A hundred dollars is a generous bribe from a couple of American tourists who don't know the local customs. Serrano might be suspicious or just plain honest. Not every cop in a country with a low standard of living is out for bribes.

"There's nothing there. You should go to Nueva Loja. There's more to see there," he says as he hands the map back to me.

"We'll keep that in mind," I let him know.

I can tell Theo wants to speak, but I put a hand on his knee, gently telling him to let me do the talking.

"The roads up ahead aren't very good. I can tell you how to take a more scenic route," offers Serrano.

"That's very kind. We'll just take this for a while."

"Okay. Have a nice day." Serrano pats the roof of the Jeep and walks away.

He gets into his police car, U-turns ahead of us on the road, and races past, waving as he goes by. I take my time folding the map to ensure he's really leaving us.

"He seemed . . . curious," observes Theo.

"Yes. I don't think they get too many tourists out this way. What does the GPS say?"

Theo pulls it from his backpack and consults the map. "We have another thirty miles. The satellite images show an unmarked road. There's tree cover over most of it, but it looks like it ends about a mile from the location."

"Were you able to find aerial imagery that shows what's out there?" I ask.

The images on Google Maps were out of date. Theo decided to do a deep dive into other records, hoping for more information.

"No. All of the public data shows jungle. I couldn't find any infrared. If there is anything, it's pretty well concealed by the jungle."

"Or the maps have been redacted," I reply.

It's not uncommon for governments and companies to have sensitive details obscured on aerial maps. Our destination could be anything from a federal prison to a secret military testing ground.

I look over at Theo and he looks back at me, wondering the same thing I am: Where on earth is our anonymous tour guide sending us?

CHAPTER FORTY-THREE
Couple's Night

As we get closer to the spot on the aerial map where we saw the unmarked road, I slow the rental and we keep a close watch so we don't miss it. The vegetation grows so thick and fast in this part of Ecuador it would be easy to drive by without noticing the exit.

"There," says Theo, pointing to a small sliver of mud between the road and what looks like a narrow gap in the trees.

"Are you sure?" I ask as I hit the brakes.

"I can see tire tracks. It may not be our road, but it's a road."

"Let's just hope this one doesn't take us to a secret zoo," I reply, making a dark reference to a very unpleasant experience we'd had the last time we followed an unmarked road.

I turn onto the muddy path and drive our Jeep down the tight passage. Brush and limbs rub against the side of the vehicle, and I hear the sound of breaking branches.

"They sure hid it well enough," I remark.

"That or we're just driving in the jungle."

A few yards later, the path clears and a gravel road is visible ahead.

"Hmm. This feels rather developed. That or the Incas were more advanced than we realized," I tell Theo.

"Next to the Romans, they were some of the best road builders that ever existed. We're about three miles away," says Theo.

I navigate the Jeep around a sharp bend and slam on the brakes.

Officer Serrano stands in the middle of the road with his police cruiser parked in front of a locked gate.

I smile, but he doesn't smile back. He draws his pistol and points it at us.

"Step out of the vehicle with your hands up!" he yells.

"Raise your hands and don't move," I tell Theo.

I unfasten my seat belt and open my door, but don't get out.

"What's going on?" I shout.

"Out of the vehicle! Now!" he yells.

I don't like this. Not one bit. The moment we step out of the Jeep, we're vulnerable.

"Can you tell me what's going on?" I ask in a pleading voice.

"This vehicle was reported stolen! Now get out. This is your last warning."

I'm ready to slam the shifter into reverse when I see that a pickup driven by a man in street clothes has pulled up behind to block us in.

I've been in more sketchy situations than I care to think about. The difference between life and death is knowing when there's a difference between life and death.

"They'll need to take us somewhere else to kill us," Theo says, thinking along the same lines I am. "They can't risk our bodies being found here. It's the first place the national police will look."

"They could always kill us and then move our bodies."

"If this was a narco hit. But this isn't. This is somebody who wants to take attention away from this place. Of course, they could just beat us unconscious right here," he replies after doing the cruel calculation.

I hear the sound of a shotgun being racked and see the driver of the pickup pointing the barrel at Theo's window.

Serrano is standing ahead of my door and has his gun aimed between my eyes. My pistol's still in my backpack. If I reach for it, they'll gun us down on the spot. Forensic evidence or not.

We have to play this very carefully.

"I have the registration. Let me get it."

"Move your hands and I pull the trigger," growls Serrano. "Get out."

I step out of the vehicle. The man on Theo's side opens the door and yells at him in Spanish to get out and get on his knees.

"You too. On your knees," Serrano yells at me.

I fall to the road with my hands behind my head. Serrano walks behind me so I can't see him.

The other man has Theo kneeling next to the passenger door out of my line of sight.

If Serrano moves to handcuff me, I'll have an idea where his gun is pointed and I might be able to catch him by surprise. *Might.*

My mouth starts speaking before my brain catches up. "If this is about the money . . . we were going to give it back," I blurt out.

"What money?" asks Serrano's accomplice in Spanish.

"She's just saying that to distract you," says Theo.

I need to explain to him again how the concept of "yes and . . ." works in improv.

"Handcuff him," Serrano says to the other man in Spanish.

Theo could have used that moment to get away from his captor. It would have left me vulnerable, but I could have used the opportunity to disarm Serrano.

I hear the sound of handcuffs being clicked and the moment is gone.

"My friend is going to take your boyfriend for a little walk, and you're going to tell me about the money. If I like what you say, we'll go down to the police station and say this was a case of mistaken identity," explains Serrano.

Sure. That checks out.

I shout over my shoulder. "Theo, don't run. We'll sort this out. Okay?"

I see the trees close in behind them as the guy with the shotgun pushes Theo into the jungle.

I may not have much time.

Serrano pushes the barrel of his pistol into the back of my head and uses his other hand to hold me by the back of my neck.

"Stand up slowly, *señorita*," he says.

I get to my feet. His hand and the gun remain in place as he guides me to the front of the Jeep.

"You're going to lean forward and place your hands on the hood and do everything I say. *Comprendes?* My friend and yours may be gone for a while."

I place my hands flat and start to make hyperventilating sounds like I'm stifling sobs.

"We'll sort this out soon enough," he says.

He lets go of my neck and starts to pat me down. First under my arm, then under my breasts. His hand starts to go lower.

I make a louder sob.

The gun barrel moves away from my skull.

I feel his breath on my neck as his hand wanders toward my waist.

"It's going to be—"

The back of my head hits his nose with so much force that even I see stars.

I spin around, push my chest into the crook of his arm holding the gun, grab the arm like a board, lever his body weight backward, then twist.

I can feel his elbow pop next to my sternum. My own elbow catches him in the jaw midscream and Serrano's out cold.

BOOM!

Shotgun blast.

"Theo!" I scream.

I pull Serrano's gun free from his twitching fingers and plunge into the jungle.

I only make it ten feet before I run into Theo.

His face is covered in blood. He's holding the shotgun in a tactical position.

"He'll live," Theo says. "The other one?"

"Alive. But if he put his hand anywhere else, he wouldn't be."

Some couples take ballroom dancing classes. We take jiujitsu.

CHAPTER FORTY-FOUR
MISSIONARIES

Serrano is lying on the ground making a gurgling sound, which I assume is his best attempt to keep breathing. I reach into his pocket and pull out his cell phone. When I redial the last number he called, I hear a ringtone play near where I saw Theo emerge covered in blood.

"I'll take care of our guests and move the truck," says Theo as he takes two pairs of plastic zip ties from the trunk of Serrano's police vehicle. He's about to close the trunk, then stops and pulls out a first-aid kit. "I'll just make sure nobody gets infected."

Serrano dialed a second number on the phone less than an hour ago. With a complete lack of caution, I decide to dial it.

A pleasant young male voice answers the phone. "Santa Fe Research Foundation. How may I direct your call?"

Damn. That's the cover name for Research Station Alpha. This was an inside job.

I look down at Serrano's blood-spattered face. "Who did you talk to? Who told you to do this?"

His eyes glance up at me in fear, but he says nothing.

I make sure Theo isn't watching and put the tip of the barrel to Serrano's forehead and whisper, "I very much want to pull this trigger right now. Give me a reason not to."

"Miguel. Miguel told me to," says Serrano through a swollen jaw.

"Who's Miguel? What else did he tell you?"

His eyes flutter and his head falls back on the loam. I put fingers to his neck and check for a pulse. He's still alive, but between the arm and the work I did on his head, he's fighting a losing battle with consciousness.

"Theo! I think I need to call an ambulance!" I shout as he drags the other man's body out to the road.

Theo leans over and inspects Serrano. "He'll make it. We'll call for an ambulance when we're ready to leave."

"Good idea. I'll do it through DC and have Gerald make the request. After we're outside Ecuadorian airspace."

"Smart. Also, how are we getting cell phone coverage all the way out here?"

I check the bars on Serrano's phone. There's only one, but that's one more than I saw on my own phone for the last ten miles.

"Good question. Maybe there's a tower in the hills?"

"Why?" asks my unstoppable question machine named Theo.

"I don't know. So the toucans can play *Angry Birds*. Let's get moving."

With both of our attackers secured, I motion to the gate and we make our way past the multilingual No Trespassing signs.

The mere mention of toucans, the colorful large-billed birds that live in this part of the world when they're not shilling fruity sugar-laden cereal to children, sends Theo into a monologue as we hike down the narrow path beyond the gate.

"They're actually another interesting example of convergent evolution," explains Theo.

"That's where two or more distantly or unrelated animals resemble each other because they fill the same ecological niche. Like marsupial wolves and timber wolves?" I reply.

"Exactly. Marsupial—"

I cut him off. "Marsupial wolves aren't true wolves and are more closely related to kangaroos than to dogs. Right? A real wolf shares more DNA with a dolphin or us than a marsupial wolf. Correct?"

Theo hacks at a vine on the trail. "I thought you usually fall asleep at that point in the lecture."

"Sometimes I like to listen to your bedtime TED Talks. Sometimes," I admit.

"Sorry. I guess I tend to mansplain."

"I've told you already. It's only mansplaining when you try to explain something to me that I know more about than you. Like magic, psychology, weapons, law enforcement, the law, pop culture, college football, martial arts, craft beers, and a hundred other things."

"And what's it called when you explain something to me that's in my area of expertise?" he asks.

"It's called me being really smart."

"Hmm. I'm still learning. I guess my point was going to be that if there are enough planets like Earth, you might find life similar to ours. But the chance of it being at the same point of evolution as ours would be very small. Glaciation, asteroids, volcanic seeps, and a number of other factors that affect things on a global scale would make it hard for life elsewhere to progress in the same manner. You might have creatures like dinosaurs and monkeys, but they could be spread apart in time much differently," he explains.

"What about dinosaur monkeys?" I joke—then realize I'm going to get an answer.

"If you're talking about a species evolving from dinosaurs and not theropods or an early reptile, the evidence is pretty scant. Someone has suggested that *Deinocheirus mirificus* went through an evolutionary stage similar to a sloth, but they were quite massive and nothing in the fossil record supports that. Although one could theorize that since we have limited fossils of modern primates . . ."

Theo suddenly stops speaking as we reach a clearing with patches of bright green grass interspersed with duller brown.

"What is it?" I ask.

"The grass is getting more nutrients," he replies.

The path continues past the clearing and into the jungle. Our GPS spot is a mile ahead.

"Do you want to investigate?"

"No. Maybe later. Whoever asked those men to kill us might have accomplices. We should keep going."

We continue hiking down the trail. At certain points it widens and you can tell that it was broader, but the jungle overtook it. Large stones poke up from the ground at certain points, suggesting this was once paved in stones and may have been an old Inca highway.

After a gradual decline that takes us deeper into the jungle, where a low-hanging mist keeps everything moist and limits visibility, the ground begins to level out.

According to the GPS, we're almost at the coordinates.

"We're getting close. Any last-minute predictions?" I ask Theo.

He checks the chamber on the shotgun he took from his assailant. "I'm still wondering if the reclusive Edward Chang sent that message or someone else did," says Theo.

"Same. I also wonder if Serrano tried to kill us because someone discovered we were here or because someone sent us here to be killed."

Theo keeps his eyes ahead. "The thought occurred to me. It doesn't seem like the most rational or efficient way to get rid of us. But I'm beginning to learn from you that people don't always think like economists trying to solve the most effective way to accomplish something."

"It's like the great philosopher Mike Tyson once said, 'Everyone has a plan until they get punched in the mouth.'"

"Didn't he lose that fight?" asks Theo.

"Yeah. It seems having no plan at all was a worse strategy."

Theo looks back at me. "So what's our plan?"

"Make sure we hit them extra hard in the mouth."

I try to put Serrano's swollen face out of my mind. The fact that he had worse coming doesn't make me feel any better about inflicting injuries and pain.

"I see a break in the trees ahead," Theo tells me.

At the far end of the path, a glow appears, literally the light at the end of the tunnel, where sunlight penetrates the thinner canopy around the clearing.

As I get closer, I squint to adjust to the brightness.

I feel a breeze absent in the jungle coming from the opening and can hear the sound of wind.

It's an eerie tone, like something out of a gothic horror novel. Isolated, constant, and somehow hollow.

"Well, damn. That wasn't in the betting pool," remarks Theo as he reaches the border of the clearing ahead of me.

CHAPTER FORTY-FIVE
Complex

"Google Maps lies," I say as I stare across a long grassy plaza at a massive—and I mean *massive*—pyramid.

It's not as big as the Great Pyramid of Giza or the Quetzalcóatl Pyramid, but still . . . a decent-size pyramid. Or is it a ziggurat?

This is the size of a sports stadium with seven levels, each twenty feet or taller. Though it's hard to guess accurately from this distance.

Vines and foliage have overtaken the structure, but I still can't imagine why it wouldn't be visible from the air.

"Any thoughts, Dr. Cray?" I ask Theo.

"That's one big ziggurat," he replies.

Of course.

"What's the delimiter between pyramid and ziggurat?"

"I guess you'd have to ask the Babylonians," he says as he starts walking to the structure.

I follow him and try to take in the size of the clearing. Stone blocks are visible under the weeds, and patches of dirt have been formed by wind and rain into small mounds.

"This is one hell of a parking lot," I observe.

"Yes, it is rather large." Theo is comparing the pyramid to the printout he made of the satellite image. "They don't even match."

I take the photo from him. Sometimes you can spot aerial camouflage by looking for features like sharp lines or repeating patterns.

Before my great-grandfather gave up magic to be a farmer, he worked with the military in World War II to devise ways to hide manufacturing plants. Grandfather liked to brag that the greatest illusion our family ever performed was making half of Los Angeles disappear so the Japanese couldn't bomb it.

It's easy to understand how some netting and fake trees could fool a high-altitude surveillance plane, but what about a military satellite?

"Any theories?" I ask Theo.

"This is your area. I guess if cartels can hide hundreds of thousands of acres of drug farming, this is doable."

"That's a hell of a lot easier. You're basically trying to make one plant not look like another. You can do that with netting and avoiding anything that looks like a farm from the air," I tell him.

"Interesting. I wonder if you could train a machine-learning model to spot drug farms from the air . . . ," he wonders aloud.

"I guess I know what your next pet project is going to be. In the meantime, let's address the present mystery?"

"Yes. I assume that since this is visible from the air that the government knows about it. And any other pilot in this region has to be aware of this. Which implies that there's a simple explanation for why we haven't seen this in *National Geographic*," says Theo.

"Or a convenient lie," I reply.

"What do you mean?"

"Like those mysterious exits you'll see off the highway in places like Nevada and Utah. Some of those are military training facilities. Others are entire airfields. When I was a rookie agent, I once had to follow a convoy from a factory in Los Angeles all the way to . . . well, somewhere and take down the license plate of every car that followed us for more than twenty miles. The purpose of our destination and payload weren't revealed to us, but it showed me how much weird stuff our government was doing."

"Aliens," says Theo.

"Missiles, nuclear materials, experimental aircraft, parts of a submarine—your guess is as good as mine. What I do know is the place we took it to looked nothing like what I saw on Google Maps. Locals were told it was munitions testing ground, which was a convenient explanation to keep people away."

"What does your federal-government brain tell you the purpose of keeping this a secret is?" asks Theo.

"Maybe it's federal property and the Ecuadorian government's keeping it a secret because it covers some kind of treasure, like a diamond mine?"

"Then why weren't we stopped by Ecuadorian military instead of a cop and his buddy doing freelance hits?"

"I don't know, Theo. I'm just making it up as we go along. Hypothetically, let's say that Theismann funded some kind of expedition, and they found a lost temple filled with treasure. Maybe he cut a secret deal with the president of Ecuador to exploit it while calling it something else. A forestry-restoration project. Whatever. This is supposed to be a biological preserve, after all."

"You might have something there," he replies.

"Well, congratulations to me. Do I pass the final exam, Professor? Do I get an A?" I mock him.

"Come to my office when this is over and we'll discuss your future." Theo stops a hundred feet from a wide gap that appears to be an entrance into the structure.

"This is some unconventional architecture. I haven't seen anything like this," he observes.

"Other than a Fry's Electronics store," I reply. "But those are ancient monuments now, too."

"Should we enter?" I ask.

"Maybe." Theo is thinking this over carefully.

"Are you worried about booby traps? We take a peek and then make a run for it at the first sign of a giant boulder or a skeleton impaled with spears."

I watch his eyes dart over at me as he tries to get the reference. Theo knows a lot about pop culture, but sometimes his brain is on some completely different track, and he has to pause to think about something completely unrelated to what is on his mind.

"Sounds good."

As we near the gap, it looks much larger than it did before. The tunnel's about twenty feet wide and at least as tall. We turn on our flashlights and step into the structure.

As the sunlight fades, the vines give up and reveal the stone underneath.

The walls are covered with dense glyphs. We take opposite sides and trace the beams of our flashlights on the carved images as we keep moving forward into the temple.

After examining several meters of carvings, I'm confused and admit, "These seem more like pictures than hieroglyphs. I mean I understand they're kind of the same, but this doesn't look like any kind of Mesoamerican style I've seen."

Theo points his flashlight at an image of a sphere surrounded by nine planets. Next to it is an illustration of what look like cells. And next to that, a primitive-looking fish.

"This is a textbook," I speculate.

"The story of creation. Or rather, a modern scientific account."

"In an ancient temple?"

Theo touches the surface of the wall. "Interesting."

"What?"

"Nothing. Just thinking."

We move farther into the temple and he inspects another section.

"This is Sumerian writing," says Theo, pointing to the wall closest to him. "And this is Akkadian."

"First question: What are they doing here? Second: How do you know the difference?" I ask.

"I saw them in a textbook."

"You learned to tell the difference between Sumerian and Akkadian writing just by reading a textbook?"

"No. I remember looking at an illustration comparing a Sumerian creation story and an Akkadian version of the same story." He points to the wall. "This is the exact illustration. Straight out of the book."

"Which is based on actual writings," I say.

"Made thousands of years ago on the other side of the world."

"It shouldn't be here."

"I'm not saying that. I'm saying there's no reason why it should be," he explains.

I aim my light farther into the tunnel and catch a glimpse of something reflective. "What's down there?"

We move past the glyphs and images toward a junction that appears to be in the exact center of the temple. Three other tunnels leading from the other sides meet in this huge chamber.

It's what's in the center that holds our attention.

Our beams catch glimpses of tiny sparkling beads suspended in a large mass. They appear to float in midair, but when I get closer, I can see thin, dark filaments running from the floor to the ceiling suspended among them.

"What is this?"

"Aim your light at the wall," says Theo as he backs up and does the same.

It takes a while for our eyes to adjust, but the ambient reflected light makes visible what wasn't apparent to our narrowly focused beams.

The entire structure forms a massive spiral filled with tiny points of light.

"Look familiar?" asks Theo.

"It's a galaxy."

"Our galaxy." He aims his light at part of the sculpture, where a bluish gem glows at the outer edge.

"That's us," I say.

"It would appear so."

I move around the structure and inspect the images on the wall.

"I don't get it," says Theo. "Nobody would believe the Incans or their predecessors knew this."

"Have you seen YouTube?" I reply. "But you're right. Especially the part about the Incans predicting the layout of Manhattan."

Theo follows my light to what's clearly a map of New York City carved into the temple wall.

His face makes a contorted look. I think I broke his brain.

Finally, he puts words to his thoughts: "I don't get it. If Theismann is trying to force a contextual reformation of reality by building what looks like the most convincing evidence of ancient alien contact, why would he add that? It would be like finding a primitive transistor in an Egyptian tomb next to a VHS tape of *The Simpsons*. Both unlikely. One completely absurd."

I investigate the map more closely. "This place may look modern, but it was built over twenty years ago."

"The foliage supports that. But why do you think so?" asks Theo.

"That image of the solar system in the front had nine planets. Now the nerds say there are only eight. And this map shows the World Trade Center towers," I explain.

Theo walks over and looks at the map.

"It would appear you're correct. Which leaves me with one big question."

"And that is?"

"What the fuck was Theismann thinking? I don't see how this fits with his hypothesis."

"Maybe it isn't supposed to."

Theo aims his light at the galaxy in the center of the room. "Then why go through all this effort? What's the purpose of this if it's his goal to talk to aliens?"

"Theo, you're not thinking like Theismann."

"Clearly, I'm not."

"What does the man want more than anything?"

"To make contact with aliens," answers Theo.

"Right. And what happens after he makes contact? Don't you see what this is?"

"Madness?"

"Well, yes. But that's not the purpose of this."

I wave my flashlight around the chamber and the connecting tunnels.

"Theo, this is a *welcome center*."

CHAPTER FORTY-SIX
PROTOTYPE

Theo is still wrapping his head around my revelation as we walk through the opposite tunnel. The glyphs here tell creation myths from Native American cultures.

Although we haven't explored the other tunnels, I assume they're stories from all the other corners of Earth. Each one explaining how humanity got to now. Or at least Theismann's explanation.

It's insane but kind of beautiful. It's a textbook that you experience, all built around a model showing our place in the universe.

I try to imagine what lies down the other passages and levels of the pyramid. More story murals? Gallery space? Meeting rooms? Interspecies bathrooms?

As we walk toward the light at the end of the other tunnel, I ask Theo a question that's been at the back of my mind. "I can sort of see how the existence of this could be kept secret. But what about the construction?"

"Hire people from remote parts of the world?" suggests Theo. "I think that was a graveyard we passed before entering the tunnel."

I get a chill, recalling the dirt mounds outside. "The women at the Colony did say their men were off building another location . . . but that would be a current construction project. I hope."

"Those graves were made in the last few years."

"Do you think . . ."

"Did they kill the workers like the pharaohs did? I don't think so. That wasn't a mass grave. That was people dying at different times, but close together. It could have been disease. We'd have to autopsy the bodies to find out. But the time period doesn't match. I think this was built in the 1980s," says Theo.

"What about that?" I ask, pointing at what's visible outside the tunnel's rear exit.

Across another wide plaza stands a series of modern structures on a hillside. Behind them tower several tall antennas and two radio telescope dishes.

A barbed-wire fence surrounds the entire complex.

"That looks way more recent," says Theo.

We reach the fence surrounding the complex and get a closer look. There are six buildings that are actually portable structures mounted on concrete foundations that look like they were airlifted in.

Next to them is a large prefabricated warehouse that was probably also brought in by air. I look back at the plaza. The surface appears to roughly serve as a runway. Or rather, helipad. I'm guessing a military-grade chopper brought all this here.

"Any idea why they have all the open space? Was Theismann planning on adding thrill rides and a gift shop?" I ask.

"Maybe it's what you said when we first saw the temple," replies Theo.

"What was that?"

"A parking lot."

"It's a lot of space for cars."

"Who says it's for parking cars? Maybe he's expecting spaceships."

I turn back around and face the plaza. "Holy shit. I think you're right. That's insane. Sheer, utter insanity."

"Any crazier than a ten-year-old boy saving a place at his birthday party in case Stephen Hawking decides to accept the invitation and show up?"

"Why not Richard Dawkins?" I reply.

"I asked him the year before. He was also a no-show."

"And if some kid ever asks *you* to show up at their birthday party?" I joke.

Theo looks down at his blood-spattered clothes and the shotgun he's still holding. "I'll contact their parents and tell them they need to have a discussion with their child about appropriate role models."

I point to a sign on the fence. "I think that's our explanation for the lack of curiosity about this place."

In Spanish and English, the sign reads:

No Trespassing: Ecuadorian Armed Forces Radio Testing Facility

"That explains *these* buildings. What about the temple?" I ask.

"It also explains the Google Maps mystery. This is all probably restricted airspace." Theo points to the radio towers. "Those are likely functional. That's a satellite uplink. Theismann or one of his subsidiaries could be providing them with digital access and communications support in exchange for secrecy."

"So all this is just a downlink?" I ask.

"It doesn't look like anyone's home. We could climb the fence and look," says Theo, pointing at the fence that separates us from the outbuildings and antennas.

The lock makes a clicking noise as I open it with a pick and tension wrench.

"Or you could just do that," says Theo.

We enter the complex and go up the steps to the first building. I open the door and we step inside what looks like a common room with a kitchen.

A hallway leads to several rooms with bunk beds that haven't been made. The closets are empty, but there're still toiletries in the bathroom.

We inspect two more modules that look exactly like the first one. Each has a kitchen, bathroom, and bedrooms.

All look recently inhabited but deserted quickly.

We walk to the next building, which is closer to the warehouse and the antennas.

"It looks like there were about twenty people here," I tell Theo as we pass an improvised basketball court amid picnic tables and a barbecue grill.

"It reminds me of a military base," says Theo.

"Yes. Something built quickly and then just as quickly abandoned."

"Although McMurdo Station in Antarctica also has the same feeling. This actually reminds me a lot of it," Theo observes.

We reach the next building and I pick the lock. It's three times the size of the others and filled with workstations. Workbenches covered in electronics line the walls under cabinets full of equipment.

Theo and I start at opposite ends, inspecting everything. So far it appears to be what the sign out front said: a radio testing facility.

"Could you somehow fake the probe signal from here?" I ask Theo, who has his nose buried in a circuit board.

"You could send a transmission from here to a probe using the radio dish out there. That would be overkill. But I can't see how you could make it look like it was coming from Neptune," says Theo.

He moves to another workstation and starts digging through drawers of components while I look for manuals with words I can understand.

"Is this anyone?" asks Theo.

I turn around and see that he's holding a photograph of a man and a woman smiling against a snowy background.

"That's David Ikeda and his wife," I reply, taking the photo from him.

"It was in this drawer." Theo points to a desk, then kneels to pull a crate out from under it. He reads documents in a binder, then sets it down. "What the hell?"

"What is it?"

"Give me a moment. That can't be right."

He starts pulling out black boxes the size of computer servers and lays them side by side on one of the workbenches. Each box has a Post-it note stuck to the top with what appears to be a serial number.

"What are those?" I ask.

"Digital signal processors. You use them to pick up a signal from background noise. Anything that communicates relies on a form of these. Our phones have several on one chip," he explains.

"Those are huge. Are they old?"

"No. They're recent. They're just really powerful. It's what you need to do radio astronomy or talk to space probes."

"Like the one the research station says they're talking to."

"Exactly. But you could also use them with fiber optics, copper. Anything with a lot of noise and a faint signal. They have dedicated processors that run complex algorithms to pick up patterns."

I nod as he picks up another box. This one has a metal case and is much larger. He unfastens several screws and lifts the outer shell to look inside.

Theo drops the screwdriver and turns toward me. I recognize that expression.

He points to the boxes. "These are three different manufactures. The US military uses that one. This is Chinese and the other's German. The circuit boards are all different. See that chip?"

I glance over at a small rectangle. "Yes?"

"They all use one like it. But they're manufactured under tight security. These kinds of boxes control military communications. They're air-gapped so they can't send signals out via the internet or any wired connection. Different on the outside but the same on the inside. Copies of the same original chip design."

"Okay . . . and?"

He grabs a pencil and points to the chip. "They're precise because they're fed two pieces of information: the signal and the position of the antenna. The antenna's position helps it separate out background noise. It uses that information to mask out interference. Don't you see?"

"Um, no. Care to elaborate?"

"The algorithms are patented and licensed to all of these manufacturers or ripped off from the patent holder because of export restrictions. One guess as to who owns the company . . ."

"Theismann. So what are you saying?"

"Glen Sexton and I looked at every inch of cable in the facility. I looked at every line of code for a hack or an exploit. But even if we found one, it wouldn't explain why the Utah facility detected the signal or what would happen if SETI or someone else was told where to look for it," he says.

"And what *would* happen?"

"They could detect it if they were using one of Theismann's algorithms, which they all do." He points to the chip. "Imagine the chip is supposed to say yes there's a signal or no there's not. But what's really going on is it's also listening to that background noise. If there's a signal coming from some other direction but it's encoded the right way, the chip says, 'Here's the signal from where the antenna is pointed.' When it's actually amplifying something from the background."

"So you could fool whoever was using one of these about the direction and content of a signal—so long as you slip the right sequence into the signal. That's a lot of effort and planning for faking aliens," I point out.

"This box is almost twenty years old. I don't think that was the original purpose. I think it was an intentional back door put in for the National Reconnaissance Office or some other spy agency," says Theo.

"Why would the government hack its own equipment?"

"One hand not knowing what the other was doing. An abandoned project. Maybe it was something the Russians planted a while ago. If you can send a signal the device thinks is trusted, you can create a lot of mayhem. This might have just been a basic hack to make it easy to hijack a GPS device. If those chips found their way into airplanes or missiles, you could send them off course. I'm just speculating."

I stare at the boxes on the counter.

"So Theismann planted a way to inject information into these two decades ago?"

"Someone did. It still doesn't fit. But he had the opportunity. So did a lot of engineers in different companies. Often subcontracting on government projects. There are secret agencies that do nothing but infiltrate cellular companies in other countries. Maybe it's him. Maybe it's someone exploiting him."

My phone buzzes with a notification.

"Anything important?" asks Theo as I check it.

"It looks like Theismann is going to hold that press conference after all."

"And tell the world he spoke to aliens? Any reason we should stop him from making a fool of himself?"

"Maybe. Maybe one big one," I reply.

PART SEVEN
CHAOTICIAN

CHAPTER FORTY-SEVEN
SIGNAL TO NOISE

Fiona Joss does not look happy to see Jessica and me. Her assistant, Teresa Bilton, was waiting at the helipad and escorted us to her office the moment we landed. Our bags are still sitting in the hallway outside Joss's office.

In a situation like this, where you're dealing with someone clearly intelligent and self-aware who also has virtually unlimited situational information, I tend to take a strategic approach—I let Jessica do all the talking.

"I wasn't aware that you were leaving the base until after the plane departed," says Joss in what could have been a conversational tone if she weren't visibly seething.

Jessica stares at her and gives a slight nod, acknowledging the fact that, *Yes, you did just make a series of sounds that were in the form of words that comprised a sentence.*

I've come face-to-face with evil. I've dealt with smooth-talking sociopaths and angry psychotics. My natural . . . objectivity . . . has allowed me to remain fairly calm and unemotional during such exchanges. But there's little strategy involved in those cases.

Here, I could deliberately try to put Fiona Joss on edge—throw out a provocative question—but I'm like a shotgun blast. Hit or miss. Jessica's an unwavering scalpel.

I don't know how much of it is her training, her background as a magic performer, a skill she picked up from peers or FBI training, a natural gift, or something she's learned from experience, but it's a talent.

Joss herself has some degree of talent for interrogation. She's a smart woman running a facility with a coterie of brilliant people and has managed to keep it a secret all these years.

Watching the two of them play conversational chicken is interesting. But I have to avoid reacting too much or else I'll become a target.

"Where did you go?" asks Joss.

"Ecuador," replies Jessica.

Joss knows this, or easily could, so there's no advantage to Jessica not disclosing this information.

"What were you doing down there?"

Great question. *Want to see the photos I took of the absolutely batshit crazy things we saw?*

But the real question is: Did Joss know we were down there?

The men who tried to kill us called, or were called by, someone at the research station. Was it her? Bilton? Somebody else?

Is Fiona Joss behind all this?

Clearly, she's the most obvious suspect. But that often means you're not looking hard enough.

"I can't discuss that," says Jessica.

"Were you acting on behalf of the FBI?" asks Joss.

"Like I said, I can't discuss that."

Joss points to the phone on her desk. "If I were to call your supervisor, what would they say? Are you here officially or in an unofficial capacity?"

"I'll give you his number and you can ask for yourself."

"I don't have to accommodate you here any further. I can ask you to leave the facility," Joss points out.

"I'm here at the invitation of Mr. Theismann. As is Dr. Cray. Has that changed?" asks Jessica.

A slight crease forms on Joss's forehead. *I think that's the answer. She* could *ask us, but that would be going against what Theismann wants—or at least what Martinez told us he wants.*

"You were invited here by Mr. Martinez. He has taken a temporary leave of absence to deal with a personal matter. I plan to speak with Mr. Theismann at the next opportunity about whether your presence is counterproductive to our work."

No Martinez? That happened fast. He might be the only one who wanted us here. Either Theismann is unaware of what we discovered in Ecuador or his scheme's much more complicated than I realized.

"Please let us know what he says," replies Jessica. "Until then, we'd like to go freshen up after our trip."

"Be advised that we might have to move you to accommodations off base to make room for the media personnel arriving tomorrow," Joss tells her.

The nearest hotel is thirty miles away. That's a cruel trick to pull. It also means the press conference is still on.

"Understood," says Jessica. She gets up to leave and I follow her.

As I reach the door, Joss calls out to me.

"Dr. Cray, I have to say that, despite your reputation, your presence has been quite . . . underwhelming."

"I hear that a lot," I reply.

"And then the fit hits the shan," Jessica murmurs out of Joss's earshot.

❧

"What the hell was that about?" I ask Jessica as we cross the parking lot with our luggage to the apartments.

"She doesn't know what's going on," replies Jessica. "She's scared. She can't read us, and she doesn't have control of everything. She loves control. The woman practically ran a cult. The idea of having people

281

with their own agenda around and outside her ability to manipulate . . . it's painful for her."

"So we don't think she's behind all this? If they weren't acting on her orders, then whose? See why she's so agitated? I'm surprised we're still on the property," I tell her.

Jessica stops at the sidewalk and faces me. "You're bright, but it's adorable how you don't see things."

"Um, thanks?"

"You're here . . . *we're* here because Thomas T. Theismann has a huge nerd crush on you," she explains.

"Me? I've never met the man."

"We'll have to talk about how crushes work sometime, Theo. The point is that more than anyone, Theismann wants to convince you—or have you convince him—that it's all real."

"But what if it's all his scheme?" I ask.

"You said the man believes in a techno-geek version of *The Secret*."

"What secret?" I reply.

"*The Secret* . . . a bestselling book that peddled old New Age non-sense to middle-aged women. Basically, it says that if you wish something to be true hard enough, it becomes true."

"That sounds like make-believe . . . and stupid."

"Yes. Have you ever been in a sports bar with a bunch of grown men wearing jerseys with other men's names on the back while they ritualistically yell at the television even though it can't hear them?"

"Okay. Fair point. But if Theismann's behind this, why keep me around?"

"I don't know. Maybe he's seen one too many James Bond movies where the villain keeps Bond alive so he can explain the plot at the start of the third act?"

"I don't think he sees himself as a villain."

"Neither do most villains. They see themselves as men with a vision. Like Stalin, Mao . . . James Cameron."

"Point taken. What do we focus on now?"

"You go get the data you need to test your theory about the signal processors. I'm going to do some more looking around and see if I can find out who the puppet master is."

CHAPTER FORTY-EIGHT
BYPASS

Rood is taking long drags on a cigarette at a picnic table alongside Glen Sexton when I approach him.

"There you are. I thought you'd reached your limit and decided to bug out," says Sexton.

"I had a couple things I needed to take care of," I tell him.

"With your FBI friend, I noticed," he observes.

I sit on the bench next to him. Rood is staring off into space and blowing clouds of smoke through his nostrils.

"Sorry, does it bother you?" Rood asks me. "I keep these around for stressful situations."

"Everything okay?"

"He's fine. Just company bullshit," Sexton answers for him.

Rood shakes his head. "By bullshit, he means I've been fired."

"Fired?"

"He's being dramatic. Joss just thinks that he's been overworked and he needs to take a little time away. It's been stressful twenty-four seven since I got here. I can't imagine what the last few months were like," says Sexton.

"Being cut out of the most important announcement of all time is kind of the same as getting fired. Your ability to spin things is miraculous," Rood says to Sexton.

"Look. Maybe Joss is doing you a favor. You've had your doubts and you wanted more time. They're not having it, so maybe it works out for you," Sexton tries to console the older man.

"Despite my reservations, I'm part of this. I'm going down or up with this ship. At least I was . . . The maddening thing is I can't even talk to Theismann about this. Joss won't let me near him. The guy hand-picked me." Rood sighs and flicks away the ashes from his cigarette butt.

"Is Theismann here?" I ask.

Rood motions toward the road. "He came in last night. He's got a little place up that way."

"I'm sorry they pulled you. This seems like the worst time to do that," I say.

"Or not," says Rood. "We haven't had a response in almost two days. The probe or whatever it is has gone silent."

"Obviously they can't blame you for that," says Sexton.

"Really? I think Joss holds me personally responsible. But I can't help it if it doesn't want to talk. Maybe our last data dump fried its circuits."

"Or made it want to go home," Sexton jokes.

"We haven't heard from it since we came back from Guatemala?" I ask.

"Not a peep. We've tried talking, but it hasn't said anything," explains Rood.

I decide to pry a little. "And the contents of the second message?"

"Math and curves we're still trying to figure out." Rood nods to Sexton. "He's putting together a computing cluster to make sense of it all."

"What's Theismann going to announce?" I ask Rood.

"That we believe we made contact. Then he wants to invite the world to solve the latest message. But Joss isn't happy about that."

"She's worried that it's a cookbook," says Sexton, making a reference to a *Twilight Zone* episode where the big reveal is that aliens want to eat us.

"That would be unfortunate," I concede.

"Or *The Communist Manifesto*. Or *Mein Kampf*," adds Sexton.

"*Fifty Shades of Greys*," says Rood, punning with a popular term used to describe the alien visitors that UFO diehards believe in.

"Joss might be into that," speculates Sexton.

Rood turns to me. "I'm sorry, Dr. Cray. Is there anything I can help you with?"

"Actually, yes. I want to know if you keep backups of all the background noise picked up by the antennas."

"Do we have backups? the man asks," laughs Rood. "We keep everything in our archive."

"What do you need *that* for?" asks Sexton.

"I just want to see if there's any kind of frequency leakage."

"Frequency leakage? What do you mean by that?"

I point to the chain-link fence. "Right now, that's absorbing Wi-Fi and cell phone frequencies. Which also means that it resonates slightly as it moves."

"You're talking effectively zero signal," says Sexton, "and we ground everything here."

"I know. I'm just curious," I reply.

Rood stubs out his cigarette on a rock and tosses it in a garbage can. "Let's go take a look in the data archive."

"Didn't Joss pull your access?" asks Sexton.

"News to me. I still haven't cleared out of my office." He pulls out a white key card. "Let's see if this still works."

I follow Rood across the parking lot to the main building. He's got a quick step and seems a little less depressed than before.

"In some ways, I feel like I'm about to miss out on the event of the millennium. Like the first atom bomb. But then I realize I might also miss out on having to be part of the aftermath." He walks up on the sidewalk and continues his thought. "Or it could just be a dud."

"What does that scenario look like?" I ask.

Rood uses his key card to let us into a side door. "It could be another *Wow!* signal. Well, maybe a little more complex. *Wow!* didn't contain any discernable information."

In 1977, researchers at Ohio State's Big Ear radio telescope picked up a signal in the direction of the constellation Sagittarius that to this day hasn't been explained and is considered the strongest candidate ever for an extraterrestrial transmission. The scientist looking at the readouts wrote "*Wow!*" next to it. The signal generated a considerable amount of excitement in the space community and helped launch efforts to search for more signals like it, but in the nearly half century since then, nothing else has come close.

We've discovered and solved many other mysteries since then: fast radio bursts, stars with peculiar rotations, binary stars, and lot and lots of extrasolar planets. But no more signals.

Rood leads me to an elevator. The doors slide open and we enter. He presses a button for the basement.

"We have one level below us used for storage and backups," he explains as the doors close.

A moment later the doors open to a long gray corridor. Rood leads me to a doorway at the end and opens it with his card.

The room is filled with racks of computer servers and a glass cabinet on the far wall holding shelves of DVDs.

"It's about twenty degrees cooler down here. Sometimes during the hotter nights when we have to shut down the air-conditioning units to limit the EMF for calibration, I'll come down here and sleep," explains Rood. He indicates the racks of servers. "Everything gets stored there first. Then we transfer it to disk for long-term storage."

"Do you do any off-site storage?" I ask.

"Oh, yes. AWS, Google Cloud, Azure. We back it all up everywhere we can."

Rood pulls a hard drive down from a shelf and plugs it into a computer workstation. "It'll take a little while to do the transfer. There should be another chair around here somewhere. Grab a seat."

He slides his chair over to a mini refrigerator. "Beer?"

"I'll take a diet cola if you have one."

"I do."

I pop the top of the can and take in the room. The amount of information stored here is enormous. Most of it mere static.

"I remember when I started out and a tape drive was high tech. I once lost a year's worth of research on a Zip drive that wiped itself. I learned my lesson. The moment data comes in, we make a copy here and send them to a remote server," he explains.

"You set all this up?" I ask.

"Yep. Joss runs the facility. I run the hardware. Or at least I did. She hates the amount of money we're spending on cloud services. When she heard the proposed cost of the TSC, she about had a heart attack."

"The TSC?"

"Oh, right. That's still proposed. The Theismann Supercomputing Center. There's a plan to build the world's most powerful supercomputer to sort through every single piece of radio-astronomy data ever collected. There're also plans to build ten more facilities like this and let AIs guide the search. Basically, move the antennas around a lot more and see if you can use machine learning to find candidate signals," explains Rood.

"That sounds incredibly ambitious."

"Maybe too ambitious for Theismann."

I'm curious what qualifies as too ambitious for a man who's already built a giant pyramid and an alien welcome center.

"It seems right up his alley," I point out.

"Yes. But over the last few years, he's been more and more worried about his legacy. His advisers have told him he should be spending more money on Earth problems or basic science research."

Interesting. I'm beginning to see an angle here for Theismann to suddenly be presented with an alien signal.

"I guess Joss is pretty excited about the prospect of running a much larger operation," I say.

"Joss? Computers aren't her thing. This was outside her sphere of influence. The entire proposal was brought to Theismann by one of his other companies."

"So who would run this?"

"I don't know. Not me. Theismann keeps things extremely compartmentalized." Rood checks the computer. "Looks like we have your data."

He unplugs the hard drive and hands it to me. "If Joss asks where you got this, tell her it fell off a truck."

We walk back to the entrance, and Rood swipes his card across the access panel. An angry red light starts blinking. He swipes again. Same light.

"*Now?* They revoked this now?" he growls.

"Is there another way out?"

"Other than going berserk with a fire ax? I have to send an email on the computer and hope some dingus upstairs sees it and lets us out." He sighs. "In the meantime, you want that beer?"

CHAPTER FORTY-NINE
DATA LEAK

After an hour-and-a-half wait in the archive, I was tempted to have that beer but held out because I wanted to stay sharp and the bathroom facilities in the server room were limited to an empty Gatorade bottle.

I've endured worse, but I don't think I could handle the irony of having to relieve myself in the equivalent of a chamber pot while surrounded by so much advanced technology.

When one of the station's staff members rescued us, it turned out it wasn't Rood's card that was the problem but the accidental reset of the entire security system.

As soon as I make it to the parking lot, my phone blows up with messages from Jessica.

I call her immediately.

"Where have you been?" she asks.

"Stuck in a basement with Rood for the last two hours. You?"

"I've been with Teresa Bilton, out where the staffer shot himself," she tells me.

"Looking for clues?"

"No. She asked me to come check it out. But she was acting weird. She kept asking me nonsensical questions . . . Where are you now?"

"In front of the main building. I was going back to the apartment with the background-noise data to check it out."

"Do me a favor. Go to the control room. Just wait there until I text you. Okay?"

"Understood."

I can recognize a no-questions-asked situation when I see it.

I walk over to the main building and into the control room. Some of the others are there looking over data on a screen.

Urbina sees me first. "Dr. Cray? Anything we can help you with?"

"I wanted to talk to you about Guatemala," I improvise on the spot. "Your latest thoughts."

"I'd love to go into them at length. But right now, we're preoccupied with something. Perhaps later?"

"Sure. Sure." I back up but stay in the control room and look for someone else to talk to so I have a reason to be here.

Trevor's in a small glass conference room off to the side. I poke my head in. "Got a moment?"

He closes his laptop. "Absolutely. This is driving me nuts. How are you?"

"Still trying to process everything. I understand the probe hasn't sent another signal."

"Yeah. That's a bit frustrating. I was just putting together a report for Theismann, explaining my thoughts. Have you done yours yet?"

"I haven't been asked."

"He might want to talk to you in person. That'd be a compliment, by the way. If he asks you for a paragraph, you're not that important. A page is a sign that he thinks you're smart. An entire white paper is either a sign of respect or else he's trying to find one reason not to banish you to some lesser project. But an in-person conversation? That's the real ticket."

"Have you had many of those?"

"I'm a one-page consultant who gets asked to evaluate the progress of his various projects. Not significant enough to get my own meeting. But good enough to get paid for an opinion from time to time." Trevor pauses for a moment and stares at me. "It wouldn't surprise me if he asks you what your dream project is. If you tell him looking for signs of alien influence in DNA, he'd probably swoon and build you a facility like this."

"You mean intelligent design? I don't see myself doing that kind of research without a rational hypothesis," I tell Trevor.

"Just tell him you're intrigued by his hypothesis—you think there's something plausible to it. That's what just about everyone else did. Other than the true believers . . ."

"True believers?"

"People like Joss." He points through the window at Urbina and whispers his name as well. "People who see this as a religious mission."

"What about you?" I ask. "Are you a cynic or a believer?"

"Neither. I'm a sanity check for Theismann. That's why I'm only visiting. My main job is chasing down grants to catalog a backlog of artifacts my university's collected. This is a fun distraction." He shrugs.

"No research facility for you?"

"If I had a single reason to believe anything in my work could plausibly be explained by alien contact, I'd do it in a heartbeat. And trust me, I've looked deeply into every comet, every supernova recorded by ancients, for something I could claim was evidence of contact. But I can't. I'm stuck with a semirespectable reputation and a modest 401k that I'd gladly trade for infamy and a fat pension if I knew I were only slightly compromising my values."

My phone buzzes with a text message from Jessica.

The Sheriff's Deputies are coming to talk to you. Do what they say, but don't give them anything other than yes or no answers. Ask for a lawyer if they want your phone or anything personal. Got it?

For heaven's sake.

Yes.

I look up from my phone at the sound of heavy boots entering the control room. Two deputies are standing at the entrance.

The taller one, with a thick black mustache, calls out, "Is Dr. Theo Cray here?"

Urbina looks in my direction.

I walk out of the meeting room. "I'm Dr. Cray. What can I do for you?"

The man's name tag says "Cauldron." His female partner's name is Krizan.

"We have some questions we'd like to ask you," says Cauldron.

"Sure. Should we find a conference room?"

"Let's speak in your hotel room," he replies.

Technically it's not a hotel room. But fine. "Okay. Follow me."

We march across the parking lot, with the deputies flanking me on either side. It's almost as if they're waiting for me to make a run for it.

Which would be dumb because there isn't anywhere to run to out here, and I don't have a reason to run. At least any I know about.

I get to my door and pull the key from my pocket.

"May I?" asks Cauldron, taking the key from me.

"Sure? Is everything okay?" I ask.

"Wait outside," he warns me.

"Would you move over here?" requests Krizan, trying to get me away from the doorway.

"I have a computer and some personal belongings. I'd like to keep an eye on those. I haven't consented to them being searched," I say as neutrally as possible.

"We don't need your consent to search this room since you're neither the owner nor the renter," says Cauldron as he walks into the room, opens the closet, and uses his flashlight to search inside.

"I believe my personal belongings are excluded, and I can call my lawyer if you need clarification," I tell him.

"Do you have an attorney?" asks Krizan, challenging what she thinks is an empty boast.

"Me? You're asking me if *I* have an attorney?"

"Dr. Cray is very familiar with courtrooms," says Cauldron as he searches the bathroom.

Satisfied or perhaps not satisfied, he walks back into the bedroom and kneels to look under the bed. He gets back up on creaky knees.

"Dr. Cray, would you please have a seat on the bed?"

"Okay," I reply, remembering Jessica's instructions.

"When was the last time you spoke to Nicholas Hendricks?" asks Cauldron.

"The head of security? Two nights ago. Right here with Fiona Joss when I caught his employee trying to plant evidence."

Cauldron studies me. "And you haven't spoken to him or seen him since then?"

"No. I heard that he left very shortly afterward."

"What else have you heard?"

"That was the end of it. I've only been back here for a few hours."

"Hey, what's going on?" asks Jessica from the doorway.

"Stand back, ma'am. We're conducting an interview," says Deputy Krizan, moving to block her from entering.

Jessica has her badge out and gets in the deputy's face faster than I can blink. "Great. I'd like to ask some questions, too. Mind if I call Sheriff Jorquera to check this out?"

"Be my guest," says Cauldron. He gives his colleague a nod. "I think we're done here."

"What was this about?" asks Jessica.

"Just checking up on something. You all have a good day. Krizan." He motions to his partner that they're leaving.

Jessica steps aside, and the two deputies exit the room, leaving us alone.

"What was that all about? Why did you send me to the control room?" I ask.

"I—" Jessica steps to my side and whispers in my ear: "I needed you somewhere visible while I got rid of the body."

CHAPTER FIFTY
STRANGE ATTRACTOR

"Body? What body?" I ask, looking around my room for signs of violence.

"Hendricks's body. It was in your closet until fifteen minutes ago," she says as she locks the door.

I stare at the closet. "What did you do?"

"I didn't do anything. Bilton keeping me away from the station had me suspicious. When I found out you'd been locked in the basement for two hours, that was just too much. I had you go to the control room so whoever is behind this would have their attention on you.

"Then I checked our rooms and found Hendricks here, ice-cold, dead for hours, wrapped in plastic with a bullet in his head. And since I'm pretty sure I'm not living with a serial killer, it looked like another obvious frame-up," says Jessica.

"It wouldn't have lasted ten minutes. They'd have taken me down to the sheriff's office and checked my alibi, spoken to you, and they'd have known the time line didn't match up," I reply.

"Theo. It's not about framing you for a crime. It's about getting you out of here. And me, too, since you're my ticket to snoop around. Theismann may like you, love you, or tolerate you. But he'd have to draw the line if you were suspected of murdering someone here," she explains.

"Who hates me enough to do that?" I ask.

"Everyone here hates you, Theo."

"Yikes."

"Okay, not everyone. But most of them. Joss, Urbina, and the fanatics are afraid you'll convince Theismann this is all bullshit. Riley, Anna, and Trevor are probably secretly worried you'll convince Theismann that there's a better way to direct his money. Rood's afraid you'll make him see the light, and Sexton envies you like crazy," she explains.

"Sexton? He seems nice enough."

"In the same way a guy that's hitting on me will be nice to the other guy he thinks is my boyfriend," she explains.

"I'm confused by that analogy. Who am I and who's the girlfriend in it?"

"Theismann is the girlfriend."

"I've never met him."

"He still passed you a note in class and invited you to the party."

I shake my head. "This is getting very confusing."

"Don't you see? *Theismann* sent you the copy of his hypothesis. It was like a schoolyard note that said, 'Do you like me? Check yes or no.'"

"Theismann sent it?" I ask, still trying to sort things out.

"Keep up, babe. People want to kill us. Martinez brought you into this because he realized you were the one person Theismann might actually trust," says Jessica.

"How come he hasn't spoken to me, then?"

"Because he doesn't want to get his heart crushed. Imagine if Richard Feynman told you that your research was silly."

"One, I'd compliment him on cheating death. Two, I'd tell him it's a field that barely existed when he was alive. And three, I'd cry like a little baby and curl up in the corner. Ah . . . I get it."

"God, I hope so. The short version is that you have to figure out whatever the hell is going on and get to Theismann before he makes his big announcement," she explains.

"Why is that important?"

"I know you're a man, but you may not be aware of how men's egos work. Once they say or commit to something, there's no going back."

I risk feeling stupid by asking another question: "Just so we're on the same page, we're thinking that Theismann *isn't* the architect behind this whole hoax?"

"TBD. He might be. But the fact that you're here and Martinez isn't makes me think otherwise. *His* personal emergency was that his son was found with cocaine in his locker. Shocker, right? It was an anonymous tip. These people play hardball. The bodies are piling up, so they have to try tricks like that and . . . well, piling up bodies they can blame on someone else, like you."

My head is still spinning. "I'd like to make a flowchart and maybe a time-series database to track this all."

"That ain't happening. You gotta figure out how they did what they did. And I'm going to try to figure out who *they* is."

"Do I even want to know where Hendricks's body is?"

"I'll put it this way: If I don't move it before the maid arrives for her shift, you're going to hear some loud screaming. I need to put it somewhere else," she says with a sigh.

"Let me know if you need help. Corpses are kind of my thing."

"Please never say that again. I'm going to see if I can find the rightful owner . . . or rather *killer* . . . and return it."

"Any idea who?"

"I have a feeling that the 'Mike' I heard about at the Colony and the 'Miguel' the crooked Ecuadorian cop mentioned are the same person. But I haven't seen him around here."

"Rood mentioned that Theismann has a place up the road."

Jessica thinks it over for a minute. "That adds up. My fear is that whoever is behind this might have an in with someone close to Theismann."

"That could be Mike," I reply.

"Maybe. But he sounds more like a facilitator working with a master planner."

"Think he's tight with Joss?" I ask.

"Maybe. She has cult written all over her. The fanatics are looking pretty suspicious . . . but that could be by design." Jessica goes to the door. "But you got all the signal data, right?"

I nod.

"Good. Don't let anyone in. And get to work."

CHAPTER FIFTY-ONE
FREQUENCY

The concept of mechanical computers has been around for almost as long as humans have known about sticks and needed to count things.

The earliest computers were probably lines etched into the dirt and rocks used as stand-ins for cattle, crops, wives, or whatever else was being traded.

There's an uncanny similarity between a grid used to count items and the electronic spreadsheets we use today.

Computers evolved as our ability to make things improved. The Greeks had simple devices that could keep track of astronomical events, and the abacus was an Eastern invention that effectively created a portable version of the lines-and-rocks-in-the-dirt method of accounting.

Clock making helped improve mechanical calculators, and the real potential of them was finally realized when Charles Babbage conceived of the Difference Engine and the more advanced Analytical Engine, which shares mechanical DNA with the devices we use today. His colleague Ada Lovelace saw the connection between the machine and the patterns produced by weaving looms and realized that a computer could be used for more than numbers and symbolic representation. Had the Analytical Engine ever been built, she could well have been the first-ever computer programmer.

Despite the potential some saw in computers, their mechanical complexity and cost was prohibitive. There was no major undertaking to build them until World War II, when the challenge of accurately plotting the trajectories of projectiles directed at and delivered from airplanes meant winning or losing the war.

Along with this interest in using computers for weapons came the realization that mechanical devices could also be made to decode the encrypted messages of Nazi Enigma machines.

British scientist Alan Turing helped improve upon a Polish decoder and then went on to design one of the first modern computers. Before his untimely suicide, he developed theories about computation that are still in use today.

On my screen are the diagrams for the signal processor that I think is the secret to why some very intelligent people think that they've spoken to aliens.

I have to convince them otherwise, because I now believe I understand the master plan: we're never going to hear from Seeker again.

Pulling off this trick over and over again runs the risk of discovery. Somebody would get a little too curious and build their own processor from scratch.

Like one of Jessica's magic tricks, you don't repeat it. Otherwise, the second time around the audience will look for clues as to how it's done.

My window of opportunity is very limited.

I'm also hindered by the fact that I don't have access to a physical machine.

I not only have to figure out what algorithms were used to spit out fake messages, I also have to find a way to transmit a signal of my own.

The latter problem is challenging, the former borderline impossible.

The processor only takes a few bits of data every millisecond. I ran the numbers to see how long it would take me to "crack" the algorithm by sending it random information, and the best estimate is three hundred thousand years.

I don't have to check my watch to know that I don't have that kind of time.

Despite that, I'm contemplating seeing if I can go "borrow" one of the signal processors from the station, then hopefully think of a time-saving solution on my trip back across the parking lot. And you know, maybe solve quantum gravity and find some dark matter.

I could also try to steal access to boxes that are on unsecure networks. There might be a few hundred I could hijack, which would lower the time needed to crack to about ten thousand years, which would also be approximately the length of time I'd spend in prison for doing that.

Another possibility would be to overclock one of the machines and make it run much, much faster.

The challenge there is I'd still need the machine, but after running the math with however much energy is required to finish in a reasonable time frame, I'd melt the machine.

I might be able to build a cooling system that works directly with the chip that has the algorithms. But that would require more time and resources than I have at hand.

I lean back and visualize the chip in my head and the stubborn transistors hardwired to do the computation. How do I get access to them?

I really only need . . .

My forehead suddenly hurts, and it takes me a moment to realize that I just slapped it.

Theo. Idiot.

The chip design was copied from earlier iterations, which means its circuitry is well known. But the actual minutiae of each logic gate isn't understood, nor was what the algorithms are actually doing. All that mattered to the users was that it worked.

I load a microchip emulator into my computer and import the files for the signal chip. One of the things Alan Turing demonstrated was that a simple computer could emulate any other computer—just much more slowly.

In theory, I could emulate my computer emulating another computer emulating another until the whole thing came to a crawl—but still emulated.

However, the signal processor is a much simpler chip. It's designed to work with higher voltages but can be completely replicated inside my computer and at a much faster rate.

I do a speed check.

Much, much, much faster.

Hours, not the length of time *Homo sapiens* has been on Earth.

I start my frequency generator and let my computer go to work.

Time to solve problem number two.

Assuming I can crack the code, how do I get it into the system in the first place?

Looking at it from another angle, how did someone send a Trojan horse that tricked the signal processor?

Despite Jessica's order that I stay in my room, I need to take a walk and think about this.

It's dark out, and the radio antennas are lit up from underneath, their dishes pointed hopefully at the sky.

I desperately want to find intelligent life out there and to ask it questions. I'm also eternally suspicious about the things I desperately want to be true.

I think that's the line between myself and a believer. The more I want to believe, the more suspicious I am.

I spot a man walking from the array and recognize Kaz Patel, the engineer who keeps the dishes running.

I intercept him before he enters the main building. "Hey, Kaz. How are you?"

"Dr. Cray. Good to see you."

"Dumb question. How do we monitor for flyovers?"

I think I already know the answer, but I want to be sure. A small plane going in a circle could fake an approximate signal. The signal in Guatemala may have been caused the same way. But the signal processor would still have to be hacked to make it look like it was coming from space.

"We have a radar dish on the building. It's good for up to a few meters across," says Kaz.

"What about drones?"

Kaz gives me the grin of someone who has heard this a thousand times. "Listen for a moment."

I hear the sound of a flag rustling by the road, the chain-link fence rattling, and the wind.

"I have a drone that I use to inspect the dishes. You can hear it from miles away on a quiet night, if it's not too windy. You'd know."

I think about what he just said, and something clicks in the back of my mind.

I make a split-second decision that I can trust him.

"Kaz, I have a favor to ask."

After talking to Kaz, I walk back to my apartment before Jessica catches me breaking curfew. I'm so preoccupied with my next steps I don't notice the older gentleman sitting alone at the fire pit until I walk past him and he calls out my name.

"Dr. Cray," he says. "Do you have a moment?"

I turn around and see Thomas T. Theismann warming his hands by the fire.

CHAPTER FIFTY-TWO

FANATIC

We study one another for a long moment. Theismann appears to be collecting his thoughts. I'm trying to catch my breath.

The man was purely theoretical until he became real.

"What do you think of our little operation here?" he asks, breaking the silence.

He has a strong face with bushy eyebrows and intelligent eyes. He reminds me of a senior politician who still has the vigor to debate much younger opponents.

There's still fire inside this man.

"Impressive," I reply.

"What do you really think, Dr. Cray?"

"Theo. Just Theo. I can think of worse things than sponsoring something like this," I answer.

"But do you think it's a waste? Theo?"

I try to be cautious with my words. "If the signal is real, then clearly it's not a waste."

"And if the smartest minds I can gather are wrong and it's some kind of fake? What would you say then?"

"The outcome is irrelevant if the question is worthwhile. You can't do science by only betting on things you're certain are going to be true.

It's not really science. It's confirming what we already know. I think someone needs to be asking these ultimate questions."

Theismann doesn't say anything. He studies me for a while, then finally speaks again: "I was elated when I heard we finally got a signal. It's something I wanted my entire life. But then I got a sense of dread. What if it was too good to be true? That's why I asked Mr. Martinez to contact you. I wanted you to be . . . my skepticism."

"I'm flattered."

"I don't know that it's a compliment. You just seemed like the kind of man that would persevere no matter what." He takes a breath and lowers his voice. "I know what kind of people I've surrounded myself with. I've gotten a little better over the years, but I'm still a wealthy man with . . . unique ideas that tend to attract people willing to pretend to share them."

"I think some of these people are quite sincere," I say. "A man like Rood is here because he believes in the potential for the idea. Joss as well. Urbina. And, if I may say so, I think your fanatics are the most honest of all."

If not the most ethical . . .

"Fanatic. I guess that's the right word. Tell me, what did you think of my pyramid?" asks Theismann.

Two things come to my mind. The first is, would he know what "nucking futs" means? The second, how much does he know about our trip to Ecuador? It was his plane, but does he know what else we found, or who we encountered?

"It was impressive," I reply.

"I was very hopeful when I built it. Perhaps I jumped the gun a bit. I'd like to go down there and see it again. I'm told the Ecuadorians are using it for military training. Perhaps they'll make an exception," he muses.

Does he not know, or is this a ploy?

"Actually, there's a satellite uplink facility and research lab there. Your people were occupying it until quite recently."

Theismann contemplates this. "Really? Perhaps the accountants figured out a way to get a tax credit in a development zone. I'll have to ask."

Is he truly unaware of what happened?

"Two men tried to kill Jessica and me there," I tell him.

"Kill? Maybe they were private security who were a bit overzealous."

"No, Mr. Theismann. I'm a pretty good judge of intent. These people wanted to kill us, and one of them had just spoken to somebody at this facility. *Here.*"

"I don't think I understand," he says.

"The concept of death?"

"You have a glib tongue . . . Theo."

Wait until you meet Jessica.

"I also don't exaggerate. But I think you know this."

"I'll make inquiries. There may have been a communications issue. I'll also find out why the facility is being used for that purpose. You have my assurance."

"Thank you," I say, trying to soften the tenor of the discussion.

"Now the real purpose as to why I'm here. I believe someone gave you a copy of my thesis. Did you by chance read it?" he asks.

Jessica's analogy comes to mind: *And did I check "yes" or "no" for liking you?*

"I did. Much of it was over my head. The speculative parts were interesting but, as you know, hard to quantify."

"You're dancing around the question."

"No. You asked me if I read it. I said that I did. I'm dancing around the question you *want* to ask me."

Theismann stares at me, and then his face breaks into a broad grin. "Few people have the balls to talk to me that way."

"I don't want anything from you," I point out. Except maybe answers.

"I'm not going to ask if you accept all of it or even agree with the premises. I just want to know if there's something there."

I choose my words carefully. "Mr. Theismann, I'm a microscope man. I have an expectation of what I'm going to see inside it, and either it's there or it isn't. Your hypothesis is much grander and far more complex than my world. If there's something we can test, then let's test it. Beyond that, I leave it to the string theorists and pure mathematicians."

"What if we *could* test it?"

"You mean like what you're doing here? Looking for supportive evidence of alien contact to reshape our world?"

"Not quite. I get suggestions all the time about what to do with my money. Build more arrays. Cure a disease. Invest in rocket ships. The older I get, the more voices I have telling me what to do. And to be honest, I'm kind of sick of it." He waves his arm at the radio telescopes behind him. "I'd be delighted to find out that this was all a clever hoax to attempt to convince me to spend more money on this pursuit. Because then I'd know it was time to do something else. But if I can't be shown evidence that it's a lie, then I have to commit my resources to this path and nothing else."

This is interesting. Theismann doesn't seem the evil mastermind or gullible fool that I suspected.

"What else would you rather spend it on?"

"Something I'd very much like you to be a part of."

Predictably, Jessica was right.

Theismann continues, "Your knowledge of biology and computation is intriguing. It's a field that was only nascent when I first put down my thoughts. But now it creates new possibilities." He looks me in the eye. "How deeply did you read my hypothesis?"

"Enough to understand your idea about rewriting reality," I reply.

"I've evolved my thoughts a bit since then. But I'd say that's an accurate assessment. I still think it might be possible to create a kind of reverse quantum experiment that changes our universe and doesn't split it into two different outcomes. I believe the key is actually quantum computers and using them to create a system with a greater fidelity than our own."

"You want to build a quantum computer to create an artificial universe to test your theory?"

"Not quite. I want to use quantum computers to do something a bit grander. I want to see if we can break our own universe. And for a project of this scale, I'd like your help. For a first step, I plan to build the most powerful supercomputer in the world."

Second time I've heard a version of this today.

"That's a very intriguing offer. Although I'm not sure what a successful outcome would look like," I reply.

"Neither am I. Let's find out."

"So, if I blew this whole alien-contact thing apart, you wouldn't be upset?"

"I'd welcome it. What do you say?"

I'd say I'm going to put his claim to the test.

CHAPTER FIFTY-THREE
No Strangers

By the time I fully awaken to the sound of a loud knock, Jessica's already beside the door with her gun drawn. She managed to slip out of bed like a cat set to pounce.

We didn't know what to expect last night. After the attempt to kill us and frame me, it was clear that someone or some people wanted me out of the picture.

My hope was that they'd exhausted all their chances and were going to let things run their course.

Jessica called this naive and joined me so we could sleep in alternating shifts in case someone decided to pay me a visit.

"Dr. Cray? Are you awake?"

"It's Bilton," Jessica whispers across the room to me.

"Yes?" I call out.

"There's been a new signal. Mr. Theismann has requested you be there when it's decoded."

"Okay. I'll be there shortly," I reply through the door.

"All right, and if you could also tell Agent Blackwood, that would be helpful."

"Will do."

Jessica watches her walk away through a gap in the curtain.

"She seemed jubilant," observes Jessica.

"Yes. Which makes me think she's just a fanatic and not a plotter."

We've started using the term *plotter* instead of *believer* or *skeptic* to determine who we think is in on the conspiracy.

We've also decided that it's a conspiracy because, well, it is.

The question remains: Who are all the plotters?

I'm hoping the sudden reemergence of the signal might resolve that. For some people it will be a welcome surprise. For others it will be confusing or scary.

To make sure that this signal wasn't kept secret, I made sure that Theismann, an early riser, would be in the control room when it came through.

Unless he is the master conspirator, I saw no way he'd let Joss and company keep the next signal a secret.

"Are you ready for the show?" asks Jessica as she puts on a sweater vest.

"I'll do my part. You do yours."

The biggest unresolved mystery, aside from the identity of the plotters, is the location of Mike, a.k.a. Miguel.

Jessica reconnoitered Theismann's house and could not find any sign of the man. She then did a sweep of the station offices, looking for a man that met his description. None did.

Another possibility was that he was staying at the hotel thirty miles away. That was until Jessica took a look at Google Maps and found a small trailer park five miles up the road.

She borrowed a staffer's car and took a look while I got everything ready for today.

We've both gone out on some pretty shaky limbs. Hopefully it all pays off.

❧

The control room is packed when we enter. Theismann is sitting in a chair flanked by Joss, Urbina, Bilton, and several other fanatics.

Trevor, Anna, Riley, and Sexton (our skeptics) sit at the opposite end, whispering to each other.

The telescope staff are busy conferring at a workstation where Carly Nicholson, the head of computer engineering, stares at a screen with 0s and 1s scrolling from top to bottom.

Rood's here, too, sitting by himself. I'd requested that he be here as well.

I study each face, trying to decide who looks guilty. The problem with that is, both parties are naturally anxious.

For the fanatics, this could be the big moment where we receive wisdom from across the stars. For the plotters, the unexpected signal means their game could be up. And for the skeptics . . . enlightenment?

I catch Theismann out of the corner of my eye watching me. I had a long discussion with Jessica about whether he really wanted me to debunk this.

Her opinion was that it was mostly bullshit he'd tried to convince himself of. He's always wanted this to be true, she reminded me. He might have talked himself into plan B, but his heart's always been in plan A . . . as in *A* for *Aliens*.

Nicholson suddenly exclaims, "Got it!"

Joss leaves Theismann's side to see what's on the screen, pushing staffers out of the way.

Nicholson swivels around in her chair to address us. "We sent instructions in the primer on how to encode various data. It appears they've figured out video and sound."

Murmurs rise in the control room. The plotters claim they still haven't deciphered the second signal. Nor do I think they ever will. I believe it's data designed to look like it can be decrypted but containing nothing intelligible. A mystery to keep the resources flowing, like being a water-pump salesman on Oak Island.

"Let's hear it," says Theismann.

"I'd like to spend more time examining it first," says Joss.

"Enough with the secrecy. We can't keep this hidden anymore," says Theismann, very much like a man who doesn't want to be talked out of this.

Jessica's phone buzzes, and she excuses herself to a conference room. She exchanges a few words, then comes back and sits down next to me.

"Good news?" I whisper.

"For us. Yes."

Nicholson takes her place back at her workstation and types in a command. "It should appear on the overhead screen."

The video image goes from black to static and for five seconds emits a high-pitched screeching sound.

Slow it down, I think to myself.

"Let me try slowing it down," says Nicholson.

I study the people in the room once more. They're all engaged and look curious. I still can't tell who's ready to bolt for it—although I don't expect anyone to do that.

"Okay. I think I got it," announces Nicholson. She taps her keyboard.

This time a blurry image appears, and the audio has more bass but is still distorted. However, we can make out something that sounds like speech.

"What was that?" asks Patel.

"I think it said, 'Know strangers,'" says Anna.

"I heard, 'Know the rules,'" adds Riley.

"I thought I heard 'love,'" Bilton counters.

"Let me play it again. This time faster," says Nicholson.

She gets the rate correct this time, and every single person in the control center hears every single word.

I'd laughed when I figured out what my alien message should be. It seemed perfect. That didn't prepare me for the look of horror on everyone's faces.

Jessica is shaking her head. "Why, Theo?" she whispers. "Why?"

Theismann speaks up. "I think it's a beautiful message. Why is everyone so upset?"

Bilton says something in the old billionaire's ear.

Theismann seems confused, then asks the room: "Who the hell is Rick Astley?"

CHAPTER FIFTY-FOUR
CONTACT

Everyone is sitting in stunned silence. The believers. The skeptics. The plotters. And the computational biologist who thought it would be funny to perpetrate the biggest Rickroll of all time.

I'm an asshole.

But I sure showed them I'm the smartest guy in the room.

When I thought about the message, I was thinking only about the conspirators. I didn't consider the people who've earnestly worked their whole lives for this moment.

That's not to say I had to let the lie continue, but there were better, less arrogant ways to achieve my purpose.

Jessica can see the look on my face.

"It's okay. There was no easy way to do this," she whispers.

Regardless, I have to own up to it—and also see this through. One or more of these people conspired to commit murder.

I stand up. "My apologies for the way this was done, but I needed to illustrate that these signals are fake," I tell the group, acting as if this were all part of the plan.

"What do you mean?" asks Joss.

I point to the frozen frame of Rick Astley's blurry face on the overhead screen. "I sent that message."

"What?" says Nicholson. "We triple-checked everything."

"Trust me. Aliens didn't Rickroll you. I did."

"Maybe they sent it as a joke," says Bilton, pitifully, or so it seems to me. She's in such a state of denial that she's not even hearing my words.

"There should be a random sequence of twelve zeros and ones every 244th digit," I tell Nicholson loudly enough for the whole room to hear. "Can you display that?"

A sequence of 0s and 1s appears overhead:

```
01010100   01101000   01100101   01101111
00100000   01000011   01110010   01100001
01111001 00100000 00111010 00101001
```

"Good. Now convert that to alphanumeric."

Nicholson types away, and the corresponding text appears overhead:

Theo Cray :)

"I added my signature just in case," I tell the room, as if it weren't completely obvious by now.

"How?" Joss almost screams.

"There's a back door in all the signal processors that use Mr. Theismann's algorithms," I explain.

"I did no such thing!" Theismann protests.

"No. You didn't, but about twenty years ago, somebody added it to the designs. It's actually a simple hack. Easily overlooked because it's not designed to get information out. Just to corrupt it." Before anyone can ask what the hell I'm talking about, I explain. "This happens more than people care to think. Even military-grade encryptions have had these. But instead of using the back door to steal information, someone figured out it was an easy way to fake the signal."

"But we know the direction of the signal. And even looked off-axis," protests Nicholson.

"The signal processors can tell the alignment of the antenna from the background noise. If it's pointed in a specific direction, it gives you what you think is an alien signal but is actually local."

"How? From where?" asks Joss.

"From a transmitter attached to one of the meteorological balloons you use to measure the wind. A piece of fishing line holds it in place."

I glance at Patel. His eyes go wide as a small mystery is solved for him.

"What about Sierra Sky Watch? They confirmed it," asks Joss.

"Same thing. Somebody spoofed them, too," I reply. "You could pull the whole thing off for a few hundred dollars. The signal in Guatemala, probably just a transmitter on a plane. Make it a few thousand bucks."

Theismann rises from his seat. "Who? Who did this?"

"I wish I could tell you, sir. Unless someone wants to come forward and save us the trouble . . . ," I suggest hopefully.

Jessica speaks up. "We know it was an inside job. The FBI will want to speak to everyone here. Some more than others."

The attendees exchange wide-eyed glances.

"And if you don't speak up," Jessica continues, "I'm pretty certain that Michael, a.k.a. Miguel, a.k.a. Mike Highfield will. The sheriff's department pulled him over twenty minutes ago and found a body in the trunk of his car."

I scan all the faces to see how this information hits them. Jessica intentionally didn't say whose body, thus avoiding an emotional reaction.

"Mike?" says Theismann, incredulous. "I've known the man for forty years."

"What did he do for you?" Jessica asks him.

"He . . . he handled problems."

Jessica nods, staring into the old man's eyes. "And did you always ask how?"

Theismann shakes his head. "I just thought he was . . . persuasive."

"Apparently, when David Ikeda didn't want to cooperate and a trip to the Colony didn't set him straight, Mike decided to kill him."

Theismann drops back into his chair and puts his face in his hands. "This is . . . this is . . ."

He can't find the words to finish his sentence. The poor man has witnessed what he once thought would be a triumph transform into a nightmare.

"Well, I'm impressed," says Sexton. "How the hell did you figure the signal part out?" He notices all eyes are on him. "Hey, now, wait! I'm not the bad guy here, doing the slow clap. I'm curious as hell. Actually, my pride is hurt. I should have figured it out."

"So should someone else." I turn to Rood. "You had me convinced."

His face is white as he nervously plays with an unlit cigarette. He simply bobs his head up and down and says nothing.

"Why?" asks Bilton.

Jessica answers: "Mr. Theismann was thinking about stopping all funding for ET research. But Rood knew if he had a signal, just one incontrovertible signal, he'd throw everything he had at it."

Bilton glares at Rood, her shock giving way to hurt and anger.

He stares back at her. "Because I believe, Teresa. I believe all this has a purpose." He points his cigarette at Theismann. "For him, it's just one of many crazy obsessions. For me, it's . . . my life."

"Will somebody please explain the time-traveling cosmonaut?" asks Trevor as Rood trails off.

I shrug. "Your guess is as good as mine. Maybe Dr. Rood designed something so blatantly stupid that nobody would think to connect him to all this."

Rood raises an eyebrow but remains silent. He knows he's already dug himself in deep enough.

"What a goddamn waste," says Theismann, his red-rimmed eyes pinning Rood.

"Agent Blackwood?" the sheriff calls out from the back of the control room, flanked by four well-armed deputies. "Who should we talk to first?"

EPILOGUE

For an old man, Theismann's extremely animated as he talks to Theo.

He gestures inside the cavernous climate-controlled warehouse, where technicians are unpacking crates filled with complex computer systems. At the center of the space stands a shock-absorbing pedestal wide enough to hold a car.

"That's where the quantum computer is going," says Theismann. "It's very exciting. There are only three like it, and Google got the other two. I had to sign an agreement that I wouldn't use it for financial forecasting. Can you imagine?"

He'd invited Theo both to show off his new facility and also to lure him into joining his insane project.

Theo described it to me as a supercollider made of zeros and ones. Instead of smashing particles together, it would try to use mathematical functions to crack open the universe. Not figuratively, but literally. It's a system designed to find cheat codes, like what players exploit in digital games.

Theo invited me along, I suspect, to serve as an anchor to keep him from getting swept up by Theismann's enthusiasm.

The FBI closed its books on the investigation several weeks ago. Theismann was extremely forthcoming about everything. Ultimately, the man was a victim of his own curiosity.

The hardest part for him was the realization that one of his closest friends, Mike Highfield, had been duping him for decades. From the moment Highfield met him in the '70s, he'd attached himself to Theismann as a guru and fix-it man.

While the jury is still out on whether Theismann ever knowingly had Highfield "fix" things illegally, it's abundantly clear that Highfield had been stealing from him for decades, then funneling the money to bogus projects and friends of his.

For Theismann, the theft only constituted a rounding error in his finances. He may have suspected Mike of being a little sticky-fingered, but the benefit of the friendship seemed worthwhile.

The elusive Edward Chang came out of hiding after I explained to his wife that his testimony could help us put away the people responsible. He was able to corroborate that Theismann had become a victim of his own machinations. If anything, Theismann was guilty of being too trusting.

Theismann sees me watching from the side. "You don't seem impressed."

"This could pay for a lot of children's hospitals in poor neighborhoods," I reply.

"Exactly," he says, missing my point.

"I mean literally use the money for that instead," I explain.

"I get your point, Jessica. Let me pose an alternative question: What if, because of this machine, children never have to go to the hospital? I'm sure Otto Schott seemed odd to people with his fascination for various chemical compounds and his obsession with trying every conceivable combination. And yet here we are today. His discovery of borosilicate glass is why children's hospitals have thermometers and test tubes that can be autoclaved to prevent the spread of disease. His correspondence with Carl Zeiss helped us build telescopes to see the edge of our universe. Big things take root in the unlikeliest of places," he explains.

"Fair enough." I could challenge him further, but who am I to tell him what's the right pursuit and what isn't?

"And what if this doesn't work out?" asks Theo.

"I doubt I'll live long enough to find out that it didn't. I used to think the existence of aliens was our principal scientific question. Now I believe it's this. But who knows what will come next? Do you?"

Theo shrugs.

"Seriously? Don't you have some big unresolved question?" probes Theismann.

"Other than how to tell if Jessica wants me to just listen to her problem or try to solve it for her?" He shrugs again.

"The answer is *listen*, Theo. It's always to listen. I've never been a great success with the women in my life, but even I know that part."

🦋

"Well?" I ask Theo in the executive airport lounge after Theismann's driver drops us off for our flight back to Virginia.

"Impressive. That's an awful lot of computer," he replies.

"What about the idea of working with him?"

Before we left, Theismann made an impassioned plea for Theo to come aboard the project, basically offering a blank check for whatever Theo needed to make it happen.

"It's compelling . . . but . . ."

"But?" I ask.

"I give it a nonzero chance of succeeding, with the emphasis on zero."

"Yes, but if it does, it could change the world," I challenge him with Theismann's argument.

"True. But this isn't like space exploration, where it's a matter of when, not if, we'll go to other planets and ensure the survival of life in the universe. I put the chance of Theismann's new endeavor succeeding at less than one in ten billion. There are approximately 7.9 billion people in the world. So, either I can put my effort into something with a one in ten billion chance of helping everyone or go help one person who needs me, with an almost one hundred percent chance of success."

"And that one person?" I reply.

A television in the lounge is tuned to cable news. The program cuts to a woman dabbing at her eyes as tears pour down her cheeks. The text across the bottom reads: ". . . the search continues."

Theo glances up at the screen. "Well, we could start with her."

ABOUT THE AUTHOR

Andrew Mayne is a *Wall Street Journal* bestselling novelist and creator. He starred in the Discovery Channel's Shark Week special *Andrew Mayne: Ghost Diver*, where he swam alongside great white sharks using an underwater invisibility suit he designed. He was also the star of A&E's *Don't Trust Andrew Mayne*.

He's been nominated for the Edgar Award for his book *Black Fall* and the Thriller Award for *Name of the Devil* and *The Naturalist*—an Amazon Charts bestseller that spent six weeks at the #1 spot for all books on Amazon.

In addition to writing, Andrew works for OpenAI on creative applications for artificial intelligence.